HIS EYES

MARK CHARLES POWERS

Unless otherwise noted, Scripture quotations are from the Holy Bible, King James Version, Cambridge, 1769.

Paperback- ISBN 979-8-9997452-1-7
Hardcover- ISBN 979-8-9997452-2-4
Audiobook and E-book also available

Cover design and interior formatting by *Hannah Linder Designs*

I dedicate this book to my wife, Kay Ward Powers, the love of my life. For over forty years as a public-school teacher/administrator and guardian ad litem, she has shown compassion and grace to children and parents navigating crises.

ACKNOWLEDGMENTS

SPECIAL THANKS:

My deepest thanks to these beta readers: Wildred Powers, Jeremy Powers, Lauren Cason, Cathy Strickland, Doc Hanberry, the late great Mike Patsolic, Martin Wiles, and Pam Gibson.
Tim Thornton for detective expertise.
Melinda Eargle for honest insights into losing a child.

ACKNOWLEDGEMENTS:

Larry J. Leech II- writing coach extraordinaire; Hannah Linder, Linder Creations- cover design; Christy Distler, Avodah Editing- proofreading and storyline consultant; Catherine Posey, Linder Creations- formatting; Miguel A. Rodriguez, voice over professional- audio book advice; Vincent Davis, BookSalesPro- self-publishing guidance.

Bryan Duncan, writer, and owner of the song "You're Never Alone," gave me written permission to incorporate his lyrics into this book. Bryan became an acquaintance when I produced one of his concerts. His credits include eighteen solo albums featuring sixteen number one radio hits in the Contemporary Christian genre and more than 1.2 million records sold.
BryanDuncan.com

CHAPTER ONE

On the day of the snake in 1997, someone shot my little brother in the chest.

I remember his eyes. He looked up at me from the ground, and my heart broke. I expected to see fear, anger, or betrayal. But I only saw love. I can't explain. And I won't try.

Yes, the sheriff ruled the shooting an accident. And yes, it happened a long time ago—over twenty-five years ago, to be exact.

 ...hat moment, though, no one could determine who pulled

 ...t didn't seem to matter then. While he lay there,

 ...d—the look we held between us. A look I

 ...day haunted us all, tested

 ...a downward spiral. The

 ...elationships.

 ...hose as a sixteen-year-old

 ...lve-year-old brother, Jacob.

 ...n much older. And not a day

 ...t gunshot changed all our lives.

 ...Mike—Mike Judson. But in my

heart, I still hear voices from long ago calling me Michael. Deep down inside, tenth-grade Michael still stands in my front yard holding a hot gun, wondering what happened. After all these years, I can finally tell the story of the weeks surrounding the accident. My life would never be the same.

When my mother died last year, a discovery shook me to my core. She kept a journal during the weeks following the accident. The old leather journal stayed hidden in the same bedside table drawer that I retrieved the gun from. I've included her journal entries within my story to help you understand her struggle.

I often recall the day of the snake—Saturday, April 12, 1997. That day remains etched in my memory in high definition.

Easter came early that year and brought warm weather. After months of winter in our new town, we couldn't wait to be outside in the sunshine.

We played our weekly baseball game in the cul-de-sac. I pitched to Jacob, my sixth-grade brother. A middle schooler— need I say more? My best friend, Lucas, played catcher. If we hit the ball carefully up the hill, it rolled right back down the street to us. Mr. Charlie, our retired next-door neighbor, puttered around in his front yard and poked fun when we swung and missed. Mom kneeled in the pine straw and planted spring flowers on the berm between our yards.

Then Mom screamed.

We dropped our bat and gloves when she leaped to her feet. My heart rate accelerated to warp speed. Mom pointed towar the magnolia tree in the middle of the berm. Her other h half-covered her face.

She screamed again, took a step toward the tr cowered backward two steps, waving her hands in fea a snake on the tree. The thing is huge. It might be po

A few feet from Mom, the reptile had slinked the pine straw and glided up the magnolia. It the bird nest we discovered the week before, to

Jacob and I sprinted to Mom, with Lucas right behind. Mr. Charlie trotted into his garage, hurried out carrying a rake, and hustled to the tree. We stopped alongside Mom and stared at the light gray snake with dark blotches along its body.

Mr. Charlie whistled and used the rake to point. "That's a rat snake right there. He's not poisonous. He's trying to get a hold of those robin eggs." Charlie ducked when a bird swooped close to his head. He chuckled. "That mama bird is not happy. Watch what she does."

The mama bird screeched and dove to fend off the snake. Undeterred, the snake continued tracking its prey.

Lucas's eyes grew big as those bird eggs. He shuddered. "Yep, that's a rat snake. I've seen 'em on our farm. They come after my chicken eggs. That one there is the biggest I've ever seen."

"Wow," Jacob said, "that snake is scary big, longer than me. That bad boy's gotta be over five feet long." He glanced at me with a horrified look.

I held out my hand palm down and motioned for him not to worry. But worry overcame me too.

Mom hated snakes more than she loved birds. And boy, did she love birds. She thrust both hands toward Mr. Charlie and pleaded, "Quick, knock it down with your rake before it gets to the eggs. When it's on the ground, we'll stomp it to death."

Charlie arched a brow, sighed, and stepped up to the tree. He crouched in attack mode and held the rake like a weapon. His hands shook.

Mom stepped behind him to shield herself.

I had a better idea. I mean, I was the big brother and the man of the house since Mom and Dad divorced. Mom depended on me to protect her and guard our home. And I wanted to save Jacob from having snake nightmares.

I whispered to Lucas and Jacob, "Come on," then turned to Mom and stuck out my chest. "It's okay. We're gonna get that snake." I ran toward the house with the other two following close.

"Michael, where are you going?" Mom shouted. "I need your help. Get back out here right now."

Mr. Charlie pulled the rake down and yelled at our backs, "You boys afraid of a little old rat snake?"

But we were gone. I ran straight into the house to Mom's bedside table and opened the drawer. Pushing tubes of facial cream, old keychains, and a box of tissues out of the way, I saw the glint of steel in the back corner.

I grabbed her .22 Magnum revolver and shielded it from Jacob and Lucas's view, then turned it over in my hand. Dad always said, "Don't pick up a gun unless you intend to use it." I hesitated a split second and held out the gun like a prize trophy.

Lucas and Jacob caught their breath and looked at each other. Their mouths hung open in awe, impressed. That made me proud.

I fished around until we found the box of bullets hidden in an old sock. We grinned at each other and raced back to the tree. I felt like a superhero. "Here you go, Mom." I held out the gun. "Shoot that nasty snake."

She gasped. "You're not supposed to know where I hide my gun. What in the world are you thinking?" She stepped back, shaking her head.

"Come on, Mom." I raised my voice above the screeches of the mama bird. "You're not gonna let that evil snake eat your birds, are you?"

She stared at the pistol—her mouth turned down in thought. The concern on her face melted into resolve when she looked back at me. "Okay, you're right. Give me the gun." Mom took it and gulped. I handed her a bullet. With shaking hands, she flipped open the cylinder and shoved bullets into the chambers one by one.

A bullet slipped through her nervous hands, and I bent to

4

find it in the straw. She checked the snake's progress. "Just leave the bullet there. Give me another one." We finished loading the gun.

Shaking his bald head, Mr. Charlie stepped toward Mom, his face lined with concern. "Now, Susan, don't you think the gun might be overkill? Snakes eat bird eggs . . . this is how nature works. Maybe we should just walk away."

Mom would not take her eyes off the snake. "Not on my watch. Not if I can save my birds. Rake that snake down into the pine straw so I can shoot him." She flashed Mr. Charlie an impatient look. "Please?"

He sighed. "Okay, but that snake's going to be a moving target. And when it hits the ground, it might come at us. I hope you can handle that gun."

Jacob glanced at me with raised eyebrows. I shrugged and turned my attention back to the snake.

It slithered to within inches of the nest. Mr. Charlie raised the rake, took a deep breath, and jabbed at the snake. It clung to the tree and hissed. He tried again with the same result. On the third jab, he dislodged it from the tree. The huge rat snake tumbled, twisting in slow motion. All five of us sprang backward at the same time.

The snake hit the pine straw and headed straight for Jacob. He squealed with fear. Mom stepped forward and pointed the gun an inch above the menacing snake head. She fired twice in rapid succession.

The sharp sound of the gun startled me.

The snake lay in the pine straw under the tree. Mom's point-blank shot had pierced his head.

We all cheered. Mom flashed a look of satisfaction, and I smiled.

Then the snake writhed, its body convulsing in a seizure.

Jacob pointed, screaming, "He's still alive! Give me the gun. Give me the gun." He lunged for the pistol.

Mom jerked the gun away. "No, Jacob. Let go." They struggled for control in a desperate tug-o-war.

Jacob shouted again, "But the snake's still alive!"

I jumped in and clutched the gun too. "Stop it, Jacob."

The three of us yanked back and forth.

Mom screeched, "Stop, you're gonna—"

The blast from the gun stunned us. We stopped tussling.

I stared at the gun in our hands. Jacob's hands fell away. Mom's hands flew up to cover her mouth. I still held the gun by the barrel.

The heat from the gunshot stung my hands. I gasped and tossed the gun into the flowers Mom had just planted. My hands felt dirty. I wiped them on my jeans.

Mr. Charlie turned away and muttered, "Oh God."

Lucas whispered, "You shot Jacob."

Mom shrieked, "Jacob! No!"

That's when I saw the wound in his chest.

He trembled. His body sagged, crumpled, and fell. Blood trickled from his mouth, along with a whimper.

But his eyes. They looked straight into my soul.

CHAPTER TWO

Eleven weeks earlier

Slivers of sunlight filtered through the trees, stirred by the icy wind, while I wandered in the woods behind Mr. Charlie's house.

The voice—not angry, just easygoing and spooky—came from the shadows. "Hey. What you doin' in my woods?"

I jumped behind a tree and picked up a rock to defend myself. I peeked around the tree to see who spoke.

A kid I'd noticed once or twice at school stood several steps away. His clothes looked like mine, but less cool and a little more worn. He stood with his shoulders slumped and sported a mullet haircut.

I tried to sound brave, but my voice trembled a little. "Who told you these woods belonged to you?" Stepping halfway out from behind the tree, I kept the rock hidden in my other hand.

He drawled, "My grandpa."

"Whatcha mean?"

"That land you're livin' on used to be my grandpa's farm. We live in the old farmhouse through the woods." Hands shoved in his pockets, he stood staring, expressionless. He sighed. "Grandpa sold the extra land to somebody who built all those houses. So we kinda think these woods are ours."

We held a staring contest, waiting to see who would make the next move. Crystal patterns on the damp ground crunched under my new winter boots while I shuffled my feet, not sure what to say.

He broke the silence and introduced himself as Lucas.

I dropped the rock behind the tree and stepped into full view. I told him my name and waited for his next move.

He looked me up and down with a half-smile. "Yeah, I watched the moving van put all the stuff in your house right before Christmas. I've seen you around school too. You're the new kid who's real smart, right?"

"Smart?" I laughed. "Yeah, I make A's and B's. No biggie." I didn't want to talk about that. "Why don't you show me the old farmhouse where you live?"

"Okay." He shrugged. "If you promise not to laugh. It's not modern like your house. But it's okay for an old farmhouse." His eyes brightened. "We raise show chickens if you wanna see 'em."

I did my best to appear nonchalant, but curiosity won me over. "Sure. I guess."

Lucas turned and crunched across the crystallized dirt. I followed in his tracks. The sound of our footsteps floated through the winter air. I grew up accustomed to the warm beach climate of our former home. The winter air in Arradale chilled me to the bone.

I caught up with Lucas. "My next-door neighbor, Mr. Charlie, told me and my brother there's a trail to the river through these woods."

"Yep, nice trail . . . goes to the county park on the river."

A smile crinkled my eyes. Jacob would be so jealous. We talked last week about exploring this forest and hiking to the river someday. But that dream would never happen.

In a few minutes, we came to Lucas's house—a typical farm-house with gables and porches. Scattered around the property lay old sheds and other buildings. Against the back fence sat an abandoned car with smashed-out windows. We climbed into the front seat and sat in uncomfortable silence. Lucas didn't talk much. But hanging out with him sure beat boredom at home.

After a few minutes of sitting in the old car, we chatted a little about school. When we got bored with that subject, Lucas led me across the yard and behind a weather-worn shed. He stopped beside a large pen with chicken coops, smiled, and pointed. I turned, staring at the fanciest chickens I'd ever seen.

"These 'uns are Chinese 'uns," he said with a note of satisfaction in his voice.

I cringed at his choice of words but grinned at his obvious pride.

"Oh, wow. I've never seen chickens like that." I stepped up to get a better look.

Lucas leaned on a fencepost and smiled. "Yep, they're strange ones. When we sell 'em, Dad gives me some of the profit since I'm the one who raises them." He spat on the ground. "But most times, they're a pain."

I spent the next half hour trudging behind him while he shuffled back and forth across his yard, showing me stuff. Following behind a grumpy old man would be more fun. From his mullet to my bowl cut, his patched jeans to my khakis, we seemed like total opposites. But Lucas would become a lifelong friend.

After an hour with Lucas, we said goodbye, and I headed home through the woods. I thought back to the past two months. Mom, Jacob, and I moved to Arradale during the Christmas holi-days. On January 2, Mom reported to her new office. A few days later Jacob and I started our new school.

The three of us craved a fresh start.

Mom and Dad's marriage fell apart three years ago, just after

I turned thirteen. Dad moved out. But we determined not to let Dad's unfaithfulness force us to leave our coastal home on the bay. Then Dad got remarried. And things got nastier.

Last fall, when Mom's real estate company asked her to transfer, she jumped at the chance. Arradale sat four hours inland and in the next state over—a small town located across the river from a medium-sized city. Rolling hills rose all around and mountains stood tall in the distance. Arradale had good shopping, nice restaurants, and a small hospital. I don't like to think about the hospital.

When I got home, Jacob shouted down the hallway, "Where ya been? I wanted you to play some video games with me."

He pouted like crazy when I told him about Lucas's farm. We played video games together for the rest of the afternoon anyway.

In days to come, Lucas and I connected several times at school. Although we were both in the tenth grade, the guidance office assigned us to different classes. I asked him about his chickens each time I saw him, and he would smirk.

A week after our farm tour, Lucas strolled over to me in the lunchroom. I nodded at a chair, and he sat while I ate my sandwich.

After a few moments of silence, he cleared his throat. "You wanna come over to the farm again this Saturday? We'll figure out something to do."

"Sure," I said, wiping mustard off my mouth.

"You wanna bring your little brother? We can show him my chickens."

"Well . . ." I put my sandwich on my tray. "Jacob's a pain sometimes. But I know he'd like to see your Chinese chickens." I shrugged. "I'll invite him."

That afternoon, when I got off the school bus and walked into the house, I yelled, "Hey Jacob, come here. I got an invitation for you." I wandered into the kitchen and dropped my bookbag on the table.

He jogged down the hallway and into the kitchen, eating my favorite potato chips. "Yeah, whatcha got?"

I glared at the chips. Jacob mooched all the good snacks because his school bus got home earlier than mine. Just one perk of still being in middle school, I guessed.

"Lucas wants you and me to come over to his house on Saturday and hang out."

Jacob hitched up his jeans and smiled. "Cool. Now I get to check out the farm. About time." He threw the chip bag onto the kitchen cabinet. "What we gonna do?"

"He wants to show off his Chinese chickens. After that, we can explore the attic over his garage." I grabbed the chip bag and stuffed a handful in my mouth.

Jacob nodded. "Sure, tell him I'll come."

Not to be outdone, he snatched the bag and taunted me by gobbling a couple more chips. He sprayed crumbs from his mouth onto my shirt, catching me by surprise. I shoved him in the chest.

He chuckled and ambled away, mumbling, "Cool. Now I get to see Lucas's farm. And check out his strange chickens."

CHAPTER THREE

Midafternoon, Saturday, April 12, 1997

Dropping to her knees, Mom intertwined her fingers and pushed down on the gunshot wound in Jacob's chest. Mr. Charlie raked the dead snake away from Jacob and glanced up the street. I followed his look. Some neighbors had come out into their yards and stood staring, some with a hand over their mouths. Great. Now we had an audience. I looked away.

A neighbor across the street shouted to Mr. Charlie that he had called 911. Mr. Charlie shouted his thanks. The ambulance wailed from a long way off.

Mom slapped me on the leg and shouted, "Michael, get your jacket and put it over him! Raise his head. They'll be here any minute."

Lucas dropped to his knees and lifted Jacob's head. Mr. Charlie hurried out into the street to flag down the ambulance.

I broke out of my trance and headed to get my jacket from the curb, where I had dropped it to play ball. My arms and legs moved in slow motion, bound by imaginary ropes of fear. I shook them off, grabbed the jacket, and hurried back to kneel beside Jacob.

His eyes stared. Blood trickled from his mouth and he made gurgling sounds. I struggled not to panic while I pressed my jacket against the bleeding. The pool of red grew bigger. I pressed harder.

A plea echoed through my mind over and over. *God, save him. Don't let him die.*

The siren pierced our neighborhood. When it turned the corner at the top of the hill, I cringed at the increase in intensity but kept my hands on Jacob. The ambulance screeched to a halt beside the curb. Mr. Charlie pointed toward us with both hands. The passenger door flew open. A female medic grabbed a bag from a side compartment and ran to Jacob.

When she reached us, she nodded to me, Mom, and Lucas, then went to work. Her partner kneeled on the other side of my brother and opened his crash bag. He grasped Mom's hand for a second when she reached out to him. "A police car is on the way to assist, dispatched by 911," he said. He dropped Mom's hand and removed an oxygen tank and IV kit from the bag.

While the female medic opened gauze and put it over Jacob's wound, she peppered Mom with questions. "How old is he? Were you here when he got shot? Who fired the gun?"

Mom answered each question. Her voice sounded shaky, but she maintained control. The other medic placed a mask over Jacob's nose and started an IV. Keying his shoulder mic, the medic alerted the hospital of a pre-teen gunshot victim, then radioed the police officer enroute. He went back to work to save Jacob.

Two minutes later, a police car sped down the street and stopped beside the ambulance. A wiry uniformed officer with wide shoulders emerged. He shoved his hat onto his head and headed for us. With hunched shoulders, he surveyed the situation and jotted some notes on a pad.

Mom pulled me into a desperate hug. "Michael, what have we done? God, help us." Her body trembled with gasping breaths. Tears poured down her cheeks, dripping onto the front of my shirt.

I held her tight, wanting to cry too, so the horror in my heart could flood out. But I determined to be strong for her and Jacob.

The officer approached Mom. "Mrs. Judson?"

Mom turned and wiped the tears from her face. She confirmed our names to the policeman.

"I'm Officer Parker. The EMTs' radio report told me your younger son got shot. I know you're distraught and want to stay close. But can we all step back so the medics can work?"

We moved back two steps.

Parker thanked us. "I know this is a terrible shock. What else can I do for you?"

We shook our heads, too overwhelmed with concern for Jacob to think of ourselves.

He turned toward Mr. Charlie and Lucas. "And did you two witness the shooting?"

Both glanced toward us and gave a solemn nod.

"Okay, please stay close and don't leave the scene. Detective Thorne is on his way and will interview you."

Lucas shot me a terrified look, and Mr. Charlie gulped.

The officer turned toward me and Mom. "If they decide to transport your son to the hospital, you can follow in your personal vehicle. After the detective investigates the scene here, he'll come to the hospital and speak with you and your son."

Mom turned to me and grasped my hand.

The officer unrolled yellow plastic tape that read "Crime Scene—Keep Out." He looped the tape in a wide circle around the magnolia tree.

I shuddered when I saw it. The crime scene tape gave me the creeps. The gun fired by accident. Nobody committed a crime.

The female medic stood and addressed her partner. Her voice

sounded urgent. "We can't do anything more here. We need to transport him immediately."

The male medic asked Officer Parker to bring the gurney.

After they eased my brother onto it, I dared to look at Jacob's face.

But I couldn't bear to look into his eyes.

CHAPTER FOUR

Ten weeks earlier

I walked into the kitchen to grab some breakfast.

Mom sat at the table in her robe, staring out the porch window, her strawberry-blond hair pulled up in a topknot. A gentle smile crossed her face each time a bird landed on the feeder outside. She folded the newspaper and pushed her half-eaten bowl of oatmeal aside. With raised eyebrows, she glanced at me. "Well, look at you, already dressed, with your hair combed on a Saturday morning. Where are you going in such a hurry?"

I walked to the fridge and poured a glass of milk. "Lucas invited me and Jacob to hang out at his house today." I grabbed a muffin from the pantry and sat across from her to eat.

Mom glanced at me with a twinkle in her eye. "I don't recall anybody asking my permission." Her gaze returned to the feeder. "I've got housework today if I can get myself going. It's been a long, busy week at the office. But you boys can go to Lucas's house. That's okay with me." She patted my arm and smiled at me. "Go have some fun. I'm excited you two are becoming such good friends."

I thanked her and devoured the muffin so we could head out.

Jacob stuck his head out the hall bathroom door, toothpaste foaming from his mouth. Struggling to speak through the foam, he said, "Lucas wants me to see his fancy show chickens."

Mom snickered. "He wants to show you his fanny Joe Christmas?"

I doubled over in laughter. Jacob's loud spitting and coughing in the bathroom got Mom laughing too.

Jacob hurried into the kitchen with a big grin on his face. "No, Mom." He emphasized each word. "He wants to show me his fancy show chickens."

Mom shook her head and shot him a look. "Well, that doesn't make much more sense than fanny Joe Christmas, if you ask me. Let's just take a step back and catch our breath."

Jacob thrust his hands out with palms up. "Mom, you say that all the time. What does that even mean?"

I smiled at her predictability, stood, and gave her a hug from behind. While I put on my jacket, I explained how Lucas and his family raise Chinese chickens to sell.

Mom rose from her chair and picked up the newspaper. "Okay. Go and have a good time. Just be nice and come home for lunch by one thirty." She gathered her bowl and coffee cup. "I might like to go over there and see those chickens myself some time." A grin crossed her face.

Jacob took off running to get out the door first. I ran after him and called over my shoulder, "See you later, Mom. Thanks. Love you."

An icy feeling from the frosty night still clung to the air. Mr. Charlie had walked out to retrieve his newspaper from the box by the street. We waved and shouted a quick greeting. He and his wife seemed so old to us. I realize now they were in their mid-sixties. She battled cancer. Coming and going, we always waved to each other. But she struggled to wave back when he brought her home from treatment.

Mr. Charlie served as a deacon at his church. I guessed a deacon was supposed to invite people to church because he invited us a lot. One Sunday, we joined him for the worship service there. That pleased him.

Jacob and I pushed through the woods and talked about things we might find at Lucas's farmhouse. We walked side by side. My blond hair and tall lanky frame towered over Jacob with his dark brown crewcut and stocky build. With strides matching step for step, we crunched through the frozen moss where Lucas and I met a few weeks earlier.

When we hurried out of the trees into his yard, Lucas sat on the front porch watching for us. We exchanged a wave, and he ambled down the steps to meet us.

I introduced my little brother to my newfound friend. They nodded at each other but didn't speak.

Lucas and I caught up on the latest school news.

Jacob got antsy. "Come on, Michael. Are we gonna see the chickens or not?"

Lucas led us around the toolshed and pointed out the chickens in their coop.

"Wow," exclaimed Jacob. "What is that thing on their heads? It looks like some old-fashioned lady's hat or something."

Lucas smiled. "It's their crest. That's what makes 'em special, along with those fancy feathers on their legs."

"It looks like they're wearing fuzzy boots." Jacob stared wide-eyed with his mouth hanging open.

Lucas walked around me and stood beside Jacob. "These chickens have five toes instead of four, like most chickens. They're called Silkies. Truth be told, they're a lot of trouble. But I guess it's worth it when I get paid for raising 'em."

"Cool, you get money for them?" asked Jacob.

Lucas rubbed his first two fingers against his thumb and

grinned. "Oh yeah, we make good money. We raise them to sell to people who want them as pets."

Jacob laughed. "Pets? Won't they fly away?"

"Nah, they can't fly."

I smiled and elbowed Jacob. "Hey, I know what to buy you for Christmas now—a Silkie chicken you can pet and cuddle. I'll put a gift-wrapped chicken under the Christmas tree with a red bow around its neck, just for you." We got a good belly laugh imagining that scene.

When we got bored watching the Silkies, we showed Jacob around the farm. Lucas led us into the shed, where rusted tools hung on nails—saws, screwdrivers, hammers, and even some we couldn't identify. The scarred wooden handles intrigued us, not like the tools with plastic handles we used at home. Lucas said his great-granddaddy worked with these tools back before World War II. We took turns feeling the wood, worn smooth by the sweaty hands of generations of working men. Next, we wandered into an old barn housing rusted farm equipment. We had a blast climbing on the old broken-down tractors.

After we left the barn, we found the old Chevy and climbed inside. I couldn't wait for the day I could drive, so I hopped in the driver's seat before the other two. Jacob took shotgun. Lucas climbed into the back seat. In our minds, we were three wild and crazy guys, flying down the highway and waving at pretty girls.

When we completed our imaginary drive, Lucas said, "My mom doesn't want us playing in the house. Let's go explore the attic over the garage."

"Sure." Jacob hopped out of the car, eager to see more.

"What's up there?" I asked and clambered out of the car behind Lucas.

"Lots of stuff." He turned and shuffled toward the garage.

Jacob leaned over and whispered, "Man, you didn't tell me Lucas had a mullet haircut." He raised his eyebrows.

We grinned at each other and hurried to catch up.

The wooden garage sat next to the side door of the farm-house. Lucas swung open the creaky wooden doors and led us across the dirt floor. He stopped and pointed. We looked up into the corner of the ceiling above. A trapdoor loomed overhead, with a thin rope hanging down.

"Come on." Lucas tugged on the rope, and the hinged door flopped open with a thud.

He unfolded the wooden steps attached to the attic door and flipped the dirty light switch. Jacob and I stepped forward. We squinted into the mysterious cavern above. A lone hanging light bulb glowed in the dark attic. It looked ancient.

Lucas pushed us from behind. "Y'all gonna be Chinese chickens, or you gonna go up there with me?"

I summoned all the bravery I could muster. "Sure, let's go for it."

Taking the lead, I climbed the steps with caution. Jacob followed, and Lucas brought up the rear. When we stepped off the ladder and onto the plywood attic floor, we saw a museum of old stuff spread around in all directions—dry-rotted cardboard boxes, moldy suitcases, abandoned toys, and faded furniture. I also saw several antique wooden trunks at the back where the light ended.

Jacob spun around in circles and stared in amazement. He whispered, "This is duh bomb."

I grabbed his shoulder and pumped my fist. "Booyah. I told you Lucas had a cool house."

Lucas tried to hide his smile. "Okay, let's see if we can find some good stuff up here." He stopped and pointed. "But, hey, stay back from the trapdoor. My dad will be ticked if anybody falls through."

I felt a shiver run up my spine. "Yep, that's gotta hurt."

We began our treasure hunt. Jacob found a discarded boom box stereo with a cassette tape player and radio. We hit the power switch. The batteries still worked, so we tuned in our favorite station for background music. I explored a box or two. Jacob poked through some long-lost toys while Lucas opened a moldy trunk. A puff of dust went up like a smoke signal.

Jacob stared into a back corner. "What's in that box with the train picture on the front?"

Lucas headed over to look, careful not to step on something valuable. He bent down, picked up the train box, and laughed. "Wow, this is my dad's electric train from his childhood." He picked it up and blew away the dust, then carried it back into the circle of light. "It might still work. I remember it from way back. Dad and I came up here and played with it about the time I turned eight."

I envied him having a dad who spent time with him.

The three of us spotted a worn braided rug and unrolled it in the middle of the floor. I took the model train from its crusty box, and we took turns holding the engine, coal car, freight cars, and caboose. We worked to fit the track pieces together, forming an oval on the rug.

I held up the engine. "Let's get this thing running."

Lucas took the lead in his unassuming way. "I'll find the transformer. We'll plug it into the outlet on the light bulb socket up there. You guys can set the cars on the track." He rummaged around in the box until he found the transformer, dusted it off and hooked up the little wires.

Jacob and I finished our assignments. We watched, holding our breath.

Lucas pushed the transformer lever up the dial slow and easy. At first, the engine sat and made a humming noise. Then the train inched forward.

Jacob shouted, "It works! It works!"

We laughed and slapped each other on the back.

Lucas pushed the lever forward to test how fast it could go, and the engine gained momentum. Round and round the train sped. We shouted at each other like award-winning inventors at a science expo.

But he pushed the limit too far. The train began to wobble and tilt. I reached out to steady the engine but realized my hand could cause an accident. I pulled back and held my breath. The crash came anyway. In the next turn, the whole thing tumbled sideways and fell apart.

The three of us gasped and groaned. For a moment, we sat stunned.

I sighed. "It's okay. Put it back on the track. We'll rev it up again."

And we did, for another fifteen minutes. We laughed and watched in wonder.

When we got bored, I got an idea. "Hey, let's find something to add to the track."

"Like what?" Lucas asked.

"There're some wooden logs and building blocks in here." I opened the trunk I had explored earlier.

Lucas rolled over and crawled across to look inside. He reached in and pulled out a faded cardboard cylinder filled with brown log-cabin blocks. Reaching in again, he grabbed a net bag of wooden pieces labeled "Sunday school blocks." Jacob grabbed the wooden logs to build a train station. Lucas and I agreed to build a bridge across the track.

When we finished building our station and bridge, we ran the train round and round through our creations. But Jacob got bored again. He stood and rummaged through more antique treasures.

"Look," he called "here's a baby doll that wants to ride on the train." He held up a tiny plastic girl doll no bigger than the palm of my hand. Her curly blond hair and overalls showed years of wear and tear.

I chuckled. "Looks like a little farm baby to me."

Lucas waved us off with a smirk. "That's my sister's stupid

doll. She used to yell at me if she suspected I might touch it. Sheesh. I had forgotten about that thing."

Jacob plopped down on the rug and pantomimed the baby doll walking up to the station. He made his voice sound like a cartoon character. "Okay, Mr. Conductor, give me a ticket to Arradale. I have money to pay. I want to party with my baby friends."

Lucas and I glanced at each other and snickered. But Jacob's silliness intrigued us too. We could see the drama unfolding in his twelve-year-old mind.

"I'm going to hop this train and ride into town aboard the coal car. Engineer Lucas, give it some juice and take me uptown."

Jacob balanced the doll on the coal car, then Lucas started the train. The train picked up speed, and so did our laughter. The baby held on for dear life while the train went to town. But the bridge we fashioned from the wooden blocks knocked the doll head over heels. She slid across the rug and sprawled face first against the train station.

Jacob shouted, "Stupid baby."

Fits of laughter filled the attic while we rolled on the rug. Our laughter rang for another hour, and late morning dissolved into early afternoon. We played Stupid Baby with every variation we could invent. Soon my growling stomach grabbed my attention. I reminded Jacob we needed to head home for lunch.

Over the years, I've been desperate to hold that day in my memory. But it continues to erode.

I long to hear Jacob's laughter again.

CHAPTER FIVE

Late afternoon, Saturday, April 12, 1997

Mom drove to the hospital faster than I had ever seen her drive. I sat in the passenger seat and tried to control my fear. She struggled to keep the ambulance in sight while it careened through intersections and sometimes crossed into the other lane. She moaned and wiped away tears and pushed her speed to the limit. I stared straight ahead, my heart pounding.

Vague prayers wove their way through my mind amid the echo of the gunshot and the siren in my brain. I could picture Jacob in the back seat where he usually sat and talked our ears off. But I saw him now like a ghost, still and quiet.

Reality hit hard. Jacob lay in the ambulance in front of us.

I reached across and put my hand on Mom's shoulder. Through tears, she looked at me with a grimace. So I kept my hand there.

We couldn't keep up with the ambulance. But we knew our destination—Arradale Hospital. Mom raced into the parking lot and parked the car. She sprinted through the emergency room entrance with me close behind.

Mom ran to the desk and blurted, "Where have they taken him?"

I caught up with her, and we looped arms together.

Smiling, the desk attendant looked at us. "I'll be glad to help you. Who are you inquiring about?"

Mom cried out, pointing to the side door, "The ambulance—the one right there. It just brought my son Jacob from our yard. Jacob Judson." She gasped, choking on the words. "He got shot in the chest. Purely by accident. I'm his mom, Susan Judson. Please"—her voice cracked—"tell me where he is."

The attendant frowned. "I am so sorry, Mrs. Judson. Let me check with the nurse to find out where he is. Hold on just a minute." She picked up the desk phone and dialed. When someone answered, she asked about Jacob, listened for a few seconds, replied, and hung up. "Okay, the ambulance crew called ahead, and our staff took him direct to surgery. They are doing everything possible to care for your son." She patted Mom's hand. "I'll call you when we have some news. You two can sit over there while you wait." She pointed to a row of plastic seats and picked up a clipboard. "And I'll need you to fill out these forms for me. If you need anything, let me know."

Mom stared at the lady without moving. More tears streamed down her face.

I sighed and grasped her limp hand. "Come on, Mom. Let's go over here and sit together." I picked up the clipboard and led Mom by her arm to the row of plastic chairs. "I'll help you. You give me the information, and I'll fill it in."

She muttered, "I can't do that right now. We'll get to it later." She slumped into a chair.

"Okay, we can wait." I put my hand on her arm and gave a gentle squeeze. She looked me in the eyes. I whispered, "Mom . . . I love you." Dirt from the flower bed streaked her face, smudged by tears. She pushed her hair back, but it remained in tangles. I felt more protective of her than I ever had.

We sat and stared at the waiting room wall, oblivious to other people coming and going. The Game Show Network played an irritating episode on the waiting room TV. I zoned out and lost track of time. Forty-five minutes later, I realized I still held the clipboard and pen.

My hands trembled, but I held out the clipboard to Mom. After a few seconds, she took it from me in a half-stupor. She read the forms. I leaned back in my chair and stared at the ceiling. The feeling of ropes binding me to the waiting room chair grew even stronger than the feeling I had in our yard.

"Susan Judson?" The voice, deep and self-assured, came from above our heads.

I gasped and sat up when I saw the large hand resting on Mom's shoulder.

"I'm Detective Thorne," the man said.

Mom sucked in a breath and stared at the middle-aged detective hovering above us. She thrust the clipboard back into my lap.

He gave her shoulder a pat and stood straight. "I apologize for intruding during this stressful time. The medical staff and I conferred by radio on my way here. They told me they took your son straight to surgery. So I know this is a difficult time, sitting here waiting for news." Detective Thorne stepped back and sat on the edge of the chair across from us. He wore a rumpled shirt, necktie, and navy-colored chino pants. With elbows on his thighs, he leaned forward. "While everything is fresh in your mind, I need you both to tell me what happened. No pressure, very casual. You talking to me, one-on-one." The detective's curly dark hair bounced up and down with each statement. "And now is not the time for forming opinions about anything. So put your mind at ease. I only need simple facts. Any questions?"

Mom looked skeptical and pulled herself upright. "Interview? Are you sure this is not an interrogation? Because the shooting happened by accident. I'll swear to that."

I glanced at her, shocked at her reply.

Thorne sighed. "Yes, ma'am, I promise. This is simply an interview. I investigated the scene with Officer Parker. We interviewed the two witnesses. I kept the gun and entered it as evidence. Looks to me like an accident. But I'll ask each of you a few questions for my report, then leave you to focus on Jacob."

She nodded and tried to smile. After a deep breath, she said, "Yes, sir, I'll do my best." With a shaky hand, she pointed to me. "This is my son, Michael. He'll help me."

Thorne gave me a smile, then scanned the waiting area. "I'll tell you what. Since no one else is close by, I'll conduct the interview right here. But I need Michael to move a few rows away so I can interview you separately from each other. I'm sorry. That's just how things work." He pointed across the room. "Okay, Michael, scoot over there for me. You and your mom can trade places in a few minutes."

Mom shrugged and slumped into the chair. I didn't know how to feel. But I stood and walked a few rows away, then sat close enough to watch and listen.

The detective reached into his pants pocket and produced a mini-cassette recorder. He pressed play and set the recorder aside. "I'll record our conversation. That way, I won't have to take notes and slow things down."

After maybe ten minutes of casual conversation, Thorne motioned for me to return. Mom and I traded seats.

With a gentle smile and unhurried pace, he questioned me. He asked me the same questions I heard him ask Mom, but with a slight difference in wording. I wondered if he might try to catch us in conflicting accounts. But his casual and caring attitude won me over and relieved my suspicions. His primary concern focused on Mom's gun stored in the bedside table because it had no lock. I hadn't wondered about that, but I tucked the question away for future reference.

Just above his head, the wall clock counted the seconds. After twelve minutes passed, Thorne switched off the recorder and tucked it away. "Michael, thank you. You've provided some very helpful information." He motioned for Mom to return.

She came back, sat, and resumed her dead-eyed stare.

Thorne's eyes met Mom's. "Mrs. Judson, I'm very sad about this terrible tragedy. I promise to pray for Jacob's full recovery. I'm so sorry we had to meet under these circumstances."

Mom and I glanced at each other, then she gave him a meek smile and whispered, "Thank you."

The detective stood. "I'll keep you in the loop. For now, you focus on your family. Call me if you need anything or have questions. We'll talk soon." He flashed a polite smile. Mom managed to return his smile before her face turned downward again.

I stood and shook his hand, and he gave me his contact card. I watched him stride to the front desk. After speaking to the receptionist in a hushed tone, he exited the ER.

Mom's shoulders sagged, her head down, eyes closed. I slid back into my chair and tried to settle in.

Another game show episode droned. The haunting crack of the gunshot echoed through my every thought.

Despite the noise in my brain, disturbing questions invaded and threatened to plunge me into panic. *How could this happen? Am I to blame? Why did I run inside and get the gun? And why no lock on it?* I pushed those thoughts away, pulled myself up straight in the uncomfortable chair, and shook my head to clear my mind.

I needed to focus on something other than those haunting questions. The clipboard lay in the chair beside me. I roused Mom from her trance. Helping her complete those forms became my immediate task at hand. Filling in the forms took longer than expected, but we finally finished them. My legs felt like gelatin when I returned the clipboard to the lady at the desk.

She thanked me and gave me a sympathetic smile.

I nodded and returned to my chair beside Mom.

A wall clock's incessant ticking measured our agony. Minutes dragged by. Two hours had come and gone since our arrival.

The lady from the desk walked over and offered us a coffee or soft drink. I glanced at Mom. She sat like a statue, stiff and unresponsive, staring straight ahead. When I shook my head at the lady, she returned to the front desk.

So we continued to sit and wait. For someone to tell us if Jacob would live or die.

CHAPTER SIX

Mom's Journal: Entry One- Sunday Evening, April 13, 1997

Jacob? Where are you? It's been twenty-four hours. And I'm still asking, "How can you be gone?"

Yesterday afternoon, after the gunshot, we spent two hours in the hospital waiting room. Agonizing. Finally, they called us into the back hallway. I struggled to leave the security of the waiting room. But the thought of seeing you smile, hearing your voice, and taking you home pushed me forward.

Directed to a room, but you're not there. Michael and I holding back tears. I pleaded, "Sir, please take me to my child."

The doctor pointed to a chair. "Have a seat, ma'am. I need to give you an update."

We sat across from him.

He looked me in the eye. "We did everything we could. Jacob is a fighter." He stared at the floor for a full ten seconds, shaking his head. At last, he looked up. "Mrs. Judson, I'm so sorry. We lost Jacob."

Michael and I stared in shock.

The doctor continued in a whisper, "He's gone. We couldn't save him."

I screamed. My world shattered into a million pieces. Michael lifted me when I slid to the floor. We held each other tight, weeping. Pain ripped through my heart like an exploding bullet. Fragments of my soul flew against the walls and splattered on the door.

Then a stifling silence overwhelmed me. I heard and felt nothing. Could I be in shock? Probably.

A chaplain came and talked to us. I heard nothing. Michael crumpled in his chair, his body trembling. I saw him wailing but couldn't hear a sound. The silence inside me felt vast as an ocean.

Jacob? Where are you? Where have you gone? Silence.

Nothing remained to be done at the hospital. I didn't want to see your body. So we drove home. Not a word between us. Nothing to say.

Michael went to his room. I sat in the den and looked out the window. There, across the yard, stands the magnolia tree. I will call it by your name. The Jacob tree. But I cannot focus on that tree today. Much too painful.

I went to my room. Lay across the bed. Sadness, anger, resentment, hopelessness, helplessness, and nagging questions all overwhelmed me. But in my heart . . . only silence.

Please break the silence. Call me from your bedroom.

Leave clothes strewn across the floor. Laugh at the dinner table. Shout in the backyard. Sing in the shower. Rattle dishes in the kitchen. Something. Anything.

Please come back and fill my silence with sounds of you.

I will call your name. You will answer. Your brother will yell at you. You will yell back. Can you yell at me now? I'm dying to hear your voice. Try it. I'm waiting. Please? Go ahead.

Please.

CHAPTER SEVEN

Afternoon, Friday, April 18, 1997

After the day of the snake, Sunday, Monday, and Tuesday became even more of an ordeal.

The phone call from Dad on Sunday morning made everything worse. Of course, he asked lots of questions. But something in his voice sounded angry rather than sad.

Mr. Charlie's pastor stopped by on Sunday afternoon to pray with us. Mom asked him to officiate Jacob's funeral. We scheduled the service for Wednesday at the funeral home.

Monday and Tuesday, people dropped by our house all day. I don't know how we survived all the well-meaning visitors. Endless questions from neighbors and Mom's work colleagues threatened to smother us. The burden of repeating the story over and over made me want to scream. I could tell Mom felt it too. But she seemed insulated, like someone had wrapped her in bubble wrap. She held it together, did her best to thank everyone, and wore her smile like a mask.

Me? Not so much. I struggled to survive and make it to

Wednesday. Of all the people who stopped by, Mr. Charlie and his daily visits comforted me the most. I wasn't sure why.

By Tuesday afternoon, exhaustion overtook Mom and me. I never knew how tiring grief could be.

Later that afternoon, Detective Thorne stopped by. At the sight of him, the last visitors left. We invited him to sit in the den. To our relief, he confirmed that the sheriff's investigators had declared the shooting an accident. We had been desperate to hear this news. When Thorne headed out, I hugged Mom as tight as possible. She hugged me too, and my spirit soared. Then I went to my room and stayed hidden, trying to prepare myself for the funeral the next day.

Wednesday morning arrived. Mom and I walked arm in arm into the funeral home. From the corner of my eye, through the window, I noticed Dad's car. He steered the new sports car into the parking lot, leaving a vacant space on both sides of his beloved automobile. He could not resist the obsession to display expensive trophies. Once upon a time, Dad considered Mom and me his trophies. Not anymore.

Mom and I stood in the parlor and greeted those expressing their sympathy. I stood beside her in a dress shirt and necktie, tugging often at my collar to breathe. Mom made me proud, though. Her hat and stylish black dress on her tall slender frame looked elegant and disguised her broken heart.

Dad slipped into the side door, and I caught him staring at us. We gave each other a subtle wave, then he turned to someone and began a conversation. I stepped toward him, but Mom pulled me back. I glanced at her in surprise. She turned away.

When the pianist started playing, we took a seat inside the chapel in the first row. Jacob's casket sat front and center. Dad broke away from his conversation and made his way to the front. He stopped at the casket, placed his hand on it, and bowed his head for a moment. His stocky build and dark brown hair reminded me so much of Jacob that my heart sank.

Dad walked up the center aisle, nodded to me and Mom, and slid into the row behind us. Mom leaned over to me and growled under cover of the piano music, "Yep, a new designer suit. Exactly what I expected." She shook her head and refocused her attention on the lone flower arrangement at the front. Mr. Charlie and his wife had sent it.

Regardless of Mom's feelings toward him, I wanted to speak to Dad. I turned to greet him. He sat glaring at Jacob's coffin. When I saw his frown, I shifted forward again.

The funeral service seemed like a dream. And since we had only moved here a few months ago, few people knew us and even fewer attended. Most everyone we knew had already come by our house to offer condolences. Mr. Charlie's pastor didn't know us well, but he did the best he could. I wish Jacob had gotten a better memorial.

At the burial service, I sat under the funeral home canopy, as close to Mom as possible, shoulder to shoulder, holding her hand. The pastor shared a few thoughts and read some Bible verses. To this day, I can't remember anything he said. We walked away before they lowered the casket into the ground.

At home after the funeral, Dad put on his salesman act and chatted up the neighbors who brought lunch. He frustrated me with how he took all the attention for himself and ignored Mom and me. On his way out the door, he hugged us and said a few well-rehearsed lines.

I watched Dad through the window blinds when he turned his back on us and walked away. Detective Thorne had come to offer his condolences, and Dad met him. When Thorne went to his police cruiser, Dad veered straight for him with one of our neighbors in tow. The detective and the neighbor engaged in a quick conversation. Then Dad stepped in. After a few minutes of intense discussion, Dad punched his finger into the investigator's shoulder and leaned into his face. I couldn't watch anymore. I nodded to the guests and headed to my room.

During the next two days, I holed up in my room, only coming out to eat. Pain pulsed through my whole body into my soul. Excruciating. I felt repulsed by the thought of seeing or talking to anyone, even Mom. I became resentful of Mom's guarded responses and careful replies. The small portable TV in my bedroom became my mindless distraction hour after hour.

When moments of anger overwhelmed me, I would grab my pillow and beat the bed. Other times, I pounded the pillow with my fists until my arms ached. After the fits of anger, I felt numb and empty. Staring at the television, the remote hanging limp in my hand, I longed for the pain to go away.

The anger felt terrible, but the haunting questions felt worse. Who shot Jacob? Me or Mom? Or did Jacob pull the trigger himself when he grabbed the gun? No way of knowing. But that didn't help. My mind rewound the shooting on continuous play-back, analyzing every detail.

Why did I run to get Mom's gun? What was I thinking? Why hadn't she secured it with a gun lock? I knew deep inside that I wanted to show off. To be the man of the family and impress Jacob, Lucas, Charlie, and Mom. I thought the gun would prove my adulthood.

I was dead wrong.

And now Jacob was dead.

Friday afternoon, after hiding for two days following the funeral, I needed to get out of the house. I grabbed my ball and glove and headed out the front door. Mom lay napping on the den sofa.

My favorite afternoon diversion consumed my attention, throwing the baseball against the brick wall under the front window. When it bounced back, I fielded the ball, wound up fast, and threw it back against the wall. Mom often complained about the sound the ball made inside the house. Today, I hoped the noise would rouse her to cook dinner so we could get back to normal life.

"What's up, Michael?"

I turned to see Mr. Charlie waving from his yard. I'm sure I looked dumb as a rock, standing there staring at the wall. After returning his wave, I trudged across the pine straw berm into his yard. I didn't dare look toward the magnolia tree in the center of the flower bed.

"Just getting ready to play ball-on-the-wall," I said, using my made-up name for the game.

Mr. Charlie gave a gentle nod. "Wanna throw the baseball together?"

"Sure, I guess. I didn't know you had a ball glove."

"Oh yeah." He grinned. "Everybody's got a ball glove." He pointed over his shoulder. "Let me run into the garage and get mine. I'll be right back."

I chuckled when he said he would run inside. Mr. Charlie probably couldn't run anywhere at his age. While I waited for him, I tossed the ball high in the air, up through the late afternoon shadows, and caught it. My spirit lifted with every throw, free from the prison of my bedroom.

Mr. Charlie emerged from the garage with his glove, and I tossed him my ball.

"Okay, Michael, catch this one, then chuck it back to me." Mr. Charlie pitched the ball to me with a crisp throw.

I caught it with ease, wound up, and threw it back. My throw soared a little high, but he reached and caught it in his old glove. Nice catch.

The afternoon sun gleamed on his bald head. And while the ball zipped back and forth, the concerned wrinkles on his round face gave way to a warm smile. I felt relieved he had not mentioned Jacob.

Mr. Charlie's old-fashioned way of throwing the ball took some adjustment on my part. His circular arm motion reminded me of those old black-and-white videos from long ago, shown on the new cable TV sports channel. But I liked his style and thought it looked cool.

"What in the world is that glove you got there?" I asked.

"Come on over and have a look."

I trotted to him while he took the glove off his hand and held it out.

"This old ball glove belonged to my granddaddy. He played baseball in the Army during World War II." He handed it to me with pride.

I turned it over with respect. "Wow, it must be an antique."

Charlie smiled. "Yep, an antique. Just like me. It's a Nokona glove. Made the same year as my birth—1935."

"Can I try it?"

"Sure, why not? See if it fits you."

I tried it on, making sure I respected this prized possession. His glove had short, stubby fingers, much different from my long, slender glove. My hand clutched and unclutched the ball in the glove. "This feels so soft."

Charlie smiled. "I rub it with oil every year to keep it that way. If you want something to last, you gotta take special care of it. That's true with people and baseball gloves. That glove's over sixty years old." He grinned. "Go ahead. Try it out and I'll use yours."

I ran back to my side of his yard and faced him. We threw the ball back and forth. It took me a few catches to get used to the short fingers in the antique glove, but I felt pretty special that Mr. Charlie's grandfather wore this same glove so long ago and now he let me use it.

After fifteen minutes, we traded gloves again. We threw the ball, and our conversation flowed until the sun slid behind the trees. The rhythm of throwing and catching comforted my soul. And thankfully, Mr. Charlie didn't mention the day of the snake.

But I soon learned this relaxed feeling wouldn't last. A sense of dread hovered in the back of my mind about what lay ahead.

CHAPTER EIGHT

Mom's Journal: Entry Two- Friday Evening, April 18, 1997

Funeral. My heart will not allow my mouth to form that word. My lungs will not expel the breath to speak it. I wrote it here. But I cannot wrap my mind around the concept.

Now, the house is empty. Just me and Michael here. I'm so relieved. I know those who came wanted to comfort us. At times, though, the constant procession of people overwhelmed me. I needed a break. And now I have it.

No mother should ever have to face the burial of her child. Especially her youngest. And even more when that child is only twelve years old. I hope I'll wake up soon and find this is a dream.

But this is no dream. More like a nightmare. Invading every waking moment.

I do find myself thinking about your memorial service, meditating on what the pastor said and who attended. But I can tell you, no way this feels real. As if none of this actually happened. As if you are still alive, safe in our home. As if, as if, as if . . .

In my mind, the gun is still in my bedside drawer, hidden away in the back corner. With the bullets tucked in that old, discarded sock where they could do no harm. And you, still here . . . knocking on my bedroom door—begging for help with homework, needing a bandage for a scraped knee, or asking what time dinner will be.

A return to normal is what I crave. But I fear normal days are gone and will never come back. Normal died with you.

So, we observed your memorial service today. Observed. Such an apt way to express my emotional detachment. Observing. Seeing—seeing yet insulated from feeling. I observed your casket from the front row. Observed other folks' reactions, wondering if they felt detached too. Observed your brother grieving.

If I had a choice, I'd prefer to be an outside observer. But that's not possible. I'm now "the mother of the deceased." That's how the funeral home director introduced me to Mr. Charlie's pastor. The funeral director and his staff were all business, not much warmth or sympathy. Maybe since death is their livelihood, they survive by observing, with emotions in check. I understand. I'm doing that myself.

The director seemed unaware we had already met the pastor. Remember? First, when you, me, and

Michael visited Mr. Charlie's church. We spoke to him at the front door and shook his hand. You liked his message about trusting God. We talked about it in the car on the way home. How trusting God could help us adapt to this new town. So we gave our best effort to trust God more in the days that followed. But here we are.

The second time we met with the pastor, you were already gone. He visited our house this past Sunday. We sat together in the den. Michael and I shared memories of you. The pastor shared those today at the funeral. Only a few people heard them. Sad.

I appreciate the pastor's care. The conscientious way he tried to honor you. He doesn't know us. But he did his best.

Despite his effort, the service seemed like a farce to me. I know that's a harsh thing to say, but that's how I felt. Most of those who came didn't even know you. And what about your friends from school? None came. Maybe we're too new in town. And the school day probably kept your friends from being there.

Your dad attended the service. He made a grand entrance, of course. Typical. Then we all became observers. Of him. Talk about a farce. Wow. But let's not go there. You understand. I know you do.

If only I could have planned the service and turned it over to the pastor. Then I could have stayed home, sitting in the backyard, watching my birds. Everyone else could have attended and left me alone.

But I couldn't do that. I had to be there to put my

arm around Michael, give a sad smile to Mr. Charlie, thank the few neighbors attending, and accept condolences from a couple of coworkers. Michael made me proud. He's strong. We've drawn strength from each other. He's becoming the man of the family. I love him so much.

If I'm honest with myself, I needed to be at the funeral . . . for me. The pastor told me funerals are for the living. "The service should help you accept death and find peace," he said. But I sure don't feel peace . . . or acceptance. Yeah, sure. I smiled and shook the pastor's hand. But my heart shouted, "No! I'll never accept this. I can't. Forget it, sir. Nice try."

Ultimately, I had to be there for you, Jacob. You don't deserve this. All three of us wrestled with the gun. We may never know who fired the shot. We all share the blame. But I deserve the greatest blame. The gun belonged to me. I'm the mother. Your mother. Why didn't I secure the gun with a lock? No excuse. No acceptable reason.

And now you're gone.

So I had to be there for you. I stood over your casket and whispered, "I'm sorry, Jacob." My tears dripped onto your cheek. I wiped away my tears. They were your tears too. But you lay silent, eyes closed.

At the service, the pastor told us you're in heaven. I don't know. Oh, how I wish I could know. I want to believe in heaven. But I just don't know.

Now eternity separates us. Eternity? That's a lot of separation. I can't deal with that right now. Another day, I'll figure out how to cope with eternity. Not now.

After the graveside service, we walked away just before they lowered you into the ground. The whole world fell silent around us. But inside, every particle of my being screamed, "No! Please, no."

And then . . . I said goodbye.

CHAPTER NINE

Morning, Monday, April 21, 1997

S unday night, I announced to Mom that I wanted to go back to school the next day. What else could I do? I couldn't take lying on my bed any longer while waves of unending questions assaulted me. Also, I couldn't bear another day of Mom and me avoiding each other around the house.

Mom reclined on the den sofa reading a book when I walked in to declare my plan. She closed the book and sat forward to look me in the face. Her forehead wrinkled with concern. "Are you sure you can handle this? We've been through a lot."

I stared out the front window at the Jacob tree. "I'm not sure, Mom. But the time has come to get back into a routine. Regardless, I gotta get out of the house."

Of course I didn't say it, but I also needed to escape her. Her sadness lay like a heavy quilt atop the blanket of my own grief. Guilt tugged at me for feeling that way. But I pushed it aside and took a seat in the chair across from her.

She looked away and twisted her hair around her index

finger. "Well, I guess that's a good plan. But you might not be that strong."

Trying to look brave, I sat forward and straightened my back. "I'll have to face it step by step. What can happen? It's just school —same people, same place. I'll be okay."

That assumption proved to be wrong. So wrong.

On Monday morning, I pressed forward onto the school bus, into the school building, the hallway, and my classroom a few minutes before the bell. Chaos ruled in my homeroom, like usual. As I navigated to my desk, the ropes of grief threatened to bind my arms and legs again. Classmates stared while they continued their conversations and antics. But no one spoke to me.

My teacher came into the room and demanded that everyone calm down. After he organized his desk and sat, he called my name and waved me over. I walked around the outside of the other desks to avoid eye contact. Loud conversations gave way to whispers and stares. My teacher motioned for me to come stand beside him.

He dropped his voice and caught my eye. "Michael, I'm glad you're back. We're all so sorry for your loss. None of us know how to help. But if you need anything, you just tell me, okay? I'm here for you."

I nodded but couldn't speak. When he sighed and looked away, I turned and headed back to my desk, glad to have that encounter behind me.

Morning classes slid by, but I couldn't concentrate on anything the teachers said. I felt like the thick fog had followed me from home. The cloud of grief engulfed me, and I couldn't shake it.

At lunchtime, I sat alone in the cafeteria and stared at my food. None of my classmates wanted to talk to me anyway. No one seemed to know what to say. I understood, but it hurt. It would mean so much if only one came over to sit with me, even without saying a word.

After lunch, we always wandered outside to the schoolyard before returning to class. The warm sunshine hinted at summer's approach, and I breathed in the aroma of spring. I leaned my elbows on the fence, turning my back on my schoolmates. Across the parking lot shared by our three Arradale schools, cars delivered little kids for afternoon kindergarten. The cheerful voices of the children entering the elementary building annoyed me. I could not bring myself to look at the middle school building. Jacob should be there, not in the cemetery. Behind me, the chatter of my classmates grated on my nerves too.

Then I heard one voice shouting above the chatter—Brandon, the bully. Like water to a cracked brick wall, that's Brandon. He could find the slightest weakness in a person's confidence, looks, or coordination. Then Brandon would expose that weakness until the object of his scorn cracked open and fell apart.

I couldn't stop myself. I turned to see why Brandon shouted. The other students hung out and schmoozed. But not Brandon. He and his sidekick, Derek, shouted accusations at a kid. Derek grabbed a football from another student and tossed the ball to Brandon. He began pounding the kid with it. The kid getting pounded arched his back and covered his head in self-defense. Conversations ended, and everyone's attention shifted to Brandon. Each time Brandon threw the ball at his target, Derek picked it up and threw it back for more. Derek egged Brandon on and laughed. School rules did not allow such bullying, of course, but Brandon and Derek didn't care.

I gasped. My fists clenched.

The kid getting pounded? My friend Lucas.

I ran. And yelled, "Knock it off, Brandon! Lucas hasn't done anything to you. Leave him alone."

The schoolyard fell quiet. Everyone watched to see who dared to challenge the infamous bullies.

Anger rose like a volcano in me. White-hot heat, ready to erupt. Lucas spun. Our eyes met. He caught his breath— shocked, I guess, to see me at school. I stopped and gave him a quick nod.

Brandon smirked. "So you wanna be next, punk?" He took a menacing step, jabbing a finger toward me. "You try to tell me what to do, and you know you're gonna get hurt." Brandon caught the ball when Derek tossed it back to him.

Derek laughed and swaggered over to Brandon. He shouted for all to hear, "Yeah, Michael, you dumb jerk! You can't tell us not to hurt anybody. You're the one who shot your little brother. You're the murderer." His lips curled in an evil smile. "Michael Murderer." The bullies exchanged a high five.

Derek's words hit me like a wrecking ball. Tension hung heavy in the air. Every eye stared at the tear trickling down my cheek. Derek looked at Brandon and they fist-bumped. Then they strutted toward me, shoulder to shoulder. The volcano in me returned even stronger, ready to erupt. My heart raced in anticipation of a fight. I pushed Derek's devastating comments from my mind and braced for a physical attack.

From ten feet away, Brandon wound up to throw the ball in my face. I cringed and covered. The school kids took a collective gasp.

He faked the throw.

The bullies bent over, laughing. The onlooking crowd giggled, and I saw embarrassment on their faces.

My body sagged. My anger dissolved like powder blown away in the breeze.

Derek walked by and hit me in the chest with his forearm. Brandon followed and dropped the ball at my feet. They walked away laughing. I gave the ball a swift kick across the yard into the far corner.

My classmates turned their backs and whispered to each other. No one spoke to me or Lucas.

I stumbled back to my corner. Lucas followed without a word and leaned against the fence alongside me, his face buried in his hands.

The bully's words rang in my mind and stabbed my heart. Me? A murderer? Everyone in the school yard heard Derek's accusation. Could it be true?

CHAPTER TEN

Afternoon and evening, Monday, April 21, 1997

When I arrived home from school, Mom sat at the kitchen table. Messy hair stuck out from under her rumpled baseball cap. She wore the same scruffy tracksuit she had on when I left that morning. I wondered how long she had been sitting there, staring out the back window.

She turned in my direction and mustered a slight smile. "Everything go okay today?"

"Yeah, it went fine." I couldn't tell her what happened. The bully's attack would make her even sadder. "So, did you have a good day, Mom?" I asked, even though I didn't want to know.

"Okay, I guess." She stood and shuffled to the sink with her cup. She rinsed it without looking back. "A friend from work stopped by on her lunch break. I got a few phone calls. Not much going on."

"Glad you had a restful day."

She turned to grab her purse from the kitchen counter. "I'm

going to the grocery store, then to get some takeout for dinner. Be back in a little while."

I didn't feel like talking, so I just grunted. I grabbed a snack from the pantry and headed down the hallway to my room. On the way I stopped at Jacob's door to check on him. Then I dropped my head. No one there.

My room—a welcome retreat. I stumbled inside and shoved the door closed. The clock radio provided background music while I started my homework. I needed to catch up after missing a week of school. The bullies' attack invaded my thoughts and interrupted my focus. My heart pounded each time Brandon and Derek came to mind. I pushed those thoughts away, trying to focus on my assignments. But my attempt to push the pain away failed.

That evening, after another quiet dinner with Mom, we hung out in the den. She read her book and I watched television. That worked for me because I didn't want to talk. At nine thirty, Mom went to her room, and I gave up and headed to bed. But sleep seemed miles away.

As I lay there restless, my mind raced. Derek's words flashed through my brain like ambulance strobe lights: "Michael, you dumb jerk! You can't tell us not to hurt anybody. You're the one who shot your little brother. You're the murderer. Michael Murderer."

The questions started again, punctuated by the image of Jacob's eyes while he lay dying.

I tried to calm myself by imagining a walk on the beach in our old hometown. But the seagulls and the waves kept crying, "Jerk." I pictured the baseball thumping against the house when I played ball-on-the-wall. But the ball and glove whispered, "Murderer."

At ten thirty I got out of bed, my T-shirt soaked with sweat from a lingering nightmare. I allowed myself a vigorous shake of the head to clear my brain, then slipped into my jeans and tennis shoes, changed my shirt, and tiptoed down the hallway. I didn't have a clue where to go but knew I couldn't lie in bed any longer. The front steps provided some shelter, so I sat and let the night breeze refresh my sweaty face. A few minutes later, Mr. Charlie's garage light flipped on and glowed across the flower bed into our yard.

With a deep sigh, I forced myself to look. The Jacob tree stood silent, glowing in the light from next door. I turned my face away. Sadness flooded my heart. I tried, but I couldn't resist looking. My gaze returned to the magnolia and the pine straw under it. The vision of Jacob lying there bleeding overtook me. I had to move. I stood and stretched. Maybe I could take a quick walk up the street.

But the tree overcame my resistance. I headed straight for it. The bird's nest perched overhead. With every ounce of determination, I avoided looking at the pine straw beneath. Grief threatened to reach up and grab me. So I focused on the stars. The image of Jacob looking at me loomed from above. I stared into his eyes.

I gasped and spun. Something had touched me on the shoulder. Mr. Charlie stood there with an embarrassed grin on his face. I let out a sigh of relief. "Mr. Charlie, you scared me to death. What are you doing out here?"

"I saw you standing here and wondered the same thing. It's late, you know. You okay?" He squinted into my face. "I saw you get on the school bus today. How did that go, being back at school?"

I looked away. "Awful. I thought I could handle it, but I couldn't."

"Oh no. I'm so sorry." He looked away and shook his head. "How did your friends react?"

"My friends ignored me. But the school bullies sure didn't." I glanced back at the tree and shuffled my feet. "So, what are you doing out in the garage this late?"

"Well, with my wife's cancer, I don't get to do chores until she's in bed. And to be honest, after caring for her all day, I need some time to myself."

"Is she okay?"

"Some days are good, others are bad. Today . . . very rough."

"I'm sorry. How long has she been sick?"

"The doctors diagnosed her with breast cancer about two years ago. Watching her go through this is a long, hard road. But she's a tough one." A slow smile spread across his face, and he pointed toward the bird nest. With a note of sarcasm in his voice, he said, "We're both tough old birds. And we're not giving up."

I chuckled. "How in the world do you keep going? Don't you get tired?"

He shrugged. "We both get tired, but we keep believing."

"Believing? In what?"

He looked into my eyes. "Oh . . . believing in lots of things. Believing God is real and cares for us. Believing the treatments will make her better. Believing the two of us are strong enough to see this through." He paused and looked thoughtful. "I've been meaning to ask you something. What kind of music do you like?"

"I like a little of everything. Mostly, I listen to the local Top 40 radio station and my rock CDs . . . Van Halen, Motley Crue, KISS, Ozzy. Why do you ask?"

"My wife and I have a song that's been our theme through this cancer thing. I'll let you borrow it. Maybe you'll hear something to help you know you're not facing this alone."

I chuckled at the thought. Mr. Charlie suggesting a song to me? How would he know what speaks to a teenager? I decided I'd go along with it just for fun. "Sure, I'll give it a listen sometime if you don't mind lending it. I'll do my best to take care of it."

"Alrighty then. We night owls gotta get some sleep, so follow me."

We strolled down the driveway into the garage. I waited while he stepped into their kitchen. When he returned, he held a small plastic case containing a cassette tape.

"It's the one called 'You're Never Alone.' Let me know what you think."

I accepted the case and stared at the cassette inside. Years of handling had worn away the print, proof this song held special meaning for them. I smiled. "Thanks, Mr. Charlie."

He smiled back and yawned. "Now, you scoot back home and get some sleep. Those bullies won't go away anytime soon. But you'll figure out how to handle them. We'll talk later."

I smiled and gave him a thumbs-up. "Thanks for coming out in the dark to check on me. I guess I needed to talk to somebody after all."

He nodded and patted my shoulder, turned, and walked in the kitchen door.

I headed back home.

The Jacob tree still shone in the garage light. But this time, I felt no need to look. When I reached my front door, Mr. Charlie's garage light went out. I headed to my room, undressed, and climbed back into bed.

Sleep overtook me in about ten minutes. I woke up once during the night, shaken awake by another dream. This one I remembered. In my dream, the tree called out my name.

But the voice belonged to Jacob.

CHAPTER ELEVEN

Mom's Journal: Entry Three- Tuesday morning, April 22, 1997

Good morning, Jacob. I need to apologize. In my last journal post, I said, "Eternity separates us."

Not true. You will always be here with me. And I will always be here for you. When I wrote that last post, I felt confused and uncertain about what's real and what's not. So I said, "Another day, I'll figure out how to cope with eternity. Not now."

At the time, my feelings refused to be organized. The constant pain defied my understanding. My head hurt round the clock. My body ached. Emotion and confusion swirled through my mind and never let up. Like the real estate market I attempt to manage every day, my feelings rode high, then plunged into the depths. Back and forth, day to day, hour by hour.

I shared my pain with Mr. Charlie's pastor after the funeral. He handed me a brochure about grief. I gave it a quick scan yesterday. The title of the pamphlet read "The Five Stages of Grief: Denial, Anger, Depression, Bargaining, and Acceptance." I tore it up, crumpled up the pieces, and put it in the trash. Gone for good, out of my life. I don't need somebody giving me a neat outline for my pain. My grief won't fit into their categories.

So, I stepped back and took a deep breath . . . your favorite saying of mine, right? My solution? Eternity is not real. Death is not real. You are here. I refuse to let you go.

See? Your mother is taking care of the situation. Isn't this an excellent solution? I think so. And once I came to that conclusion, the weight of eternity lifted from my heart. Relief flooded my soul.

Here's the plan: I'll keep your room untouched. I haven't been back inside yet. The door is half open just like you left it. But to me it is closed. Locked.

I stood in the dark hallway yesterday afternoon and ventured to look into your room. The glow of sunset through the window cast shadows inside. I smiled at the sight of your clothes lying on your chair. Your video game controller is on your desk. Your pillow holds the impression of your head. I promise not to touch anything. Because you live there. You are my son, and I am your mother. My heart will keep you alive.

I know you are okay with that plan. How do I know? I just do. Moms understand what no one else knows. Why would you want to live anywhere else, be anywhere else, do anything else?

So you are here. For eternity. Your mom is always

here for you. And we'll always be together.

I have it all figured out now. I have our solution. No booklet about grief needed.

Your dad always said I'm too analytical. His sarcastic pet name for me is "the little engineer." I hate that. But you know what? I say that's my strength.

Now, I've engineered eternity. The gunshot is not real. Your death is not real. Separation for eternity is not real. There it is. That's my plan.

Plus . . . I engineered a little extra help from a doctor. I called and got an appointment at a family practice. We never had one, didn't need one . . . until now. They gave me an emergency appointment. I confess, I told them our story, and they bumped me to the front of the list. So I went late this afternoon. The doctor listened and empathized. Then she prescribed something to help.

The prescription should help calm the storm and smooth some waves. I'm confident this med will work hand in hand with my analytical strength. I'll be in control of my thoughts and feelings again. At least my emotions will be normal, even if nothing else is normal. Like I said, your mother is taking care of the situation.

Michael doesn't know about the appointment . . . or the prescription. I told him I had to go get groceries. After I saw the doctor, I got the prescription filled at the grocery store. Then I picked up some dinner there, just like I told Michael. Smart, right?

See, I'm not a liar. You boys can trust your mom.

So, here we are. You and me. In this house. In this life. Together. We'll talk, we'll live, we'll walk through our days, hand in hand. I already feel your hand in mine.

You will always be my son, and I will always be your mom. No one can take this from us.

No bullet can stop my heart beating for you.

I love you, Jacob. For eternity.

CHAPTER TWELVE

Morning and afternoon, Tuesday, April 22, 1997

The next day at school, Lucas wandered over to my corner of the schoolyard after lunch. We exchanged a nod and settled into uncomfortable silence.

After a minute, he broke the quiet. His words dripped out like pancake syrup. "I'm kinda surprised you came back to school yesterday. But I sure am glad you came to my rescue. Thanks for getting Brandon off me."

"You're welcome." I looked up at my friend and smiled. "How are you?"

"I'm okay. I got some nice bruises on my back from that football, though."

"Yeah, Brandon and Derek are brutes."

Lucas glanced over his shoulder. "I've been avoiding them all day. I saw them in the hallway, but I made a quick turn and hid."

"You should be safe now. They always move on to another target."

"Yeah, maybe." He spat on the ground and looked back at

me. "But you and I both know they'll get back around to us. Just a matter of time. Nobody's safe."

I kicked the chain-link fence several times and wondered when our number would come up again.

Lucas looked down and cleared his throat. "How did you handle coming back to school yesterday? I mean, besides what happened with the bullies?"

"Weird. Nobody spoke to me. They said nothing. Just stared. It felt strange, like an out-of-focus movie or something."

Lucas stood up straight. "Well, of course it's weird." He threw his hands out and emphasized each word. "None of us knows what to say to you. Plus, we're afraid we'll say the wrong thing." He relaxed his arms but continued to stare.

I shrugged. "Yeah. I guess so."

A sudden surge of anger rose in my chest. I jerked my head around, face-to-face with Lucas. "Mean old Derek. He sure didn't worry about saying the wrong thing, did he?" The intensity of my voice shocked me. "I couldn't even sleep last night. His words kept replaying in my brain. So I gave up on sleep, got dressed, and went out to the tree where it happened."

Lucas shot me a look of surprise. "Whoa. That must have been tough."

I took a deep breath. "Yeah, spooky, for sure. But I couldn't help it. Some invisible hand pulled me out there. Then Mr. Charlie walked up behind me and touched me on the shoulder. I almost jumped out of my skin. Freaked me out."

"Wow. What was he doing out there in the middle of the night?"

"Working in his garage. He saw me by the tree. So he walked out to see what brought me out in the yard so late." I turned and leaned back on the fence. "We talked a few minutes, and he gave me a song on an old cassette tape. He said this song might help me believe things are gonna work out." I shook my head. "But we don't have a tape player anymore. I asked Mom this morning.

She donated it to the Salvation Army when we moved." I draped my arms over the fence and stared out across the parking lot. "I guess I'll take the tape back to him."

Lucas leaned beside me. "I have a tape player. We could listen to the song together." He looked me in the eye and waited for my response.

I turned away. What if the song made no sense or I hated the style? I wouldn't know what to say to Mr. Charlie. So I didn't answer.

Lucas scooted closer and dropped his voice. "If you don't want to hear it, I'll listen to it myself, without you. Then I'll report back. Does that work?"

"I don't know." I let out a slow breath. "Well . . . maybe I should give it to you and let you check it out. Then you can tell me if you think it's any good."

"Okay." He tried to look uncaring but couldn't hide his curiosity. "I'll come to your house this afternoon and get it."

I gave him a thumbs-up. We headed to class.

"Mom, I'm home!" I shouted when I came through the front door.

No answer.

I went to my room and dropped my bookbag, walked into the kitchen, and crossed to the back door. She sat in a lawn chair in the middle of the porch, her back toward me.

I stepped onto the porch. "Mom, I'm home." I walked around the chair. A closed magazine lay in her lap. She stared at the bird feeder mounted on the corner of the porch.

With a slow smile, she lifted her head, squinting at me. "Hey, honey. I'm just watching my birds. Glad you're home." She refocused her gaze on the feeder and paused uncomfortably. When she continued, her words slurred. "That wren keeps knocking the birdseed out of the feeder. The doves must be paying him extra. They just walk around the porch eating what he scatters." She giggled. "A little while ago, a titmouse, a house finch, and a family of cardinals kept me company." Still smiling, Mom turned and gazed at me.

A strange sensation rippled through my chest. I struggled to recognize this lady sitting in my backyard. Something about her seemed different. I wasn't sure what. I shook it off and went on, "That's cool, Mom. You relax and talk to your birds. Lucas is coming over in a little while."

She nodded, with that goofy smile stuck on her face. "That's good. He's a great friend. But you boys be careful, okay? Real careful." She waved me over, gave me a big hug, and held me tight for a few seconds.

When she released her grasp, I stood and looked down at her. She had already returned to watching the birds. I shook my head and went inside, then grabbed a soft drink from the fridge and went to my room. Mr. Charlie's cassette tape lay on my desk, where I left it last night. I flopped onto the bed and started today's homework.

An hour later, movement caught my eye outside the bedroom window. Lucas ambled across our yard toward the front door. When the front doorbell rang, I grabbed the cassette and headed down the hallway. I opened the door and held out the tape.

Lucas stood there with a blank look without taking the tape. "Come over and listen to the song with me."

"What?"

"Come on." His face remained expressionless. "Don't you even want to know what it says? It must be an antique if Mr. Charlie has it. It might be like a trip back in time or something." Lucas waited and crossed his arms.

I snickered and took a deep breath. "Okay, dude, you got me. I'll come over. We'll listen to it together. Besides, if I let you listen first, you might try to sing it to me. I couldn't take that." I shoved him with a laugh, then shouted to Mom that I would be at Lucas's house.

The path to the farmhouse felt familiar now. We settled into a comfortable conversation. But a haunting awareness lingered in the back of my mind. Jacob walked with me the last time I came this way. I avoided the thought with all the strength I could summon. The comfort of having a friend like Lucas helped.

When we walked out of the woods into his yard, I asked, "Are we going inside to listen to the tape?"

"No way. Mom doesn't want us in the house, remember?"

"So where is the tape player?"

Lucas stopped walking and faced me, his look solemn. "You know where it is. It's the boom box in the attic, over the garage. We listened to the radio when—"

I turned my back on him. "Oh man. I can't do that. The attic . . ." Tears welled and emotion clutched my throat.

Lucas tapped me on the shoulder and waited. I swallowed hard. After about a minute, I faced him again. He extended his hand and I handed him the tape. He resumed walking toward the garage.

My heart convulsed like Jackie Chan had kicked me in the chest. I stood still and watched Lucas walk away. Looking to the heavens, I shook my head in disbelief. Then I followed him.

He walked into the garage, grabbed the rope to the trapdoor, and pulled. I took a deep breath and stared into the darkness looming overhead. For a moment, I heard Jacob's laughter echo from above. A shudder went through my body. Deep inside my soul, I found the courage to follow Lucas up the steps.

CHAPTER THIRTEEN

Afternoon and evening, Tuesday, April 22, 1997

The train track lay in the same spot we left it. Jacob's log station stood quiet, keeping watch alongside. Our block bridge still spanned the track around the bend. Stupid Baby sprawled beside the derailed train and stared at me.

My eyes locked on the doll. Emotions too many to name raced through my soul. Memories of Jacob's laughter echoed through the old attic into my heart.

Lucas stepped beside me and held out the cassette. "You wanna hear the song?"

Words wouldn't come. I nodded.

He kneeled beside the old boombox, opened the plastic case, and removed the tape. With the two holes balanced on his first and second fingers, he studied it.

I muttered, "What's it say?"

"Hard to tell. The print is just about worn away. Looks like a guy's name on it. Bryan something. I can't tell. Mr. Charlie and his wife must play it a lot."

A quick push of the eject button and the tape holder popped open. He inserted the tape.

"Maybe it'll work. We'll see."

I remained standing. "Mr. Charlie said it's the last song on side two. Number nine, maybe."

Lucas peered through the window of the cassette player. "Looks like he left the tape set on that song for you."

"Wait." I leaned down. "I'll do it." I pressed the play button and raised the volume.

The spindles turned inside the window. Music filled the attic. Lucas and I sat cross-legged on the rug beside the model train and listened. The guy on the tape began singing.

The words spilled out of the stereo and washed over me:

Though smiling, you silently weep in perfect disguise.
So clear by the distance you keep, protected by lies.
And me with so little to say, what can I do?
Lost to know how I should pray. Hurting for you.
No matter how hopeless it feels, you're never alone.

At the instrumental break in the middle, Lucas looked up. "Kinda old-style, isn't it? You sure Mr. Charlie said it's the last song on the tape?"

I nodded. "I'm sure that's what he said."

The singer started again. I focused my attention on the words, looking for a message in the lyrics.

You're never alone. You're never alone. That's all I know
to say.

Over and over I heard, "You're never alone." I shook my head and sighed. "I'm not sure what that means. When I return the tape, I'll ask Mr. Charlie."

The song ended, and Lucas hit the stop button. "I'm not sure either. Cool music, though."

I struggled to my feet. "Yeah, but right now I need to go home. This place and that song have me spooked." I shuddered.

Lucas stood, stretched his legs, and headed for the ladder. While he climbed down, I looked around.

I felt heartbroken to be back here. And my heart broke even more to leave. When Lucas disappeared down the steps, I grabbed Stupid Baby and shoved her in my jacket pocket. I didn't know why. But I knew I couldn't leave her in the darkness of this cold, dusty attic. Back in the garage, I said goodbye and thanked Lucas for helping me with the song. I headed home.

Dread rose in my chest. Mom's recent state of mind had me very suspicious. I snuck in the front door and peeked into the kitchen. My mouth dropped open. Mom had prepared dinner and sat at the table waiting.

She smiled and stood to give me a hug. She had changed clothes and combed her hair. I felt relieved.

"Wow, Mom, you fixed dinner. Thanks."

She patted my shoulder. "Yep, I hope you like it. Go wash up."

On the way down the hall, I glanced back to make sure Mom hadn't followed. Then I swung into my room and took Stupid Baby from my jacket pocket. The top shelf of my desk made a perfect perch for her to watch over me. I hurried to the bathroom and washed my hands and face.

Dinner tasted delicious. Beef stew and rice with fresh veggies —my favorite. The tension between us melted away while we ate. This felt like old times. Except without Jacob.

Then, during dinner, Mom took a medicine bottle from her purse. She swallowed the pill with a swig of iced tea and went back to eating.

"What medicine are you taking, Mom? Are you hurting . . . or sick?"

She smiled but didn't look up. "This is just a little medication the doctor at the hospital suggested I take when he told us about Jacob. He said these will help ease the pain of the weeks ahead. I'll be fine. Eat your dinner."

I stared at her, concerned. She kept eating, acting as if nothing had happened. Could she be hiding something—or worse, lying?

"So, is that why you've been so goofy lately? From the pills?"

Her fork hit the plate with a loud clink when she dropped it. She glared and shouted, "Listen, mister, you don't need to worry about me! And you have no right to question your mother and call me goofy. I can handle this. So step back and take a deep breath right now. Got it?" Her intense stare resumed, and I squirmed to avoid it.

I raised my hands in surrender and leaned back in my chair. "Yes, ma'am. I got it."

She sniffed and looked away. In humiliation, I lowered my head. Her reaction shocked me. But in a weird way, I felt glad she cared enough to defend herself.

We didn't speak to each other for the rest of the meal.

When we cleared the dishes, Mom stopped. She stood still, looking at me with raised eyebrows. *What just happened? I wondered.*

"By the way," she said, "I got a call from your dad today. He wants to drive over here tomorrow and talk to you after school."

"Dad? Drive over here?" I frowned. "That's strange."

"Well, you know your dad." A smirk crept across her face. "He thinks he's the only one smart enough to figure out what happened to Jacob. And who's at fault." She walked to the sink to load the dishwasher.

I held my plate, stunned. "Dad didn't hear what the sheriff said about it being an accident?"

She picked up a dish and turned to me before placing it on

the rack. "Oh yeah. He heard. He's determined to blame me anyway." She stuck the plate in and mumbled under her breath, "And don't expect your dad to drop this."

CHAPTER FOURTEEN

Wednesday Afternoon, April 23, 1997

When I got off the school bus the next day, Dad's sports car sat in our driveway. Dread and curiosity began a tug-o-war in me while I walked down the street.

I stopped on the porch and swallowed.

Dad's success came from real estate investment. He and Mom met when their companies collaborated on a big corporate deal. Mom served as office manager, while Dad led the office in sales every year. Dad always pursued the next cool thing on the horizon. I guess he didn't consider me and Mom cool anymore.

Determined to be strong, I walked through the front door. Quiet but angry voices came from the kitchen. I stopped right inside the foyer, held the front door from slamming, and listened.

Dad spoke just above a whisper, in an intense and threatening tone. Phrases like "skeletons in your closet," "pressuring the sheriff to reopen the case," "involving the state law enforcement division," and most shocking of all, "you'll end up in prison."

Enough. I couldn't bear to listen to another word. I slammed the front door and called out, "Hey, I'm home." After waiting a couple of seconds, I stepped into the kitchen.

Dad and Mom sat across from each other at the kitchen table. Anger lined her face. But Dad's expression looked downright scary. Despite the tension, I strolled up to the table and stood between them. Mom wouldn't look my way.

Dad stood with a fake smile. He reached to tousle my hair. I dipped my head to dodge him. Hey, I wasn't a little kid anymore. He laughed, then extended his right hand to me.

I shook with the strongest grip I could manage. "Good to see you, Dad. When did you get here?"

"About fifteen minutes ago, I guess."

Mom stood and hugged me. I could tell she meant to assure Dad of our strong relationship. An interesting move, considering our tense exchange last night. She exhaled a deep breath and hurried to the stove. "You two can go to Michael's room and talk. I'll get dinner ready."

Dad motioned toward the hallway. "Let's go to your room, son. We'll hang out for a little while." His tone seemed too casual. I knew he had an ulterior motive. But I agreed, and he followed me out the kitchen door.

When we entered my room, Dad noticed Stupid Baby on the top shelf. "What's with this baby doll? You playing with dolls now?" He laughed and took a soft jab at my shoulder.

Looking away, I felt my heartbeat kick into high gear. "No, it's not mine." I returned a jab to his shoulder but hit him harder than I meant to. "It's a consolation prize for a video game I play with my friends. We call it Stupid Baby. The loser keeps the doll until we play the next round." Proud of my lie, I tried to keep my voice from shaking. I fought back the emotion and covered myself with a smile. "Sounds weird, but don't worry. No sissies here. I'm not playing with dolls." Hoping against all odds he would change the subject, I took a step back and sat on the edge of my bed.

He pulled out my desk chair and straddled it backward with his hands crossed over the back. "Since we missed talking together at the funeral last week, I wanted to come by. Are you okay, son?"

I almost said that Mom and I weren't talking much either. But I caught myself. No need to throw her under the bus. "Yeah, I'm okay. My friends at school ignore me, but that's understandable. They don't know what to say. So I stay strong for Mom and try to be the good kid you taught me to be." I smiled. "I'm making it through, step by step." I looked to see if he bought my explanation.

The razor-sharp look Dad used to intimidate competitors now zeroed in on me. He scooted closer, hands overlapped with fingers interlocked on the back of the chair. "Well, you know me. I'm not afraid to talk about tough things. So, tell me what happened the day Jacob died. And don't try to be strong and protect your mother. I want to know every detail about your brother getting shot." His index finger began tapping on the back of his other hand, ticking off the seconds.

I shrugged, attempting to sound casual. "Who knows what happened that day? It all went by so fast." Looking into his dark eyes with every ounce of my will, I held my gaze steady.

Dad's laser look burned into my soul.

I hated it when Dad did this. Who would flinch first in this game of chicken? He always won. And of course, he won again today. I forged ahead. "Mom shot the snake. Jacob jumped in and grabbed the gun. The three of us had a tug-o-war. The gun went off. Jacob got shot in the chest. It killed him. I don't know what else to say." I raked my fingers through my hair and looked at my shoes. "What do you want from me?"

Dad spit his reply in rapid-fire style. "How many shots were fired? The neighbor who called 911 reported he heard four shots. But the detective found one bullet missing from the gun cylinder. Somebody's hiding something."

I raised my head and huffed in frustration. "No way, Dad. Mom only fired twice at the snake. Then Jacob jumped in, and the gun went off . . ." But my voice faltered and my sentence faded to silence.

He didn't flinch. "So who pulled the trigger?"

I managed to keep my voice quiet but intense. "I. Don't. Know. I just told you, everything happened so fast. Just a blur. Maybe I pulled the trigger. It could have been Mom. Or even Jacob. But the shooting had to be an accident. A crazy, stupid accident." My voice rose in pitch, overcoming my futile attempt to control it. "You saw the sheriff's report. There's no way Mom or I would shoot Jacob on purpose. I'm sure you know that, don't you?" My volume rose another notch. I shouted, "Why can't you let it go, Dad?"

He slid back a little and dropped his arms off the chair. His eyes never left mine. "Are you certain, beyond doubt, you are not missing any details? Completely sure?"

I took a deep breath and met his glare. I whispered with intensity, "Yes, Dad, I am absolutely certain." When he looked away, I tried to catch my breath.

He sniffed, refocused on me, and hammered his fists on his thick thighs. "Well, I am livid. To think your mother would hide an unprotected gun in a bedside table drawer." I rolled my eyes and threw my hands out, but he forged ahead. "Unimaginable. How stupid is that? If I had known, I would have bought her a gun safe. Or a cable lock to secure it."

His fists beat the back of the chair in rhythm with his next words. "This is so irresponsible of her . . . to leave a gun lying around like that." He looked at the ceiling. The room fell silent except for the sound of his heavy breathing. He refocused his laser-like eyes, burning into mine. His voice rose, and he slapped the back of the chair for emphasis. "I believe your mother had her finger on the trigger."

I stood. "Dad! Please! Give it up!" I stormed out of the room.

When I rushed into the hallway, I collided with Mom. Shocked, I reached out to keep her from falling backward. Realization hit me hard. She had been listening from the bathroom across the hall in the dark.

Meanwhile, I heard the desk chair topple and fall onto the floor behind me, then Dad hustled to catch up. Mom recovered, pushed me aside, and scooted into the kitchen.

I spun to face Dad when he burst through my bedroom doorway into the hall. We stood facing each other in a stalemate. Relief swept over me despite the face-off. Realization dawned that he had not seen Mom eavesdropping.

But before I could seize control, anger overwhelmed me again. I lost it and yelled into Dad's stone-faced expression. "Jacob's shooting runs through my mind a million times a day! I hardly sleep at night. The memory of his eyes haunts me every waking hour." I made a half turn, facing Jacob's door. My voice trembled. "Here's the thing, Dad. Who ran inside? Who got the gun? Not Mom. Not Jacob." I turned back to him. "If anyone is to blame, it's me." I jabbed my chest with my thumbs. My shout echoed up the hallway. "Meeeee!"

A violent sob ambushed me from behind. Dad stepped back with raised eyebrows. My hands covered my face. I collapsed backward, crumpled against the wall, and struggled to catch my breath. I wept while convulsions wracked my body.

After a few seconds that seemed to last an eternity, Dad leaned across the space between us and put his hand on my shoulder. "Okay, buddy, I believe you. It's okay. Thanks for leveling with me. This has been a terrible thing for all of us." He looked away. "I'm sorry it's come to this. But it can't end this way with you blaming yourself. I'll handle it."

He rubbed my shoulder, and I wiped my eyes.

My breathing slowed and became more normal. But I couldn't look at him. My voice quivered and my words faltered. "This is not how I wanted our visit to go. I just wanted to be with you. And talk." Emotional exhaustion crept through my body. "I miss you, Dad."

I looked into his face. For the first time ever, I saw tears in his eyes.

He hesitated. Then he swiveled around beside me against the wall. We stood side by side, his arm around me, and I leaned into him for support.

A full minute passed. Dad dropped his arm and retrieved his keys from his pocket. "I need to hit the road for home." He stood up straight. "Walk me to my car, okay?"

He stepped away, and I followed him down the hallway.

Before leaving, Dad took one step into the kitchen. Mom stood at the stove, stirring a steaming pot, her back toward us. "Thanks for your time, Susan. I'll call you from the road. Take care of my boy."

"Yeah, sure," Mom said without turning around. "Too bad you can't stay and eat dinner with us." Her sarcasm didn't go unnoticed.

Dad and I walked together out the front door and into the driveway.

We stopped by his car, and he turned to face me. "You know, your mom and I truly loved each other when we got married. But we are very different from each other. I'm driven. I want all the answers, and I want them now. Your mom, on the other hand, is analytical. She'll spend weeks exploring the details and thinking everything through. We loved each other, but our differences made for a lot of shouting. We just couldn't make it work." He frowned and looked back toward the house. "I regret that."

I shrugged but couldn't look at him. "Yeah, I know. I've tried to forget the shouting. Still . . . I just wish we could be a family again."

Dad ignored what I said and rattled his car keys, anxious to move on. I pulled back from him and stuck out my hand. We shook.

A solemn look crossed his face. "Thanks. This is not over. Regardless, I'm proud of your honesty, Michael. Take care of yourself and let me know if you need anything. I'm here for you."

I wondered how he could be here for me, yet three hours away at the same time. But I hugged him anyway. He stepped away and slid into his car. The engine purred with a quiet roar.

"Talk soon," he shouted through the sunroof and backed out of the driveway.

I waved goodbye, then folded my arms across my chest to protect my heart from further damage.

He gunned the engine up the hill. I watched the car slip around the corner. When the soft roar faded, I trudged back into the house.

Mom stood at the stove, stirring a pot. With a fierce turn, she faced me when I entered the kitchen. She snarled, "Isn't it a shame we had such a short time together?" Her tone stretched like a rubber band at its breaking point. "Such a fun little game of finger-pointing and accusation. Isn't your dad the most wonderful, caring man?"

I watched and waited.

She picked up the metal lid and slammed it on the pot. "So he tried to corner you into saying I pulled the trigger, did he?" Her tone seethed with anger. "How nice of him to drop by and offer such warm condolences. I guarantee you that we've not heard the last from him." She ripped off her apron and stomped across the kitchen. "Enough. I'm done. I'm going to take a pill and go to bed."

I took a quick step toward her. "Mom, no. You can't keep taking those pills. Social Services is gonna find out and take me away from you."

She halted and screamed at the top of her voice, "Oh sure! Like that's going to happen. I'm a good mom. And don't you forget it."

She wound up and hurled the apron at the kitchen chair where Dad sat. She grabbed her pill bottle from the table and stormed up the hallway.

I called out before she could escape, "Remember, step back and take a deep breath, Mom. I love you."

The bedroom door slammed.

I stood motionless in the empty kitchen. The pot on the stove hissed, and I turned. Steam billowed upward. I trotted over and lifted the lid.

Nothing in it but boiling water.

CHAPTER FIFTEEN

Wednesday Evening, April 23, 1997

Clouds moved in after Dad left. A steady rainfall started thirty minutes later.

At the kitchen table, I stared at the half-eaten sandwich I made for myself. The whole confrontation with Dad and then Mom's reaction left my stomach feeling like a raging volcano.

Mom kept to herself, locked in her room in silence. My mind remained captive to the aftershock of this afternoon. I opened the back window a crack just to have some sound in the room. The rain dripping off the roof onto the back porch measured each second. I wanted to scream.

The phone rang in Mom's bedroom. Probably Dad calling from the road—most likely from a pay phone at some fancy little restaurant on his way home. I snuck down the hall to listen. The hushed conversation sounded tense, followed by an abrupt silence. Then the sound of the phone slammed into the base. I tiptoed back to the kitchen table.

In a funk, I nibbled on the last half of my sandwich. I thought about playing some video games or watching TV. Not interested. Mom's bedroom phone rang again while I put my paper plate and cup in the trash. I didn't bother to sneak a listen this time. I knew she lay seething in the darkness of her room, her pain muted by a pill.

After dinner, I worked on my homework for an hour and a half. Darkness came earlier than usual because of the rain. After finishing my assignments, I packed my bookbag for tomorrow. Nothing else to do but sit and mope. After grabbing my rain jacket, I headed out the front door and stood on the porch. Raindrops splashed in a steady rhythm at my feet. Thunder echoed across the distant hills and reverberated in my empty heart. The conversation with Dad and my confrontation with Mom replayed in my mind. I let them play, despite the repeated punches in the chest they gave me.

Mr. Charlie's garage light clicked on, washing our yards in light again. His cassette tape needed to be returned. I retrieved it from my bedroom. Stopping at Mom's door, I called out, "Mom, I'm going to Mr. Charlie's. Okay?"

Silence, as expected.

Pulling my heavy rain jacket around me felt secure and safe. I lifted my hood as I left the porch, then ran through the rain with the cassette tucked in my pocket.

Dodging the raindrops distracted me from the tree. I entered the garage at a gallop and brushed the rain from my jacket. Charlie glanced up and greeted me with his usual upbeat attitude. I managed a half-smile and walked around to the front of his car.

A jumbled mess of yard tools hung on the side walls, with storage bins stacked in corners. But a well-organized workbench stood along the wall in front of the car. He had placed a kitchen chair upside down on the workbench. A pair of worn-out reading glasses sat perched on his nose.

I stepped closer. "What are you doing to the chair?"

"This old kitchen chair is falling apart. The support rungs are pulling right out of the legs. I must be overloading it. A diet might be in my future. Ya think?" He looked at me in that old-man way he had when he joked. His comical smile made me laugh despite my mood.

With his screwdriver, he reamed out the dried glue that once held the chair rung. Without looking up, he asked, "Did I see your dad's car in the driveway today?"

"Yep."

He raised his head. Curiosity lined his face, the screwdriver frozen in hand. "So what's up?"

"Dad wanted to grill Mom and me about the accident."

Mr. Charlie whistled. He tossed the screwdriver aside, perturbed. The screwdriver slid off the bench and clanged onto the floor. He turned to me with a raised eyebrow. "Doesn't your dad know the sheriff ruled it an accident? They dismissed the case. Hasn't anybody told him?" He sighed, bent over, and retrieved the screwdriver from the floor.

I shrugged. "Sure, Dad knows all that. And I reminded him again today. But he wanted to hear what happened in my own words. He still wants to blame somebody."

Mr. Charlie's eyebrows drew down. "Well, you know . . . he lost a son. That's gotta be tough. He's trying to express his grief the only way he knows how. I imagine he's questioning a lot of things." He stared out the garage door at the rain. "Your dad might feel guilty himself. We just don't know. Who can tell?"

I winced. "Whoa. I hadn't thought of all this from Dad's point of view." I sighed. "But I'm not sure what anybody feels. Much less what I feel myself."

Mr. Charlie turned to the chair and continued scraping. "How did your mom react to your dad's questions?"

"Not good. Really ticked. She eavesdropped on our talk. She overheard what Dad said."

He glanced over the top of his reading glasses. "And what did he say?"

"Well . . . Dad thinks Mom pulled the trigger."

Mr. Charlie stepped back and his eyebrows shot up. "That's a serious charge."

"Yep. Like I said, Dad's obsessed with blaming somebody."

"How did your mom handle that accusation?"

"She got really quiet—the way she does when she's upset to the max. Kind of like a steaming pot."

Mr. Charlie shook his head and rotated back toward the workbench. The scraping sound filled the garage again.

I took his cassette tape from my jacket pocket and held it up. "I brought this back. Thanks for lending it to me."

He took it from me, laid it on the workbench, and went back to work on the chair. "You're welcome. Did you listen to the song?"

I tried to think of a way to change the subject, but nothing came. So I told him about the cassette player in the attic and how we listened to the song there.

"And what did you think about it?" He glanced at me sideways and waited for my answer.

I dreaded the conversation but knew I couldn't avoid answering. "I, uh . . . I didn't understand what it meant. Nice music, though. That guy is an awesome singer." I pointed at the tape. "You must listen to that song a lot because you've worn off the print. Who is the singer?"

Mr. Charlie flipped the chair over and began work on the next rung. "His name is Bryan Duncan. A long time ago, he came to Arradale Community College to give a concert. My daughter loved his music, so she begged me to take her." He stopped and looked up. "My daughter went through a rough patch that year. She felt like an outcast at school. Kids shunned her because of her artistic nature. On top of that, the two of us couldn't get along."

"Man, I understand how that goes." I leaned back on the workbench and crossed my arms. "Did the concert help?"

"Oh yeah. To my surprise, I enjoyed the concert a lot. Bryan writes his own songs. They make you think—especially about hard times. Sounded like he had some hard times himself." Charlie grabbed a rag and wiped perspiration from his forehead. "Thankfully, the concert proved to be a turning point. My daughter and I had a breakthrough in our relationship. Things weren't perfect, but they got much better."

"Yeah, my family needs a breakthrough like that." I felt the familiar heaviness again. Did this ever let up? A teenager shouldn't have to deal with this much grief and anxiety.

Mr. Charlie nodded and went to work on the next rung. "That song, 'You're Never Alone,' helped her know God's always here for her. She played it over and over. My wife and I grew to like it too. When our daughter left for college, she wrote out the words for me. A gift from her I keep right here." He poked the screwdriver toward the wall above the workbench.

A dusty piece of notebook paper hung there, attached with weathered cellophane tape. The writing had faded, and the paper crinkled around the edges.

I stared at the old handwritten page. "This song means a lot to you, doesn't it?"

He flipped the chair right side up and examined it. "When my wife got cancer, that song became way too real. When her treatments beat us down, that song lifts us up. God hasn't abandoned us. He's here in the good times and the bad." Mr. Charlie turned toward me and leaned on the workbench, brushing his hands on his pants. "What did you say about not understanding the song?"

I felt my face flush with embarrassment. "I don't understand what the song means."

He looked up and tapped the screwdriver on the workbench. "Yeah, that's difficult for most any sixteen-year-old. But you've been through something that makes you different. So I think this song has a message for you." His eyes narrowed. Did he have a secret to reveal? He pointed the screwdriver my way. "God is always ready to help us, whatever we're facing. But we have to believe he loves us, then open our hearts and minds to his love."

I tried to sort through my thoughts and put them into words. The words took a few seconds to come. "So the song says God is here to love and help, even in bad times?"

"See, I knew you could understand." Mr. Charlie reached over and patted my shoulder.

I felt encouraged and relieved to give the right answer somehow. A smile spread across my face.

He gave an energetic nod and grinned. "This song is a gift to people who have experienced a terrible tragedy. No matter where that tragedy came from. Whether they caused it themselves or it happened by chance. God still loves them and is right beside them. That's the point."

I thought about that for a few seconds—that God would care about me and be here for me, a sixteen-year-old kid with a messed-up life.

But then doubt hit me square in the back of the head. "But how can God care for me after what happened to Jacob? Seems like he would ignore me, like my school friends. Or like Dad, point an accusing finger on his way out the door."

Mr. Charlie tilted his head sideways. "You've got a point there. And I've wondered the same thing about my wife's cancer. Is her illness a punishment? Is God here for us or not? Well, the answer is in the song. It reminds us of everything God already told us in the Bible."

Mr. Charlie faced the paper taped to the wall, held his glasses up to look through the bottom of the lenses, and read aloud:

Do you need to know who cares?
Is the pain too much to bear?
You can find help on your knees
Anytime you please, 'cause He'll never turn away.
He'll never leave you, never leave you,
Always love you. You're never alone.

He removed his glasses and looked at me. "What do you think?"

I shrugged. "I'm not sure. What do you think?"

"I think God created us so he can hang out with us." He watched for my reaction.

The question I had been wondering about tumbled out. "But if God made us to hang out with him, why would he allow Jacob's death and your wife's cancer?" I bowed my head and stared at the garage floor.

"Good question. The Bible tells us God is love, right? He created us so he can love us. And He wants us to love him in return. But here's the thing . . . love always has an element of freedom. It wouldn't be genuine love if God controlled us like robots, would it?" He broke out in a terrible version of the robot dance.

I laughed at his awkward movements and funny expression. Mr. Charlie laughed at himself too.

When our laughter faded, he wiped his eyes. "Okay, think about this. Your mom loves you. But she can't force you to obey her. If she forced you to obey, your relationship would be fear, not love. God wants us to choose to love him because we're free, not forced."

I shifted my weight and listened closer.

He smiled. "Sometimes—within that God-given freedom—tragedy, accidents, sickness, and hurt occur. God doesn't cause those things to happen. But he will allow them to happen. Otherwise, God is not love, he's just a bully."

I let out a nervous chuckle. "That's awesome." But then my doubt returned. "I'm still not sure how God could let Jacob die."

Charlie looked at me with a slight smile. "When you and your mom visited our church, we prayed the Lord's Prayer, remember? 'Thy will be done on earth as it is in heaven'?"

"Yes, I remember that prayer."

His face became more serious. "God's will is always done in heaven. He's in complete control there." He shrugged. "But not here on earth. Because God gives us freedom to choose or reject him, earth is a battleground between good and evil."

I threw my hands up in protest. "But I don't want to live on a battleground. Somebody could get killed—"

Our eyes locked together. Realization hit me fast and hard. I dropped my head.

Mr. Charlie reached over and put his hand on my shoulder. "It's unfortunate, Michael, but people die all the time on this battleground called life." He paused while I wiped a tear from my cheek. "Remember, though, nothing that happens on this earth surprises God. God is all-powerful and knows everything yet loves you regardless. Every step of your life, he walks with you. You're never alone." He patted my shoulder.

When I looked into his eyes, I knew Mr. Charlie had walked with God for a long time.

CHAPTER SIXTEEN

Thursday and Friday, April 24 and 25, 1997

The next morning, I stepped into the kitchen dressed and ready for school.

"Good morning, Michael."

I tried to focus through groggy eyes, wondering, *Is this a mirage?* Mom sat at the table wearing stylish work clothes, her hair fixed and makeup done. She turned toward me and laughed at my shocked look.

I stood staring. "What's up with you this morning?"

"Well, after your dad's threatening phone call from the road last night, my boss called. She asked when I could come back to work. They need me in the office with so many homes going up for sale." I took a seat at the table, and she continued. "The more I thought about it, the more I wanted to return to normal. So I set my clock for six, got out of bed, and I'm ready for work."

"Are you sure you're ready?"

She chuckled and stood. "I asked you the same thing, didn't I? And look how well you've done. You've inspired me." She carried her mug to the sink. "Besides, if I sit around the house all day, I'll get angrier about your dad's accusation. So hurry and get ready for school. I'll drop you off."

No time to eat. I grabbed a banana and a cereal bar and hustled to my room to get my bookbag. I hoped we were back on track. But I remembered the electric train in Lucas's attic. What if we got back up to speed, then a big curve in our track knocked us flat like Stupid Baby?

Mom drove me to school—a rare occurrence. In the car, she asked me if my return to school had gone well. I broke down and told her about the bullies' attack. She offered to call the school and complain, but I begged her not to. I assured her I could handle it myself. When I hopped out of the car, she called, "I love you, Michael." I walked into the school building feeling good.

I breezed through my morning classes. A slight sense of normalcy had returned. But I watched my back, knowing the bullies lurked out there somewhere.

At lunch, I woofed down the pathetic offering in the cafeteria. Friends nodded when they passed, but no one sat with me. I headed outside to my usual corner and leaned forward against the fence with my back to the other kids, staring out across the parking lot. The sun glinted off the teachers' cars lined up in nice, neat rows.

Lucas shuffled over, dodging the puddles from the rainstorm the night before. "What's up?" he asked. He joined me, leaning with his chest against the fence.

"Dad came for a visit."

"Are you kidding me? He did what? Like . . . you just saw him at the funeral."

"Yeah. Definitely crazy. He kept pushing for details on what happened to Jacob."

Lucas took a step back. "Come on, man. I thought he knew what happened. He talked to the sheriff, right? What else does he need? Sheesh."

Tension gripped my neck. "I'm sick of everybody's questions. And now Dad's pushing me with more questions." My volume increased. "He thinks Mom did it. He thinks she isn't telling." I kicked the fence hard. "Can you believe that?"

Lucas dropped his head and let out a whistle.

I looked to the heavens, thrust my arms out, and shouted, "An accident. Just an accident, Dad."

Something whacked me in the back. I hunched my shoulders and groaned.

The voice came from right behind me. "Hey, Michael, pick up the ball. Throw it back to Derek."

I spun. Brandon leered, inches from my face. He shoved with both hands and pinned me against the fence. "You getting a little over-excited, Michael? Better shout louder. Your old man's four hours away, ya know?"

Brandon laughed a loud, exaggerated laugh. Again, the schoolyard fell silent, and everyone turned to watch.

Derek trotted over and pointed to the football lying in a puddle. "Yeah, murder man. Throw me the ball. You chicken or what?"

Brandon stood a head taller than me. Still holding my shoulders, he thrust his chest against my face. Pinned against the fence, I felt pain shoot down my spine.

I pushed back but couldn't move him. His height made my eyes level with his chin. He sneered down into my upturned face. With all the courage I could muster, I glared up at him. Sheer determination welled inside me. "If your friend Derek wants the ball so bad, pick it up and throw it yourself, you bully."

"Yeah, Michael Murderer, I'll do that." He grabbed me by the shoulders and yelled, "Catch this one, Derek!" A murmur went through the crowd as Brandon shoved me toward the puddle where the football lay.

Before I could get my balance, he stuck out his foot and

tripped me. I landed face first. The splash pushed the football out of the puddle on a wave of water. I lifted my dripping head.

The ball rolled to Derek's feet. He sneered and picked it up. "Nice throw, Brandon. Thanks, Michael, you jerk."

The bullies burst out with exaggerated laughs. Snickers rippled through the crowd behind them.

Jumping up, I spit a mouthful of puddle water into Brandon's face. My schoolmates gasped and several dared to laugh. He silenced them with a scowl, wiped off his face, and shoved me hard. This time, I braced for the push and kept my balance.

He muttered, "That's gonna cost you, murder man." He turned and high-fived Derek. They swaggered toward the building, football in hand. The onlookers turned away and headed back to class.

I squeezed water from my clothes and considered reporting them. But that would make things worse. Besides, just today, Mom got up her nerve to go back to the office. I didn't want the school calling her to bring a change of clothes. Lucas ambled over and stood silent while I shook the excess water from my hair. Without a word, I headed to class.

Lucas called from behind, "Hey, wait up." He fell into step alongside me, and we plodded toward the building. He clapped my shoulder and huffed, "Sorry, man. I shoulda grabbed the stupid ball myself and thrown it back to Derek. Then grabbed Brandon and beat the snot out of him." He gritted his teeth and looked away.

I snorted water from my nose. "That's okay. Attack mode is their specialty. They sneak up, inflict damage, and walk away. Nothing anybody can do. Better to shake it off and go on with your life."

Lucas glanced at me with his eyebrows raised. "Um . . . so your dad wants to pin the shooting on your mom? Sorry to bring it up, but I'm kinda anxious to hear what happened."

Ruffling my hair one more time, I raked it into place with my fingers. I filled him in on the other details of Dad's visit. There wasn't enough time to tell him about Mom's outburst.

"Wow, dude. Totally weird reaction from your dad. You can tell me the rest later." He gave a mock salute. We entered the building and parted ways for our separate classes. The remainder of the day passed without incident, other than the stink of my clothes drying.

After I got off the bus that afternoon and headed into the house, I threw my clothes into the washer. I got redressed and headed outside to play ball-on-the-wall.

I fell into a mindless rhythm of throwing the ball against the wall, fielding the grounders, and flowing into the next throw. The continuous circle of motion drew me into a place of peace.

But after a while, my thoughts wandered back to Brandon and Derek. The more I thought about the bullies, the harder and faster I chunked the ball. I imagined their faces on the wall, and I pounded them. I threw with all my might. My fury ebbed back toward peacefulness.

A car door slammed and broke my rhythm. I turned to see Mom standing in the driveway. Her steps faltered when she started toward the front door. She stared at her hands and fiddled with the keys, her shoulders and face downcast.

I took several steps toward her. "You don't need your keys. I left the door unlocked. Did you have a good day back at work?"

She hesitated and swayed a little.

I sighed. Here we go again. I raised my voice. "Did you hear me, Mom?" I tucked my baseball glove under my arm and headed up the sidewalk to her.

She smiled and half-waved. "I'm fine. I made it through." A dark shadow moved across her face. "Of course, everybody just stood around and watched me . . . and whispered. I guess nobody knew what to say. Neither did I. Awkward. The silence felt terrible." She didn't ask about my day, just walked past me into the house.

I followed to make sure she made it inside without falling.

She hung her purse on the back of a kitchen chair and set her briefcase on the table. "I think I need to lie down. I'll get up in a little while and fix dinner." Leaning on the wall for support, she headed down the hallway.

I followed her into her room. "Mom, what's going on? Are you okay? You don't look well."

She collapsed onto her bed. Several hours later, when I went to bed, she still lay in the same position.

The following morning, déjà vu. I found her in the kitchen dressed and looking sharp. The warm smell of cinnamon filled the room.

She breezed around, nonchalant, then looked at me with a smile. "Good morning, honey. I made toaster pastries. Sit down and eat with me for a minute before you head to the bus."

I sat in a huff, rested my chin in my hand, and stared. "Mom, what's going on? From yesterday morning to last night, you went Dr. Jekyll and Mr. Hyde on me. This is crazy, living like this."

She put her coffee cup down and looked me in the face. "I keep telling you I'm fine. You and I are strong. We're going to make it." She munched on her breakfast.

I took a bite of my pastry, drank some milk, and swallowed. My brain hammered inside of my head. "Yeah, I know we're strong. What I don't know is what to expect from you. Yesterday morning, you looked like you could conquer the world. But in the afternoon, you wandered into the house like a ghost."

I dreaded a confrontation with my mom today. But everything felt uncomfortable and downright strange.

She sighed and shrugged. "Okay, Michael, I'm going to tell you the truth. I did okay at the office yesterday, despite the awkwardness. But when it came time to leave, the sorrow of missing Jacob hit me like a punch in the chest. So before I left, I took one of the anxiety pills the doctor gave me. I guess it makes me zone out or something."

I put my pastry on my plate and sipped some milk. "Believe me, I understand that punch in the chest. Losing Jacob brought terrible pain that won't go away. You and I walk around the house, sniffing all the time. But please don't let the pills take over your life. Those drugs might help short term, but they could also ruin our lives in the long run."

Mom looked so sharp, all fixed up and ready for work. This version of my mom was who I wanted—not the dreamy-eyed, slow-motion, spaced-out version.

She smiled. "Okay, honey. I'll do my best to face this without the meds. I promise." She stood and walked to the sink. "Off with you now. I'll see you this afternoon."

I decided to trust her. Now I would see if she could find the strength to deliver.

After heading to my room, I dressed at hyper-speed, then fast-walked to the corner. The bus pulled to the curb at the same time I arrived. Entering the bus, I slid my bookbag under my arm and headed to my usual place. But Lucas sat in my seat.

He looked at me with a glum expression. "Hey, man, you almost missed the bus. You better get with it, dude." A hint of a smile crossed his face while he raked his mullet into place with both hands.

I let the comment slide.

Most mornings, Lucas rode to school with his dad. But he caught the bus when his dad had to go to work earlier than usual. On those days, I would be glad to see him. But not today. My mood didn't lend itself to talking about Mom's erratic behavior. I dropped my bookbag onto the floor and slumped beside him.

Silence hung between us while the other kids talked and laughed. I stared at the back of the seat in front of me. Now Mom's drug had created an invisible wedge between my best friend and me. What else could go wrong?

I thought through my recent conversations with her. *Does she need that pill to face coming home? Is she depressed or is this just normal grief? Are the meds making it better or worse?*

I avoided Lucas at lunch. I knew he sensed my frustration. Despite that, he respected my space. And I needed that space today.

But on the bus ride home, I couldn't hold back my frustration. I told Lucas about Mom's drug problem.

After listening with a caring ear, he looked perplexed. "Isn't that, like, dangerous for her to drive home high?"

"I suppose she has it timed right, so it hits her when she gets home." I looked sideways at him.

A muscle twitched in his cheek. "You oughta grab the bottle and dump the pills down the toilet."

"Won't work. I think she took the pills to work and keeps them in her desk. I saw the name of the meds when she left the bottle on the kitchen table. Today I worked up my courage and asked the school nurse about it." I mimicked the nurse's official tone. "Doctors often prescribe that drug after the tragic death of a loved one. Don't worry, the prescription should run out soon with no refills."

Lucas threw his hands up in surrender. "I suppose there isn't much you can do about it. Sure is frustrating, isn't it?"

I clinched my fists and spun toward him. "Yes. If this keeps up, I don't know if I can stand it. I hate seeing her like this. If she doesn't honor her promise to kick the drugs, I may have to run away. My patience is wearing thin."

I sank into my seat and stared forward with crossed arms. *Run away? Where did that thought come from? I must be getting desperate to even think that way.*

That night in bed, I tried praying to God. I held tight to the truth of Mr. Charlie's song. *Can God hear my prayers? Is he here with me? Will he help Mom overcome grief without the meds?*

But even if God listened and helped, I wasn't sure Mom had the personal strength to make it happen.

CHAPTER SEVENTEEN

Mom's Journal: Entry Four- Friday evening, April 25, 1997

Well, Jacob, I returned to work yesterday.

Leaving you at home felt like a kick in the gut. In fact, walking out the front door hit me harder than anything I've ever done. My heart broke when I left you behind. Abandoning you. Betraying you.

So here I am apologizing again. I'm so sorry I had to leave you here and go to work. But my personal leave ran out. I must make a living. Living. What a strange word.

My coworkers acted nice. They stopped by my desk with kind compliments about your funeral. Some who visited complimented our home. I returned dishes to those who brought food. Still, no one knew what to say.

The rest of the day, they walked in a wide circle around my desk. No one looked my way. Whenever someone caught my eye by accident, we faked a smile and went back to work. But to tell the truth, I felt relieved to be ignored. I worked in silence. And tried not to think of you alone at home, Jacob.

Yesterday, on impulse, I tucked the pills into my purse. Had them close by in case I needed them. And I did need them. I took one midafternoon.

About 2:00, I couldn't catch my breath. Anxiety overcame me. I hurried to the restroom and took a pill. Then I sat in a toilet stall and willed my heart rate back to normal.

A toilet stall, of all places, is where I heard your voice. You whispered, "Anxiety, Mom? What are you scared of?"

Well . . . to be honest, I'm terrified you might be gone when I get home. Petrified . . . that my leaving might give you an excuse to leave me. So, yes, I took a pill. And it gave me the strength to make it to five o'clock.

But the panic attack came back. During the drive home, an ambulance passed me on the bridge to Arradale. It appeared out of nowhere. I hyperventilated at the unexpected screech of the siren. I jerked the steering wheel to get out of the way. My car swerved and came very close to hitting the guardrail. The red flashing lights flew past me in a rush. A giant unseen hand squeezed my chest and lungs. I almost blacked out.

I made it across the bridge. There is a car dealer there beside the road. I pulled into the parking lot to calm down. A sales associate walked over to check on me. He saw me gasping for breath, my head slung back, my eyes closed. I rolled down the window and tried to smile. He accepted my explanation that the ambulance scared me. No mention of you or the tragedy. I came home. Home—our sanctuary.

Of course, when I walked in the door, I knew. You're still here, waiting for me. Such an immense comfort. I took a deep breath and leaned against the wall for support. So thankful.

These last two weeks at home with you felt very special. But painful too. During these days together, I sat in the yard talking to my birds. You in your room, hanging out. And then I would come inside for our little conversations together. Like normal? No. Normal is not a word I would use to describe our lives yet. Nothing is normal. But I'm hoping for normal to return soon for you and me.

I'm thankful though. Thankful my engineering of the situation helped. The storm of pain and the fear of eternity have been relieved. And, I must admit, the med helped too. To tell the truth, quite a bit.

But the pill hasn't given me courage to enter your room yet. So far, I can't bring myself to go in. Maybe your room is my shrine to your memory. Oh no, what am I saying? Shrine? Memory? No, I'm sorry. There I go, apologizing again.

Rewind. You still live here. This is your home.

I don't go into your room because I'm fearful of disturbing your spirit. What if I move something by mistake? What if an innocent mishap made you angry, drove you away, caused you to leave?

Please, Jacob, never leave me. I cannot bear to lose

you again. Let's agree. We'll be here forever. Together.
And we'll talk every day when I get home from work.

Michael is a wonderful son. But please don't tell him
how I've engineered our reality.

He won't understand like you do.

CHAPTER EIGHTEEN

Saturday, April 26, 1997

Friday afternoon and evening, after our talk, Mom seemed better. Her old self reappeared, not the doped-up version I dreaded.

Saturday morning, I slept late like usual and woke up around nine o'clock. When I wandered into the kitchen still wearing my gym shorts and T-shirt, Mom greeted me with a cheerful, "Good morning, Michael." She stepped into the laundry room to check the dryer.

I looked around in shock. She had finished the house cleaning. Now carrying a stack of dish towels, she headed to the stove.

A smile brightened her face. "Can I cook you some breakfast? I'll make your favorite."

I grinned. "Yes, ma'am, that would be great. Thanks, Mom."

She put the dish towels in the drawer, took a carton of eggs from the fridge and bread from the pantry, and started cooking. I hurried to my room, got dressed, and combed my bed head.

Back in the kitchen, I pulled up a chair and Mom sat beside me at the table. A fried egg, cooked on a piece of toast with a hole cut in it for the egg, sat steaming on the table. We called it toad-in-a-hole.

What a surprise—a delicious breakfast with actual conversation. I enjoyed our time together and our casual talk. She asked me questions about school, and I asked her about work. When I finished breakfast, I took my plate to the sink.

She wiped the table clean. "By the way, have you seen Mr. Charlie around? Doesn't seem like I've noticed him in the yard these last few days."

I put my dish in the dishwasher. "His wife is going through a round of chemo right now. He's busy taking care of her."

Mom crossed the room to drop the rag in the clothes washer. "The weather outside is glorious. Why don't we take a walk around the neighborhood?"

An unexpected laugh escaped my lips, followed by a big smile. "Sure, let's go for it."

We headed out the door and inhaled the breezy warmth of the spring day. The gentle wind strummed the leaves overhead. My steps felt lighter than they had in weeks. In stride together, we set a fast pace, moving up one street and down the other. We laughed and talked while we circled the whole subdivision. Our time together warmed me from head to toe, even more than the brilliant summer sun.

When we arrived back at our driveway, the Jacob tree caught our attention. The flowers she planted on the day of the snake bloomed in abundance. We stopped walking and stared at the tree. Mom glanced at me with a questioning look. I nodded. We walked toward the tree together.

Standing at the foot of the tree, Mom reached over and hugged me. I savored it with every inch of my being.

Something metallic in the pine straw caught my eye. I nudged Mom and pointed. The sunlight reflected from the object, shining at us. I bent and picked it up.

The unspent bullet. The one Mom dropped when she loaded

the gun on the day of the snake. I dropped it back into the straw as a shudder ran through my body at the memory of the hot gun. Mom covered her mouth with a hand. A whimper escaped her lips. I regained my composure, bent, and picked up the bullet. She extended her other hand. A tear dropped onto her palm alongside the bullet when I placed it there. We could do nothing but stare.

The sound of hammering from Mr. Charlie's garage broke our focus on the bullet.

Mom tucked the bullet in her jeans pocket and whispered, "I'll lock this one away somewhere—a memorial to Jacob." She stepped away from the tree toward the garage. "Come on, I can't stand here any longer. Let's peek in on Charlie. I want to thank him for helping us survive these last few weeks."

We found Mr. Charlie standing in front of his workbench. He looked to be building a birdhouse.

"Hey, Mr. Charlie," I said, walking into the garage.

He turned and smiled. "Hello, Michael. Who's that pretty lady with you? Good morning ma'am. My name is Charles. I don't believe I've seen you around here in a while."

Mom laughed. "Thank you, Mr. Charlie. I started back to work Thursday and needed to get outside and get some sunshine."

I stepped over to the workbench. "How's your wife?"

"It's a struggle." Scratching his day-old beard, he shook his head. "But you know what our song on the wall says." He winked at me.

Mom raised her eyebrows. "What's this about a song?"

I answered before Mr. Charlie could. "He lent a song to me on an old cassette tape."

Mr. Charlie chuckled. "Just a family favorite. Come over and read the words for yourself."

We walked around the old Chevrolet and looked at the yellowed paper taped to the wall.

Mom read the lyrics of the first verse and chorus aloud, then looked at us with eyebrows raised. "Seems a little poetic for a sixteen-year-old boy and a sixty-something man." She pressed her lips together. But then she giggled. "I'm kidding. I like it."

She returned to reading aloud. Her voice wavered when she read the last chorus. She finished and stood still for a few seconds. A tear trickled down her cheek. Mom put her hand in the pocket where she hid the bullet and gave me a slight nod.

She cleared her throat. "Well, I can see why this song is special to your family." Her voice became subdued. "Charlie, would you let me borrow that tape and tape player? Maybe the song will help me too."

I glanced at Charlie. He winked at me again. "Sure, Susan, I'd be glad to let you borrow those."

Mom sighed and backed away from the workbench. "Thank you, Charlie, for being here for us these last two weeks. And for your encouragement to Michael." She reached over and gave him a hug.

Charlie looked embarrassed. "Nobody in the world wants to go through the loss of a child. Or a loved one with cancer. But here we are." He paused. "Now, I might be pushing my luck too far, but would you two consider joining me at church tomorrow?"

Mom and I glanced at each other. I nodded my approval.

She smiled at Charlie. "Well, I guess it wouldn't hurt. We don't have anything on our schedule."

Mr. Charlie chuckled. "Sounds great. I'll see you at church. Oh, and let me get the song for you." He stepped through the kitchen door with the energy of a young man. When he returned with the tape and player, he handed them both to Mom. "We keep this on the kitchen table and play it on my wife's treatment days. It helps us know we're not alone in this battle."

Mom thanked him and gave him another quick hug.

We walked home—me carrying the player and her holding

the tape in one hand, the bullet in the other. In the kitchen, she played the song while she prepared lunch. Relief settled in my spirit to hear those words echo through our home. I hoped the lyrics would bring Mom comfort. I even lifted a quick prayer and asked God to help.

Before sleep overtook me that night, I heard Mom playing the song in her bedroom. I hoped she didn't wear out Mr. Charlie's tape.

CHAPTER NINETEEN

Sunday, April 27, 1997

I dressed in my best clothes—khaki pants, blue golf shirt, and my newest tennis shoes. The sound of a chair on the kitchen floor echoed down the hallway. Mom was up too. I walked into the kitchen to see if she had finished getting ready for church.

She sat at the table in her best dress. But her hair. Oh, such a mess. And she had not done her makeup. "Michael, I dread going to church. I already know what will happen. They'll stand there staring and whispering, just like work. I'm not up for this today. I can't do it." Her face contorted with emotion. She gave her coffee mug a violent shove. It skidded across the table. I caught it just before it fell to the floor. "You catch a ride with Mr. Charlie. I'll stay home and avoid that entire scene." The muscles twitched in her cheek.

I shuffled around the table to her side and put my hand on her shoulder. "Mom, come on. You promised Mr. Charlie that we'd join him. We can't let him down."

Without looking up, she snorted. "Yeah, I know. But I can't

do it. I'm doing my best. It's just not happening." She expelled a quivering breath and lowered her head into her hands.

I moved my hand from her shoulder. My voice took a parental tone. "Mom, Mr. Charlie has been there for us every step of the way. We can't let him down. He's expecting us." I softened my tone. "Please, get up and finish getting ready. We'll stick together and make it through this. We can't avoid people forever. Come on, let's go."

She lifted her head and slapped the table. Her plate rattled. She shook her head with resolve, glaring at me.

I glared back. And waited.

At last, she rose to her feet, pushing up from the table. "I'll probably regret this." She swallowed a last gulp of coffee from the mug I had rescued. Her look softened. "Okay, I'll go for you and Mr. Charlie. But I'm not taking any junk from anybody." She turned and strolled from the room.

I called after her, "I'll wait right here. Hurry. We don't wanna be late." I grabbed a dishrag and cleaned the spills from the table. Having to assume the role of parent with my mom hit me hard.

When she finished getting ready, we hustled to the car and headed for church. No surprise, we rode in silence for the twelve-minute trip. But when we got out of the car, she grabbed my hand. We hesitated. The last time we walked through this door, Jacob walked alongside us. We glanced at each other, then started a slow walk toward the church.

On the front porch, several people greeted us warmly. We returned their greetings with a cautious smile. Mom shot me a brave look, and we walked through the large front door. We made it inside. So far, so good.

Mr. Charlie stood at the front of the church talking to a lady. We didn't want to interrupt. The sight of where we sat with Jacob sent an icy chill up my spine. Mom grabbed my hand and squeezed. We moved away to sit on one of the padded benches on the opposite side. Others filed in and took their seats.

Several people came over and welcomed us. Did they know who we were?

One gentleman shook hands with us. We introduced ourselves and told him Mr. Charlie invited us. When he left us, he walked over to Mr. Charlie and pointed at us.

Mr. Charlie waved with a smile and came over. "How are my favorite neighbors today?" He looked sharp in his coat and tie.

Relief swept over me to hear his comforting voice.

With a shudder in her voice, Mom said, "We're doing fine." She mustered a smile.

Mr. Charlie whispered, "I understand." He turned my way. "What's up, Michael? You okay?"

I smiled. "Yes, sir, I'm good. Thanks for inviting us."

Mr. Charlie took a seat beside Mom.

A group of people walked into the boxed-in area behind the stage. I knew from our first visit they were the church choir. A lady began playing the piano while more people filed into the pews and greeted each other. The minister walked in and sat on the stage in a large chair. The crowd became quiet. The choir sang an upbeat song, then the music director invited us to stand and sing. Mom showed me how to find the hymn in the songbook. We sang several songs about God and how much he loves us.

The minister made announcements about all the activities happening in the coming weeks. Then he led everybody to recite the Lord's Prayer together. Mr. Charlie looked over and winked at me right before we started the prayer.

We sang a few more songs. During the songs, my mind twisted around the conversation with Mr. Charlie about the battles in life between God and evil. That night in the garage, I admitted to myself for the first time that Jacob had died. And I knew he could never come back. But the words Mr. Charlie shared stayed fresh in my mind: "Nothing that happens on earth surprises God. He knows everything and is all-powerful, yet loves you anyway. He's walking with you every step. You're never alone."

When we sat after singing, the minister who led Jacob's service stood to deliver the Bible message. I remembered his interesting talk from our first visit and how he made good points. But today I zoned out. I leaned forward and put my chin in my hands. I thought about the garage conversation from many angles. So many things to comprehend. I glanced at Mom. I wondered what she heard in the pastor's message.

After the service, Mr. Charlie introduced us to more of his friends. When we walked up the aisle to exit, he asked, "How about we grab a bite to eat together on the way home? My treat."

"You don't have to do that," Mom said.

"I insist. It won't take long. We can eat somewhere quick. And I can grab some takeout for my wife."

They let me choose the restaurant, and there, after ordering, we sat in a booth near the back. Soon they called our number. When I returned from the front counter with our food, we dove in.

While we ate, Mr. Charlie explained he had been a member of his church for forty years. That's why everybody there knew him. During his wife's treatment, the church members cared for them lovingly. Of course, Mrs. Harris went to church too before she got cancer. Now she stayed home because of the fear of infection. But Mr. Charlie continued teaching their couple's Sunday school class, plus he served on several committees.

I wanted to change the subject. So when he stopped to take a bite, I jumped in. "Hey, when we first moved here, you told me about the path down to the river. Is it a long walk from our place?"

"Nah, not much more than an hour walk through the woods. Once you come to the main road, the path becomes a wide trail." He wiped his mouth with a paper napkin. "The trail leads to the county park on this side of the river. It's nice. We'll have to walk down there sometime."

Mom stopped, her fork halfway to her mouth. "County park? What do they have there?"

Charlie pushed up his glasses. "Picnic area, campground, playground, camp store . . . but the genuine attraction is the river itself. Folks like to hang out, eat, play, and sun on the river rocks. It's a pleasant place to spend an afternoon, for sure."

We all nodded and continued eating, then I stopped mid-bite, eyes wide.

From a table in the middle of the restaurant, a lady wove her way through the crowd to our booth. I noticed her staring at us while she approached. She walked up to the end of our table and put her hand on Mom's shoulder. "Hi, Susan. I'm Ellen Davenport. We met at the school open house. My son is in Michael's class."

This caught Mom by surprise. She almost choked on her food, attempting a smile.

Mrs. Davenport flashed a sad look at me, then turned back to Mom. "I heard what you dear people have been through. I just wanted to say how sorry we are about the loss of your son. What a terrible tragedy. When something like that happens, I always tell people, 'God just needed another angel in heaven.'" She patted Mom's shoulder, gave me a smile, and walked away without looking back.

Mom and I stared at each other, mouths agape.

Mr. Charlie said, "Oh, wow. I'm so sorry about that. Some people oversimplify what they don't understand. Come on, let's get outta here."

We eased out of the booth, discarded our lunch trash at the door, and left.

Another lady, closer to Charlie's age, crossed the parking lot and headed straight for us. We tried to step around her, but she cut off our path to the car.

This lady attempted to pat me on the back. I dodged her hand. She turned to Mom. "Oh, you sweet people. We live around the corner from you. We are so sorry to hear about Jacob's passing. I hope you know . . . he's in a better place, a much better place. Just think of him there and I know it will bring you comfort." She opened her purse, took out a tissue, and dabbed at her eyes. "Okay, I need to run in and meet my family. Take care and God bless you."

She turned and headed into the restaurant. In stunned silence, we watched her go.

Mr. Charlie stepped over and laid a gentle hand on Mom's shoulder. Frustration etched his face, and he pressed his lips together. "And once again, I'm so sorry. We better get to our cars before anyone else tries to comfort us."

Mom turned from watching the lady. She shrugged, downcast. Her voice sounded hollow. "They mean well, Mr. Charlie. You don't need to apologize. They're just saying what's easy. They don't know what to say." Then her face flushed and her nostrils flared. Through clenched teeth, she muttered, "So they say something stupid." She sniffed and marched across the parking lot.

Mr. Charlie and I hurried after her. When we caught up, Mr. Charlie said, "You know, Susan, they've said those same things to me about my wife's cancer. So, believe me, I know how frustrating and hurtful those platitudes are."

When we reached our cars, we stood there a moment, not knowing what to say. He broke the silence. "Well . . . I'm thankful you came to church today. It's always special to have you with me. If you need me, you know where to find me." We exchanged hugs.

On the drive home, a tense silence hung between Mom and me.

At home, I changed out of my nice clothes into shorts and T-shirt. With hands in pockets, I ambled into Jacob's bedroom—

my first time there since he died two weeks ago. The dead quiet sent a shiver up my back. The only light came from a sliver of afternoon sun filtering through the window. I didn't turn on the light. The shadows looked spooky, but they fit my mood.

Jacob and I played video games here, always trying to beat each other's score. But with Jacob gone, I didn't feel like playing. Alone, I sat on his bed. I didn't have a brother anymore. Tears welled up, so I distracted myself by flipping through cartridges of our favorite games. An aching emptiness spread through my whole body. I missed him so much.

The words from the lady in the restaurant came to mind. Could Jacob be playing games in heaven now? Did he miss being in our home, or did his new home enthrall him too much to think of us? Did he miss me like I missed him? I didn't want to imagine him anywhere but here.

Mom shuffled through the door, still in her church clothes but barefoot. Tears streaked her face, her hair hung limp. She slumped onto Jacob's bed beside me.

Realization struck me—she had not been in Jacob's room until this moment. We sat together and mourned the emptiness. Moments passed without a word. So many of his things exactly where he left them, a cathedral of memories.

In a whisper, she spoke first. "I can't get out of my mind what those ladies said. If God took Jacob from us because he needed another angel, I say, 'Give him back right now. You do not need him. I need him, and Michael does too.'" Her face took on a look of defiance, but her voice remained hushed. "If God is loving, he would never take Jacob from us, would he? Does that make any kind of sense at all? Well, I can answer that with certainty. It . . . does . . . not."

I sat still with head bowed. I couldn't think of a suitable answer to give her.

Mom clenched her fists and stood. Her voice rose. "And how dare anyone say Jacob is in a better place?" I felt her anger building, about to boil over again. "Like our home is not good enough? Like God had to take Jacob out of some kind of mess?" She cried out, "We have a wonderful family. And I am an excellent mother. People should keep their misguided comments to themselves." She flopped back onto the bed and sat next to me, sullen.

That's when the answer came to me. I mustered some courage and swiveled toward her. "Mom, you said it yourself. Those ladies didn't know what to say. They said something nice. It made them feel better. But—"

"Sure, their words helped them feel better. But those words didn't help us. It's obvious they've never experienced a tragedy like we have. Or they wouldn't say stuff like that."

I patted her arm. "Hold on a minute. Let me tell you something I learned from Mr. Charlie. He understands what we're going through." I looked her in the eye. "Do you remember when we prayed the Lord's Prayer at church today? The part where we asked for God's will to be done on earth as it is in heaven?"

She nodded and looked at me with eyebrows raised. "Of course. I've heard the Lord's Prayer my whole life. I've prayed it myself. Why?"

"Well, Charlie explained that God's will is the ultimate authority in heaven. But here on earth, things are different. You know why?" I waited to see if she would venture a guess, but she sat and stared at me. I chose my words with care. "You can't force love on somebody. And because God loves us, he lets us choose or reject him."

She nodded, "Okay, but keep going."

I forged ahead, feeling more confident. "God didn't take Jacob from us or give Mrs. Harris cancer. Those are tragedies. Tragedies happen because God gives us freedom. He decided not to make us robots programmed to only do good. We're free to choose him or not. In our freedom, bad things happen sometimes."

Mom raised her eyebrows. "Wow. That's deep for a sixteen-year-old."

I smiled at her and chuckled. "I guess so. But I've thought about this a lot lately. It really makes sense. Plus, it helps heal my pain." I swallowed. "Here's the cool thing, though. God is here for us and loves us. Especially when bad things happen. Just like Mr. Charlie's song says, we're never alone."

Mom gazed into my eyes while the seconds ticked by. She nodded. "Yes, that does make sense. And I do understand all that." Her chin dropped and her voice trembled. "But it's still difficult for me. See, I'm very mad at God right now. And I can't promise my anger is going away anytime soon. I understand he's here for us, but this still hurts so bad." She shook her head and paused before continuing quietly. "I can't help it. I need something to take my pain away." Her face crumpled. She put her head in her hands. Tears dripped between her fingers onto her lap.

I didn't know what else to say. Her heart remained broken on the floor of Jacob's room.

And mine too.

CHAPTER TWENTY

Tuesday, April 29, 1997

On Monday, Mom faced another workday. And I faced another day of school. The aftereffects of Sunday lingered like a stain on our spirits and hung between us at home. But we both agreed it would be best to move on and ignore what the ladies said the day before. So we didn't discuss that anymore.

Tuesday promised another mundane school day. And boredom felt like a welcome relief these days. When I got home, homework took top priority. I settled at my bedroom desk and focused on my assignments. A couple of hours later, the sound of Mom's car door closing broke my concentration.

My legs needed stretching and my mind demanded a break, so I went to greet her at the front door. Curious what state she might be in—stoned or sober—I opened the door with hesitation. Mom bustled through the door in a hurry.

I stepped back to avoid being knocked down. "Whoa, Mom, what's got you in such a hurry? Are you okay?"

She hustled to the kitchen, with me following close behind.

When she placed her briefcase on the table, she turned and said, "Detective Thorne called me just before I left the office. He's coming by here in just a minute to talk with us." She swiped a wisp of hair from her face. "Something's going on, but I don't know what. I'm suspicious your dad is up to something." She wrung her hands and glanced at me. "Go comb your hair and meet me in the den." Her voice carried a frantic note of worry.

Regardless, I felt relieved she wasn't under the influence of the drug. I guess the detective's call came at the right time. Sometimes you just gotta savor minor victories when you can.

I combed my hair and washed my face. The coolness of the water felt good. In the mirror, my face looked flushed, drawn, and tired. The roller-coaster emotions of the last weeks had taken their toll. I scrubbed my face a few seconds more with the hand towel. Maybe that would help wipe away the signs of fatigue somehow.

I threw the towel aside and walked toward the den. The doorbell rang, so I detoured into the foyer. I could see the detective's head through the glass at the top of the door. I glanced over to see Mom in the den, sitting stiff as a statue in her favorite chair. She forced a nervous smile, shivered, and stood.

I opened the door, shook hands with Detective Thorne, and invited him in. I hoped he had good news. Despite my best attempt, I could not read this man.

Mom smoothed her blouse and skirt and took a step toward the door. Thorne walked into the den, with me close behind. After his cordial greeting to Mom, we sat in the same places as his last visit—Mom and I in separate recliners and the detective on the couch.

"Mrs. Judson." He nodded to Mom, then turned to me. "Michael. I'm glad to see you again." He gave us a well-rehearsed smile. "I hope you're both surviving this ordeal."

"I guess we're doing okay under the circumstances," Mom answered. "What brings you here for this surprise visit?" Her hands fluttered around her lap, no doubt from fear of the answer to that question. But she looked beautiful in her dress and high heels, unchanged from the office.

Officer Thorne cleared his throat. "Well, I'm sure you know, our team studied every piece of evidence from Jacob's shooting. After gathering and processing everything, we ruled the shooting an accident. Of course, we may never know who pulled the trigger. So, no charges against anyone. Case closed."

I held my tongue, sensing an unspoken issue. I looked at Mom and saw her frowning at the investigator. With an eerie voice, she said, "Yes, sir, we understand all that. So, if the case has been closed and ruled an accident . . . why are you here?"

Thorne shifted in his seat and swallowed. "There's been an unexpected development. Your husband went over our heads to the State Law Enforcement Agency. He's bringing pressure and making lots of noise, demanding we reopen the case. It appears he enlisted the support of several high-placed officials in the agency."

Mom stiffened in her chair and glared at the officer. I released the breath I had been holding and looked away.

Ignoring her searing gaze, he continued, "Of course, we confiscated your gun on the day of the shooting. Then I did my best to cover everything in my research. And in my honest opinion, reopening the case will not change anything. But the sheriff asked us to go along. So I don't have a choice. I'm sorry."

Mom's voice trembled. "Your office already notified me I'm on probation from gun ownership. Believe me, I don't ever want to see another gun in my life." Her polite veneer split open and her anger flooded out. "But that stupid man is obsessed. He's determined to blame somebody for Jacob's death. And that someone is me." She shouted. "The case is closed. Ruled an accident. He just wants to hurt me. How can he get away with that?" She put her head in her hands and wept.

The need to comfort her welled up inside me. I hurried over

behind her chair, cupped my hands on her shoulders, and laid my cheek on top of her head.

In anger, she pushed my hands away and stood, smashing my cheek with the top of her head. I recoiled, but she didn't notice. She took one step toward the detective. With an intensity in her voice I seldom heard, she demanded, "Tell me, please. Tell me what evidence he has."

Detective Thorne rose from the sofa with a calm that surprised me. "Now, Mrs. Judson, take it easy. I know this is a scary situation. And I know it hurts when your former husband makes these accusations. I understand your concern." He gave her a caring smile. "Please, sit down. I'll do my best to explain everything. And I'll advise you what to do next." He motioned to the chair. "Please?"

I circled around to stand beside her. "Come on, Mom. Let the officer explain things. He's always been up front with us. We gotta trust somebody. Once we hear his explanation, we'll figure out how to handle this."

She wiped her eyes. "Okay. I hope you can give me some reassurance here, because I'm about to go under." She eased into her chair.

Thorne and I sat too.

"First, is there anything else that might help us prove this as an accidental shooting? Anything we might have missed?"

Mom threw her hands up. "No. I've told you every detail each time you've asked. There is nothing else to tell."

I squirmed in my chair. "Well . . . there might be one thing we overlooked."

Detective Thorne slid forward. "What are you talking about, Michael?"

"We found a lost bullet in the flower bed where the accident happened." I looked at my mother. "Remember, Mom? You said you would keep it somewhere special."

Mom gave me a thoughtful look. "Yes, we did. But I sure

don't understand why one missing bullet would be important." Mom shared a detailed explanation about the dropped bullet and how we rediscovered it on Saturday.

Thorne's eyes crinkled in a subtle smile. "That unfired bullet could be very important. Can you retrieve it for me? I need to take it with me."

Mom stood and went to her bedroom. Thorne removed a plain white envelope from his pocket. She returned and placed the bullet in the envelope he held out.

He sealed it. "Thank you." He lifted the bag. "This evidence could be very important. The revolver holds six bullets, right?" We nodded. "At the scene, I counted three spent bullets, two unfired bullets, and one empty cylinder. So the neighbor's claim he heard four gunshots puzzled me. Could the missing bullet be the fourth shot? Michael's dad used that missing bullet to demand we re-open the case." He glanced at me. "I'm so glad Michael remembered this bullet. If this bullet matches the others, we can put this four-shot issue to rest and close the case." He returned the envelope to his shirt pocket. "Okay, is there anything else that might help us? Anything at all?" His steel-blue eyes rested on Mom, then he glanced at me.

Mom and I held a look between us for a moment and shook our heads.

I spoke up. "Sir, there's nothing else to tell. That's all we got. I promise."

"He's right," Mom agreed, looking him in the eye. "That's everything."

Detective Thorne smiled and stood, and we joined him. "You've both been very helpful. And I'm sure thankful for that help." He patted his shirt pocket with the bullet safely inside. "You have my number. Call me if you think of anything else or have questions, okay? I'm here for you."

He made a slight bow to Mom, and she blushed. I stepped across the room and shook his hand. Mom escorted him out the front door and I followed. We stood shoulder to shoulder on the porch and watched while he got in his car and drove away.

For an extra moment, we stayed there and stared at the Jacob tree.

Could one forgotten bullet make a difference in the middle of so much confusion and hurt?

CHAPTER TWENTY-ONE

Mom's Journal: Entry Five- Tuesday Evening, April 29, 1997

Three days have passed since I wrote to you. Three horrific days.

Life felt more normal these last two weeks. And now, just look at me. A total mess. Just when I think I'm about to climb up on top of all the pain and confusion, something else knocks me down again.

Here's what happened. We went to church with Mr. Charlie on Sunday. At first, I resisted. But Michael persuaded me we needed to honor our promise. So, we summoned all our courage to make it through the door and into the building. Mr. Charlie sat with us and introduced us to his friends.

I felt your spirit there with me, Jacob. Michael sat beside me, and we held hands to comfort each other. But I felt you holding my other hand, which made the struggle worth it.

You would have liked the pastor's message. His sermon had a similar theme to the Sunday we attended with you. But I didn't expect how the singing would affect me. We sang reassuring songs about God's love. Those songs truly spoke to my heart. Especially after I listened to "You're Never Alone" over and over on Saturday night. For a little while, I felt very close to God. I haven't had that feeling in many years.

As a teen and young adult, I remember specific days and weeks when God seemed very close. Those days felt amazing. The awareness of his presence made my life sparkle. But over time, my sense of God's presence eroded. My life always returns to busyness, and my soul returns to emptiness. I get stuck waiting and hoping for another personal revelation to draw me back to him.

Your dad and I didn't go to church much. Just on Christmas and Easter. I grew up going to church, though. I loved church back then. But adult life encroached on church life. Our work weeks exhausted us. We slept late most Sundays, then tried to do something fun with you and Michael in the afternoon.

Everything considered, church with Mr. Charlie proved to be a wonderful experience. Regardless, my horrendous week still happened. To be fair, the church wasn't the problem. And God wasn't the problem either. I felt genuine love from both. When we left after the service, my spirit soared for the first time in a long time.

And then lunch happened.

Two ladies stopped to talk with us and said things

that shocked and upset me. Mr. Charlie tried to help me understand they meant well. But their words hurt me deeply. Regardless of the intent, their words knocked me right off the spiritual high I found at church. And I can tell you, the downward plunge ended in a terrible crash.

Now I find myself doubting everything in Mr. Charlie's song. Questioning everything the pastor said. Skeptical of every reassurance in those hymns. Uncertain whether my closeness to God actually happened.

The cliché condolences those ladies shared sent me into a spiral of endless questions. How could God love me and take you away? I don't understand. God, where are you in this? And where have you taken Jacob's spirit? Is he in heaven or not? Is he an angel now, or still here with me? I know you would never leave him in the grave. That's a horrible thought. No loving God would ever do that.

Just a few days ago, I had everything figured out, engineered with perfection. Then confusion took me hostage again. Strange enough, I long for the deep silence I felt after the accident. Instead, my mind is in a shouting match with itself every minute of the last two days.

Michael did his best to help me make sense of it all. He and Mr. Charlie have been talking about where God fits in this tragedy. Michael is smart for his age. And he grasps deep concepts. His explanations make sense to my analytical mind. Regardless, this mother's heart just cannot grasp Michael's explanation. I'm desperate to understand how a loving God could allow this. But I just don't get it.

So, after all the good vibes of Saturday and Sunday, my world crashed. No engineering on my part can answer those terrible questions. They refuse to leave me in peace.

And then, to top it off, Monday happened.

I got a phone call at work from Detective Thorne. Your father has convinced the sheriff and state police to reopen the case. He is determined to prove the shooting is all my fault.

Can you believe that? Well, I can. He drives me crazy. Why won't he let it rest? What is his problem? He knows how Michael went into the house and got the gun. He knows I used it to shoot the snake. And he knows you jumped in and grabbed the gun because you saw the snake move.

So, who is to blame for you getting shot? For God's sake, can't he see? No one is to blame. No one. Law enforcement ruled the shooting an accident. There is no other evidence. There is no case to be solved. Accidental shooting. Case closed.

I'm sorry, am I shouting? Let me take a breath and step back so I can calm down.

Thanks to your dad, more questions are now piled atop my own questions. (You know, like why I didn't lock the gun. But let's move on.) The question pile is burying me. Jacob, I'm being pushed to my limit. I don't know how to survive. I'm so glad I can talk to you. If you're an angel, ask God to send help. Fast.

Okay, I'll go take a pill. Without it, there's no way I can fall asleep. I'm too wound up. I skipped my afternoon dose because of the detective's visit. So I'm obsessing. Just a little desperate. We'll talk soon. Sorry.

Rest in peace tonight, my son. I love you.

CHAPTER TWENTY-TWO

Tuesday, May 13, 1997

Two weeks came and went. Things with Mom got worse. For several days, she tried harder not to use her afternoon pill. But the ladies' comments and investigator's visit pushed her over the edge into a downward slide.

As the first week wore on, she looked, talked, and moved as if trudging through mud. Her dependence on the medication had returned. During the days following Detective Thorne's questioning, she hid in her room most afternoons and evenings.

At school, I cruised through my classes. Friends began talking to me again. And the bullies had moved on to other targets. I kept my interaction with Lucas on the surface and avoided discussing Mom's relapse. And the chaos inside me.

At home, I hid from reality. I claimed the den couch for TV time, played video games in Jacob's room and ball-on-the-wall outside. Trying my best to stay distracted, I pushed Jacob's reopened case far from my mind.

During the second week, after work each day, Mom took up residence on the porch. She sat in her chair and talked to the birds. So eerie. I couldn't get her to speak to me, yet she poured out her heart to those stupid birds. I felt sad for her. And very frustrated.

What could I do? The pressure in my chest built like a tsunami deep in the ocean and grew until it threatened to overwhelm everything in its path. I wondered if I could escape somehow. No idea how or where that escape might come, but I knew I had to do something soon.

Tuesday, Lucas rode the bus again. Talking to him brought some relief. But I had reached my limit. A dark cloud hung over my life.

When Lucas asked about my state of mind, I stared straight ahead without answering. I managed to exhale with a low rumble and shake my head. Frustration stifled my voice. And the weight of Mom's drug abuse continued to crush my spirit.

The chatter of kids and the grind of the engine provided a monotonous soundtrack for my state of mind. But silence hung between me and Lucas, as heavy as the stage curtain in the school auditorium. Summoning a bit of courage, I pushed back the heaviness and faced Lucas.

"Remember what I told you several weeks ago?"

Lucas looked at me and tried to dredge up the memory. "You mean, about your mom?"

"Yes. I hate Mom's drug use. It drags me down like an enormous boulder on my back. I've got to get away somehow. I'm done."

Lucas frowned and dropped his voice to a whisper. "Whoa. You mean like you wanna run away from home? That's a crazy thought."

I processed his question and turned to him. With hushed intensity, I said, "I know. That's not like me. Not my normal reaction, for sure. Of course, nothing is normal right now. Everything is upside down. It's all way off the chart."

Lucas pulled himself up in his seat and focused his full attention on me. "Dude, I'm here for you. We could go together."

I snickered. "Run off together? Now that is a really crazy thought."

"Why not? We don't have to stay gone. Just get away for a day or two. Not far."

"That's not possible. No way."

He almost shouted. "Yeah . . . way." He snickered and covered his mouth with his hand.

"Whatcha got in mind?" I narrowed my gaze, my eyebrows knit together and waited.

Lucas leaned toward me and dropped his voice. "You tell your mom I invited you to spend the weekend at my house. Then I'll tell my mom you invited me to spend the weekend at your house. My mom works a lot and your mom's spaced out. So they won't check with each other. Then we'll take off for a weekend getaway somewhere nearby."

A burst of laughter escaped me before I could catch it. Several kids around us stopped talking and stared. Lucas and I nodded to them, and they returned to their conversation.

After a minute of waiting, I gave Lucas a big smile. "You're joking, right?" I poked him with my elbow.

Lucas looked miffed. "Heck no. You're the one who wants to run away. I'm just trying to help."

I chuckled. "No way, man. We can't lie to our parents. If we got caught, we'd be grounded for the rest of our lives."

I sank back in my seat, and Lucas crossed his arms with a sigh. The school bus rumbled to a stop and more kids stumbled in to claim empty seats.

Half a minute later, I sat straight up. "Okay, here's an idea. Let's just ask them. You know, get our parents' permission." I made a quick turn to Lucas. "Then we hike to the county park by the river. We can camp there on Friday and Saturday night. Mr.

Charlie says there's a camp store there. We could use the pay phone to check in."

Lucas hesitated. "Hmmm, nice idea. Yep . . . that might work."

I whispered, "So when would we do it?"

"The sooner, the better, I say. Like this weekend. Sounds like you need it quick."

The bus pulled into the school parking lot. We had to hustle to class. After grabbing our bookbags, we nodded to each other and headed to homeroom.

I didn't hear a word my teachers said all morning. My mind took off and ran with the idea of a getaway. What seemed chancy, on the one hand, felt adventurous and exciting on the other. Could we make it work? Would our parents go for it? What would we do for food, and where would we sleep?

Despite my questions, this idea seemed like a cool way to take a break from the tension and frustration at home. If I didn't catch a break soon, I might lash out at Mom or do something destructive. Maybe a simple weekend escape would release me from the maze where I had become lost.

After lunch, I circled the schoolyard, too antsy to stand in my usual corner.

Lucas came alongside and fell into stride. "Well?"

I laughed at his directness. "I'm interested. Do you have a tent we can use?"

Lucas shrugged. "We got a bunch of camping stuff. I'm pretty sure there's a tent in there somewhere."

"Cool. Let's check the weather report on that new cable channel. Then we can ask our parents tonight. After school on Friday, we'll grab some food from each house and a sleeping bag with a change of clothes tucked inside."

We walked faster. Lucas, always Mr. Laid-back, chimed in with excitement I'd never seen in him. "Okay, we hike through the woods and camp at the park Friday and Saturday night. We come home Sunday afternoon and slide right back into our routines. But you get a fresh start. I have some fun. And we keep you from going crazy." He nudged me with his elbow and grinned.

I smiled. "You got it. I get a break from Mom. She gets a break from me. We explore the river by day and sit by the campfire at night. Nice."

Lucas stopped. "So, you in?"

I hesitated, breathed a sigh, then gave a slow nod. "Yep, I'm in."

CHAPTER TWENTY-THREE

Afternoon, Friday, May 16, 1997

Friday arrived. Lucas and I had executed our plan with near perfection.

During the Tuesday bus ride home, we had discussed every detail of the camping trip. Lucas got off the bus at my stop and we sat on our front porch, scheming. We thought of answers for every question our parents might ask.

That evening, separately, we presented our getaway idea. Both of us agreed to stay cool and not appear too excited. At first, our parents had some reservations. We whispered updates to each other by phone when our parents left the room. Wednesday, we promised we'd be extra careful to stay safe. Thursday morning, we filled in the gaps where they still had doubts.

Thursday afternoon, after an agonizing day of anticipation, they gave us their permission. Lucas and I rejoiced. Our planning shifted into overdrive.

I had only camped once before, a single night in our backyard with Jacob and a friend when I was twelve. We used our neighbors' pop-up tent. Jacob had chickened out and gone back inside at ten o'clock. About an hour later, he and Dad snuck outside, shook the tent, and yelled. It scared me and my friend to death. We came running out, screaming like babies. Jacob and Dad rolled on the ground laughing. That night seemed like just a few months ago. I wished Jacob could be here now to go with me this weekend. What a great time we would have together.

After school on Friday, I hustled home and finished packing. I walked into the kitchen and laid my sleeping bag on the table. Humps and bumps poked out from the extra clothes rolled inside. I had emptied my book bag of school stuff, so books, papers, and pencils now lay on my bedroom desk to make room for camp food.

As usual, Mom sat in her favorite chair on the porch, still dressed in her business clothes. I went to the back door and cleared my throat.

She turned toward me, dream-like. I knew the routine. A slow smile crinkled her eyes. "Have a good time camping. Be safe now. You know I couldn't stand it if anything happened to you . . ." Her smile faded.

Fear for her condition overrode any fear for me. And sorrow for her helplessness welled up inside. But then deep frustration gripped me, and my sorrow became laced with anger. I deserved this getaway and nothing could keep me from it.

My emotions under control, I strode to her chair. "You be safe too, Mom. Take it easy on the pills. I'll call you tomorrow from the campground. I love you." She reached for me, so I bent to hug her, anxious to leave.

"I love you too, my firstborn." Her hug dissolved into a limp embrace.

When her arms dropped to her sides, I stood and moved fast into the kitchen, watching to make sure she didn't pass out. Then I turned and went to work. There wasn't much food in our neglected pantry. Scrounging snacks, granola bars, and juice boxes, I stuffed them into my bookbag. We would have to survive by eating whatever we had. I jogged out the front door and headed for the path.

Lucas waited in the middle of the woods, his backpack loaded and his sleeping bag tucked under his arm. A big grin crossed his face when he saw me striding toward him. "Come on, slowpoke, where ya been? You ready for Lucas's and Michael's Excellent Adventure?"

I laughed joyfully. "Are you kidding? You know I'm ready." I lifted my book bag. "I ransacked the pantry and grabbed all the snacks I could find. Not much there, but we'll make it work. And my sleeping bag has a change of clothes stuffed inside."

His eyes grew wide. "Man, you got your entire closet stuffed in there?"

I grinned. "Did you bring anything for us to eat, hotshot?"

As usual, Lucas spoke with a slow drawl, but I could hear his excitement anyway. "Hey, you don't trust me to deliver on my promise? And we haven't even gotten into the woods yet." He lifted his backpack off the ground and patted it with pride. "I got a whole package of hotdogs in here, along with some apples and those little cereal packages. I also have some bread slices and a package of bologna."

"Well, it's not steak and potatoes." I chuckled. "But that should keep us going for the weekend. Let's do this." I glanced at Lucas's camp supplies. "Wait, where's the tent?"

Lucas grimaced. "Oh, yeah . . . about that. When I pulled the old tent out of its carry bag, it fell apart. Rotten. But, hey, the weather should be fine. We'll just sleep under the stars." He raised his eyebrows, waiting for my reaction.

I shook my head and laughed. "Okay, whatever. Come on, let's get out of here. No way I'm gonna let a little thing like that mess up our weekend." I pointed up the path toward the river. "Let's go."

We slung our backpacks over our shoulders and grabbed our sleeping bags. I tried to contain the lumps in mine.

Mr. Charlie guaranteed this path would take us to the river trail. We walked this way several times each week, of course, on the way to each other's home. But halfway to Lucas's house, the river path forked to the left. We took the left turn and ventured into unknown territory. I gazed at the pine straw path stretched out before us. My shoulders felt a little lighter from the weight I carried over the last weeks. I hadn't felt this good in a long, long time. I smiled. And quickened my pace.

A light breeze rustled in the trees high above. The crunch of twigs and leaves underfoot made a nice soundtrack for our adventure. With each step, relief washed over me.

After two miles of hiking through dense woods, we stepped out alongside a busy four-lane street. We looked up and down it. I recognized where we were. Mom and I often came this way. I shuddered to realize we followed the ambulance up this road just a few weeks ago. No, I would not let that thought ruin this afternoon.

I pointed. "See that store across the road? Mr. Charlie told me the river trail starts behind it. Be careful and let's cross over."

Heavy traffic from the afternoon rush hour raced in both directions. We waited. And waited. The stoplight down the road provided a break in traffic. Lucas took off in an awkward jog across the road. I sprinted after him. Temptation whispered to head into the store and buy a drink, but adventure and limited funds overruled thirst. We pushed on toward the river.

When we arrived at the back of the store, a wide, paved trail stretched out before us. Bike riders, joggers, and dog walkers parked behind the store in a designated lot and used the trail for recreation and exercise. We smiled and nodded to them when they passed. Impatience kept our pace quick while we bounced along.

After another couple of miles, the trail crested the river bluff. From our vantage point high above the river, we could see the park. We dropped our packs and admired the view for several minutes. Years of wind and water had carved a level terrace into the ridge just above the river below. Campsites, a playground, picnic tables, and the camp store lay scattered on the riverside terrace. Enormous boulders protruded from the river and a few early season sunbathers lay on the rocks. I gave Lucas a thumbs-up and he clapped me on the back and flashed a big smile.

I inhaled the fresh air, then exhaled with a whistle. "Lucas, dude, just look at that. This park is amazing. What a great place for a getaway. This is going to be fun."

"Yeah, this place is really cool. I can't believe my parents haven't brought me here." He picked up his backpack and swung it over his shoulders. "Come on, let's go find us a campsite. And let the fun begin."

We laughed and continued walking. The winding trail cut back and forth down the steep bluff leading to the campground. We found a campsite in the far corner next to the woods. Several campers had set up nearby, but none too close. An assortment of camping trailers and large tents dotted the landscape. Since summer remained a few weeks away, large crowds hadn't invaded yet.

Lucas dropped his pack and sleeping bag beside the rock fire ring in the middle of our site. "Let's gather some firewood. We need to make a campfire and cook dinner before it gets too dark. I'm getting hungry."

I dropped my stuff across from him. "Dude, you're always hungry." Our shared laughter felt like a gift from heaven.

The site we chose featured level ground with abundant pine straw. The bluff would protect us from behind, and our campsite sat safely above the river—a perfect place for a weekend campout.

We plundered the woods and each gathered an armload of branches and sticks from the ground. We stacked the firewood in the ring. Then we found level spots for our sleeping bags. Our hands served as makeshift rakes, fluffing the pine straw into a makeshift mattress.

As a camping novice, I deferred to Lucas, who had obvious experience building a fire. He constructed a base of tree bark, kindling wood, and scrap paper, then laid twigs and sticks on top. He produced a cigarette lighter from his jeans pocket and lit the base. "Come on, help me," he said.

I followed his lead and kneeled beside the fire on my elbows and knees. We blew on it until the flames started. Then, we stacked larger sticks on top. The fire roared to life, lighting the gathering shadows of sunset.

"Wow." I sat back on crisscrossed legs. "That's a hot fire. Nice work."

"No biggie. When my dad takes me fishing, we always build a campfire to cook our catch. But since you and I don't have any fish, let's cook some hotdogs."

Lucas pulled out a small lunch cooler from his pack. So far, he exhibited a real knack for this camping thing. We took out two hotdogs each and stuck them on sticks. They bubbled and steamed when we held them to the fire's edge. The smell of roasting hot dogs floated on the breeze like a song. And that song promised a number one hit for our stomachs.

We ate our dogs from the stick, like kabobs at a fancy restaurant. When I finished, I spread out my selection of delicacies gathered from Mom's kitchen.

Lucas grinned. "Awesome, dude. You brought some of my favorites." He grabbed a juice box to wash down his hotdogs and reached for a pack of crackers and a snack cake. I followed suit.

We savored each bite as we leaned back against the large rocks that previous campers had pulled around the fireplace. The sun sank low in the sky and darkness gathered. Smiles of satisfaction crossed our faces as we glanced at each other across the dancing flames.

"How were things with your mom when you left home?" Lucas threw another branch on the fire.

I shrugged. "The same. But, hey, let's not talk about Mom, okay? I'll call her in the morning to check on her. Let's make some plans for all the fun stuff we want to do."

A loud thump pounded the ground between us. We both jerked upright. A large rock, thrown from the woods, had landed between us and rolled into the fire. Embers scattered as we scrambled backward, desperate to avoid flying cinders. Lucas and I stared at each other. A flash of fear pulsed between us.

Lucas rose in slow motion and shouted, "Who's out there?"

I strained my eyes into the shadowy woods. Nothing moved. We stayed still and listened hard. What hostile force hid in the dark, poised to attack? We heard nothing. Just the breeze and the sound of the river. A minute passed.

Then we heard an ominous sound—someone stepping through leaves in the trees just beyond our campsite. The intruder whistled a nondescript tune with no real melody. Then I recognized it . . . the *Andy Griffith Show* theme song whistled in a weird, out-of-tune way. I rose to a crouch like a sprinter on his mark.

Lucas shouted again, "Who's out there?"

I looked across the fire at him and whispered, "What are we gonna do?"

His hands trembled as he shrugged and whispered, "Beats me."

CHAPTER TWENTY-FOUR

Friday Night, May 16, 1997

T watched a horror movie at a friend's house once. The movie portrayed a camping trip full of terror. Could that movie play out in real life tonight? I shuddered.

A shout echoed through the woods, "Hellooooo!" We heard footsteps again, coming closer. No whistling this time. Instead, the intruder hummed the tune. Thinking an axe murderer might be on the loose, we remained ready to run. Both of us reached in silence and grabbed a rock to defend ourselves.

"Oh, hello, gentlemen." The stranger stopped and stared at us when he emerged from the thicket. "Got any more of those hotdogs?" He sported a goofy grin on his unusual face.

Despite the stranger's casual tone, fear gripped us. Running home was a tempting thought, even with all its problems.

The stranger kept smiling. He threw his arms out wide, took three more steps, and stopped at the edge of the firelight. "Come on, boys, I ain't gonna hurt you. Drop them rocks. How about helping a hungry homeless guy?"

We remained still. Watching.

Dirt and scars marred his dark brown face. Straight black hair hung limp around an unusual face that sported a wispy mustache and bad teeth. He wore a ragged assortment of clothes that hung on his thin body, making him look clownish. Worn-out tennis shoes wrapped in duct tape shone from his feet like a pair of new dimes.

Lucas shot me a look of desperation. "Okay, mister, we can spare a couple of hotdogs, just don't hurt us." Lucas waited.

The man took two more casual steps toward our fire ring. "I don't mean no harm, boys. Smelled your campfire and wondered what was cooking. Bad luck been tagging along with me in recent weeks. I stay out here by the river to keep away from trouble. You have nothing to fear from me, scout's honor." He held up three fingers together.

I glanced at Lucas. I detected something unusual in Lucas's expression, but I wasn't sure what I was seeing. Lucas kept staring at the man, his eyebrows knit together. He backed up, dropped his rock, and held out his open hand to me. I retrieved two hotdogs and handed them to Lucas. The man stepped over and reached for the hotdogs.

Lucas gasped and jerked the hotdogs back. "Wait a minute, I know you. You worked on our farm for my dad. I can't remember your name, but I'm sure you're the guy. Who are you?"

The man pulled himself up to his full height and struck a pose, thumbs under his arms, chest thrust forward like a rooster. "The name is Strike. At your service, my good man. And yes, I worked on your farm off and on the past few years. I remember you too. Couldn't forget that mullet, for sure." He laughed and stroked his chin.

Lucas continued to glare at him.

"Your dad's a good man. Hired the likes of me to do odd jobs. I'm obliged to him. And very pleased to see you again, I might add." He stuck out his hand.

Lucas gave him a tentative shake and stepped back. I stood watching with my mouth hanging open. Lucas realized he still held the hotdogs in his other hand. We both let out an anxious laugh and Lucas handed them over.

Strike mumbled a quick thank-you, squatted by the fire, and grabbed the stick I had used. "Now come on, boys, sit and join me for dinner."

We sat around the fire again but stayed vigilant. I kept my rock in hand, out of sight.

The hotdogs sizzled over the fire in no time while he continued whistling the mixed-up tune. When his dogs finished cooking, he stuffed them into his mouth, chewed furiously, and swallowed. Then he belched. "That's some excellent dogs, boys. Got any more?"

Lucas glanced at me, and I gave him a subtle head shake.

"Nope, that's all we've got." Lucas dropped his head.

"Gentlemen, you don't have to be worried. I won't waste your food." A glimmer of mischief shone from his eyes. "I can get all the food you'd ever want. I'm the king of this here river. And everybody in the city over there knows old Strike too. I guarantee it. So, what else you got?" He wiped his mouth and waited with anticipation.

I found my voice. "Well, mister, since you're homeless, I guess we can share. You can have a snack cake and a juice box." I quietly dropped the rock behind me and retrieved the goods from my pack. I tossed a cake and a juice to him across the fire. He snatched them out of the air and grinned.

The snacks must have been a gourmet meal to him. Strike devoured the snack cake and drained the juice box. "Now level with me, boys. What the heck you kids doing out here in my woods? You running away or just out for the weekend?"

Lucas glanced at me with a questioning look on his face.

I shrugged. "Before we tell you what's up with us, you tell us . . . what kind of name is Strike?"

He chuckled and wiped his mouth on his dirty sleeve. "Came from my dad. He used to yell at me all the time when I acted wacky." Strike sat up straight and dramatized a dad voice. "'Son, that's two strikes against ye. Don't make it three strikes, or I'll have to eject you from the game of life.'" Strike's cackling laughter rang through the darkness. "It got to be a daily habit for me to act wacky and Dad to yell at me. So my little brother started calling me Strike." He laughed again, and this time Lucas and I joined in, despite our efforts to look fierce. "Okay, now you know about my name. So what are your names?" Strike leaned back against the rock.

Lucas threw another branch on the fire and introduced us. He looked at me and winked. "We just came out here for a Friday night getaway. Headed home in a little while."

I picked up on the cautious twist to our story. "Yeah, Lucas and I are school friends. We needed some fun on a Friday night after a long week at school. We know we trespassed in your woods, Mr. Strike. Please accept our apology. We'll be clearing out of here as soon as the fire burns down. Our parents are expecting us home tonight."

Strike nodded. "No problem with the encroachment, gentlemen. Truth be told, these woods ain't mine—least not legally. Ever since that big cop across the river ran me out of town, these woods have been my home. Yours truly is the mayor of the river, and these woods are my jurisdiction. Squatter's rights." He cackled again.

His laugh sounded a little hysterical. I looked around to see if other campers heard the wild laughter. To my relief, no one stirred at the other sites.

Strike stood and shook his legs one at a time. "You boys are safe here in these woods. King Strike has guaranteed it. Stay as long as you like and come back as often as you want. Thank you ever so much for the delicious dinner." He bowed to us with an exaggerated sweep of his hand. "I shall see you on another day.

Mother nature calls." Strike turned and strolled back into the thicket.

The odd combination of cast-off clothing camouflaged him. He melted into the shadowy trees of his kingdom. We sat staring at his ghostly disappearance.

"What in the world just happened?" Lucas asked, his eyes wide and mouth hung open.

I nodded in agreement. "Yep, totally weird. That rock came soaring into the fire like a heat-seeking missile. He scared me to death when he walked out of the woods. I need to check my underwear."

We broke out with a laugh so crazy it rivaled Strike's cackle. Relief swept across our faces, and we relaxed at last.

Lucas stirred the fire with a long stick. "I sure hope Strike told us the truth when he said he would protect us. I sure hope you and I don't wake up dead tomorrow."

We broke out in another fit of laughter.

"Has he ever caused any trouble on the farm working for your family?"

"Nah," Lucas said. "Far as I know, he's a good worker with a very flamboyant personality. Dad likes him all right . . . but he tunes him out a lot."

As the fire burned down over the next hour, we sat and stared into the flames. The crickets, frogs, and cicadas provided a symphony of night sounds. One by one, the other campers turned off their lights. Our sleeping bags called our names.

We stood and stretched.

Lucas yawned. "We need to chunk our trash so we don't attract wild animals overnight."

I chuckled. "You mean more than just Strike?"

We snickered as I walked to the trash can and deposited the remnants of our dinner.

The campsite spigot provided water to brush our teeth, wash up, and get a drink.

I took off my shoes and socks and crawled into my sleeping bag. "Good night, Lucas."

He did the same and mumbled, "Yep. Interesting start to our adventure. Sleep good."

While I lay there on my back, the river sang me a lullaby. I soon fell asleep. At some point after midnight, I awoke with a heaviness in my chest. Another nightmare? No way to remember. Pushing back the sleeping bag to uncover my face, I gazed into the night sky. Brilliant stars punctuated the blackness. Hanging overhead, a bright constellation formed the image of eyes. Jacob's eyes haunted me since the day of the snake. But tonight the stars reminded me of God's loving eyes. I stared into eternity. His eyes grew larger and larger, closer by the minute.

Half-sleep gave way to deep slumber. I looked into God's starry eyes. I heard him whisper, "I'm here with you. You're never alone."

CHAPTER TWENTY-FIVE

Mom's Journal: Entry Six- Friday night, May 16, 1997

Hi, Jacob, I'm back.

I have some news. This afternoon, Michael left home for a weekend camping trip with Lucas. Lord knows, he needs a break from all my questions and doubts. This has been a terrible ordeal for both of us. He deserves this. So I hope it's a fun adventure. Michael's a good son.

Well . . . more than a week has passed since I wrote. I'm sorry. I wanted to talk to you. Kept planning to write.

So, why have I avoided talking to you? Because the silence came back. Remember when we talked last? I told you I hoped it would return. The questions drove me crazy, waging war in my brain. So I upped my dose a little. Not much, just an extra half pill each day. A tiny adjustment.

It helped. The silence returned.

The relief from the barrage of questions is nice. But the silence is more pervasive than I bargained for. And along with the silence, the darkness crept back in. I didn't expect that. Crazy as it sounds, this afternoon I craved the adrenaline rush of the endless questions. But I'll gladly accept the silence and darkness, because the hamster wheel of questioning was ruining my life.

So anyway, that's why we haven't talked in a while. Besides, I know you're okay. I'm sure life is wonderful in heaven. You probably don't even think of me and Michael down here, do you? Wait. Don't answer that. Please think about us every day. Don't forget us. Listen to your mother and do what I tell you. I love you and always will.

Which brings me to ask a favor. I need you to ask God some questions for me. I mean, you live up there with him, right? You see him every day. Will you make an appointment with God to present my questions?

Wait. Did I just hear you answer? Answer again, please.

Wow, I actually heard you whisper. I clearly heard you say, "Mom, listen to Michael. He's giving you good answers."

Okay, I hear you. And you're correct. Michael's answers do come from the Bible, so they must be from God. I should accept them as truth. I definitely should.

But no, I can't do it. I can't find the faith to accept Michael's answers. Not because they don't make sense. His answers make good sense. Something deeper always hangs me up. This analytical mind works against me. My natural tendency to mistrust overwhelms my desire to believe.

And that's where I'm at, Jacob. That's why I need you to take my questions straight to God. Can't you be my mediator? You're more real to me than people I live with every day. Make an appointment with the Big Guy, okay?

I'll sit here in the darkness and silence and wait for your answer.

Waiting.

Yeah, I hear you. I know. You always are the son who tells me exactly what you think. Now you say, "Take my questions directly to God."

That's your answer? Well, I don't like that answer. Who am I to question God?

Okay. We'll see. This weekend, while Michael's gone, I'll have some time. Maybe I'll ask God myself. Take my questions directly to him. But I've been away from God so long. Will he listen to me? Does he remember who I am?

So here we are. I hope I can survive the darkness and silence while Michael's away.

I love you, Jacob. Stay close.

If I slide too deep into darkness, come get me, okay?

CHAPTER TWENTY-SIX

Saturday sunrise, May 17, 1997

Morning snuck up on the horizon and crawled across the river. Towering clouds moved in overnight, filtering the sunrise into golden shafts shining through the trees. I pulled my sleeping bag over my head and turned away from the light. Sleep came again like a comforting hug.

When I woke up a little later, Lucas had dressed and scavenged for more wood. I rubbed my eyes, slicked back my hair, and sat up to look around. The ache from sleeping on the ground fell away while I stretched my arms and legs. The morning air filled my lungs with a rich brew of forest and river. What adventures lie ahead on this brilliant morning?

"You sleep good?" Lucas dropped an armload of wood on top of the branches gathered last night.

"Considering this mattress, I slept well." I patted the ground beside me. "Had some interesting dreams too. Kinda weird." I looked up through the trees. Just clouds and sky overhead.

Lucas built the morning fire in the ring. "What you want for breakfast? I've got apples and cereal, but we ain't got no milk."

I rummaged through my bag, then held up a juice box and a pack of crackers. "There're still some crackers, snack cakes, and juice boxes in here. We need to keep the bologna and leftover hotdogs in your cooler for later."

Lucas chuckled. "Okay. Sounds like a bona fide breakfast buffet to me." He lit the fire, and it crackled and sparked to life. I passed some food to him.

We ate and talked about ideas for our first day of adventure: hiking, swimming, sunning, exploring the riverbank. The possibilities seemed endless.

After breakfast, I headed to the river to wash my face, arms, and hands. Clean clothes awaited, so I changed inside my sleeping bag. Tight fit, but it worked.

We settled back on our rocks by the fire. In a solemn voice, Lucas asked, "Did you see those stars last night? Like an IMAX light show with nature sounds piped in. How awesome was that?"

I nodded. "Very awesome. And definitely cool. Just before I fell asleep, I thought the stars looked like Jacob's eyes—staring at me like the last time I saw him. But then, the vision of his eyes became a vision of God's eyes." I hadn't planned to say that. The words snuck out.

"Wow." Lucas sighed and looked me in the eye. "Do you think about Jacob a lot? I didn't know him for very long. But every day I still think about . . . what happened." He paused. "Heavy, isn't it?"

I looked away. "Yeah, real heavy. Seems totally unreal that it happened at all. But the hurt reminds me—it's real."

"How are you handling it?"

"It's tough, but Mr. Charlie has helped a lot."

Lucas threw a pine cone onto the fire. "Hm, I've been thinking a lot about his song lately. How did he help?"

The pine cone burst into flame. "Just being there to talk to. Helping me know God is here for me . . . and loves me."

Lucas rubbed his chin and looked sullen. "So, knowing God cares, does that help you make it through this?"

"Yep. Through all this mess with Mom's drug abuse and Dad's questions, I need somebody on my side. Mr. Charlie has been there for me. But knowing God is with me is off-the-charts awesome. Now if I could help Mom realize God's presence is the best anxiety reliever, maybe she could leave the anxiety drugs behind. No luck so far." I picked up a stick and drew a question mark in the dirt.

"Speaking of your mom, why don't you call and check on her? Go on and get that done so we can start our adventure. You can walk over to the camp store and use their pay phone."

"Yeah, I guess I should. I'll head that way and give her a quick call. Be right back." I grabbed a quarter from my pack and headed out. The store lay on the far side of the campground, near the picnic area and playground. The forest continued on the other side. I took my time and wandered along, admiring the tents and trailers. Several campers waved, and I responded with a smile.

The pay phone hung on the outside wall of the store. I fished the quarter from my pocket and flipped it in the air. Then I paused. A sense of dread to drop it into the slot and place the call came over me. Looking toward the sky, I hoped to see God's reassuring eyes. Nothing there. Only bright sunlight. So I bolstered my courage by standing tall and flexing a bicep.

The quarter slid into the slot, and the dial tone sounded. I spun the rotary dial one number at a time and held the big handset to my ear. Our home phone rang. Mom answered on the fourth ring.

I jumped right in, talking with enthusiasm, telling her all about our hike and campsite. I may have exaggerated some details. No mention of Strike, though. Eventually, I ran out of things to say and paused. She hadn't gotten a word in.

When she spoke, I heard the drugs in her voice. "That sounds wonderful. Maybe I should wander down to the river and join you," she slurred. "I wonder if I could find my way through the woods and back."

I cut her off. "No. No way you should come down here. You can't even find your way from the car to the back porch. Stay home. We're fine. Enjoy your vacation with me out of the house." I faked a laugh, realizing I may have come on too strong.

Pots rattled. Was she looking for something or stumbling around the kitchen? Her sniffles dissolved into tears.

I sighed. "It's okay. What's wrong?"

"I miss my boys. I want you both here with me."

The old hurt rose in my chest, wrapped around me, and drug me down. I slumped against the wall. "I'm sorry. Why don't I leave here now and come home to you?"

Her voice trembled. "No, no. Don't you do that. I'm just whining. You need a vacation from me. I'll be okay. Go have fun." The call ended.

I stood holding the receiver, stunned she had hung up. In a trance, I opened my hand. The receiver fell, bouncing on the metal cord connected to the phone. I retrieved it and put it in the cradle. My emotions felt like that receiver, bouncing out of control, hanging on by a slender cord.

I trudged away and felt the weight of Mom's grief pulling me down. I wandered into the forest beside the store and leaned against a tall pine tree at the edge of the river bluff. Deep sorrow snuck up and swamped me. The pain punched me in the chest and cut my legs from underneath. I crumpled in a heap against the tree.

A hand touched my head. With a violent shout, I jumped to my feet, ready to defend myself. I spun and assumed my best Karate Kid stance.

Strike stood staring. "Michael, it's okay." With a frantic wave of his hands, he tried to calm me. "Relax. Everything's alright. I'm here to watch out for you."

But it wasn't okay. His sneaking up on me ticked me off. I stared at him. I knew he felt the heat of my anger.

Strike spread out his arms and faked a smile. "Sorry, man. I promised to protect you in my kingdom. Just honoring my promise, that's all. Cut me some slack. I wasn't trying to freak you out." He took a step toward me. "We okay now, buddy?"

Lucas ran up the gravel road at a full gallop. "What's with all the shouting?" He bent over to catch his breath and stared wide-eyed. "The other campers heard it too. I knew it was you, Michael. I took off running to make sure you're okay. What happened?"

He glanced at me and then at Strike, who shuffled around in the pine straw. Meanwhile, I fought to quit hyperventilating.

I slumped, head down. "Come on, guys, let's go back to camp. We can calm down on the way back. I'll tell you everything when we're back at our site."

We stumbled together across the campground, trying to put the outburst behind us. Lucas nodded and flashed the okay sign to the other campers who watched our little parade. I kept my eyes straight ahead. Strike's smiles and waves earned some strange stares.

When the three of us settled again on our rocks at the fire ring, I started talking. I told them about the conversation with Mom and how she hung up on me. Then I explained my violent shout when Strike grabbed my head. We shared an awkward laugh around the circle.

Embarrassed, I looked at Lucas. His eyes reflected my hurt.

Strike broke the silence. "Okay, I got a distraught mom and two runaway kids. But none of the rest of that story makes any sense to this old boy. Why don't you lay it out for me real simple so I can understand?"

"Take it easy, Strike," Lucas said. "A few weeks back, Michael's little brother Jacob died in a handgun accident." Lucas told Strike the entire story and why we took this getaway.

Strike let out a low whistle through the gap in his front teeth. The serious look on his face painted a stark contrast to his zany clothes. "Okay, I'm tracking with you now," Strike said. He turned to me. "Sorry you had to go through that terrible tragedy. No wonder you collapsed against that tree grieving. I get it. My little brother died in childhood too."

"What happened?"

He shifted his weight on the rock and shook his head. "Drowned in the river during a family picnic. Me and him out swimming, our parents on the shore. Got his foot caught in a rock. The current took him under and swamped him. Before we could get there, the surge dislodged his foot and washed him downriver. They found his body the next day. Terrible. Still breaks my heart." Strike looked toward the river. "His name was Michael, just like yours."

The three of us sat with our heads down for a minute.

Lucas looked at Strike. "Did he die here in this river?"

"No. Way up north where I come from. I never went back to that stinkin' river."

I kicked a small rock toward the fire ring. "Are you scared to get in the water since that happened?"

"Nah, I take baths in this river all the time. Just what a man like me does, you know. Plus, this river's a part of my kingdom. But I still think of my little brother whenever I dip in the water. Seems like he's nearby when I'm close to the river. Guess that's one reason I like it down here."

"Wow, so sorry, Strike. I get it." I looked toward the river. "So, you ever blame yourself for your brother's death?"

"Oh yeah, I do. At least, I used to. Had to learn to let that go. Hard to do, though." He scratched his head and looked around. "Speaking of the river, how 'bout we take our groceries down there and sit on that big rock and enjoy the cool water under these here clouds?"

Lucas glared. "Oh, so it's *our* groceries now, is it?"

Strike's laugh rolled through the park and ended in a squeal. "Whatever you say, boys. Whatever you say."

He stood and swaggered toward the river. A king surveying his kingdom.

CHAPTER TWENTY-SEVEN

Saturday morning, May 17, 1997

The three of us helped each other jump from small rocks to medium boulders until we arrived at our destination —the biggest boulder on the river. I'd never experienced such a precarious journey.

I placed my backpack atop the large boulder. We tucked Lucas's small cooler inside. Now I sat still with my arms clutching my knees. My heart raced, afraid if I slipped, the strong current would beat me senseless.

Centuries of running water had carved a large indentation in the back of the huge rock. Strike pointed to the calm pool trapped in the curve. "This is the place, my friends. You're gonna love it."

Lucas explained how the boulder acted like a dam to make the pool safe—a good place for fishing and swimming. "So come on, jump in. The water's fine." He removed his shoes and socks and stuck his feet into the pool with a big grin. I loosened my grip on my knees but wasn't ready to push my luck.

I shouted above the sound of the rushing water, "Hey, Lucas, before you jump, if you got any cash on you, let's stuff it in my bookbag for safekeeping." Both of us pulled from our jeans pockets the little bit of cash and coins we brought. I shoved it in the outside pocket.

Strike took off several layers of shirts. He exposed a sun-darkened chest and a pungent body odor. The smell assaulted our senses even more when he took off his duct-taped shoes. We kidded him and held our noses. He just smiled, climbed atop the rock, and cannon-balled into the pool below, his over-sized boxer shorts flapping like wings.

We watched, wondering if he drowned. But he came shooting out of the water, laughing. His long, stringy hair stuck out in all directions. The signature laugh served notice to all— the king was in his kingdom. He dove again and surfaced with a lump of sand cupped in each hand. After scrubbing his body with the sand, he washed his head and hair. I had never seen such a thing. His flair for drama made his bath a comedy routine.

Strike asked for his clothes, and Lucas threw them in. He scrubbed the clothes with vigor, then flung them at us in a spray of water. Lucas stripped down to his shorts and jumped in. I stood and spread Strike's wardrobe to dry. Then I took off my T-shirt, counted to three, and jumped in with a big splash, still wearing my jeans. The water felt refreshing. The gentle swirl of the pool washed away the stress of the morning.

After swimming and diving for a couple of hours, my stomach rumbled. "Hey, guys, I'm hungry," I called out. "How about we snack on the cakes? We'll eat our bologna sandwiches in a little while."

They agreed and joined me atop the rock.

I rummaged through my bookbag to see what we had. "I guess we're down to a few hotdogs, bologna sandwiches, and apples. But we can make it work." I elbowed Strike. "Even though we're splitting it three ways instead of two."

Lucas frowned at our uninvited guest.

I handed out the last three snack cakes and juice boxes. We sat in a circle, savored the food, and laughed at our water antics. After our snack, we lay on the rock, warm in the sun.

"Hey, Strike," Lucas said, "tell us where you come from."

"Now, there's a good story. My dad fought in Vietnam during the war. He met my mom there. They fell in love. He brought her back home and they married. My mom birthed me up north in the big city where we lived." He chortled. "Problem was, Dad spoke English and Spanish because he came from Mexico. Mom spoke Vietnamese and a little English. Chaos reigned at our house. They cussed at me in three languages. See, I got this half-and-half face from them." He pointed toward his head and posed with a crooked smile.

Lucas rolled on his side and looked at Strike. "What's a half-and-half face?"

"Half-Asian, half-Mexican. Ain't it beautiful?" Strike cackled. "My parents loved each other but weren't much on romance. They fought like cats and dogs and worked themselves to the bone. We moved to one rough city, then another, over and over." He shook his head at the memories. "Tough life."

I rolled over and leaned on one elbow. "How did you end up here in Arradale?"

"Well, after my little brother drowned, Mom and Dad grew farther apart. They stayed together and made a marriage of it. But I didn't fit the mix. I dropped out of school about your age. Walked away. Been wandering ever since." He grinned. "Seems like I always find me a river to live on, though. It's kinda where I belong, I reckon. My little kingdom."

Rolling over onto my back, I stared at the sky. "Amazing story."

Lucas let out a huge yawn. "I'm ready for a little snooze. Tough sleeping last night on the hard ground."

The hollow of the rock seemed tailor made for napping. A

light breeze played a melody on the water and the clouds provided a sunshade across the sky. Warmth from the sun lulled me into snooze mode in a matter of minutes and dried my jeans too.

In my dreams, I heard Mom talking to Lucas's chickens while Stupid Baby rode the electric train around the attic track. That gave way to Mr. Charlie working in his garage to repair the snake we shot. The robin from the Jacob tree perched on Charlie's workbench and talked to him in a voice that sounded like Strike.

I rubbed my eyes to clear the dream from my head but then fell right back asleep. Ball-on-the-wall dominated my next dream. I threw hard at the faces of Brandon and Derek. Something grabbed my head in the middle of a throw and jerked me around. I screamed and began kicking at the wispy spirit that took hold of me. My foot connected with something solid. I kicked it as hard as I could to defend myself against the attack.

Wide awake, I bolted into a sitting position and shouted, "Stop!"

Strike and Lucas jolted awake. My backpack teetered on the edge of the rock from my kick. We watched it tilt toward the water. I scrambled on my hands and knees, the rough rock scraping skin from bone. A stiff breeze and the pull of gravity took over. All three of us cried, "No!" as I dove for it.

Too late. The backpack tumbled end over end and splashed into the river.

I jumped to my feet, hands outstretched. "No! This can't happen. There goes our food, sailing down the river."

Lucas jumped up and got in my face. "Yeah, and our money. What in the world did you do?"

"I had a crazy dream. Give me a break, man." I shook my head to clear the sleep from my brain. "In the dream, I kicked a ghost. In reality, I kicked our groceries and cash right into the river."

Lucas stepped back, and we stared at the backpack floating away.

"Stupid dream. Stupid me," I muttered.

Strike and Lucas joined me at the edge of our boulder and watched the bookbag bob up and down, riding the current. It rolled between rocks and over rapids like a roller coaster. Halfway down, the flap flew open and spilled food and cash into the river. Bologna, bread, hotdogs, and apples scattered in a little circle across the water. Several dollar bills floated alongside like a flock of seagulls. Our food for the weekend floated around the bend and out of sight.

I uttered an expletive before I could stop myself. Lucas sighed and plopped down on the boulder. I looked to the sky in frustration. Then I slumped down on the rock beside Lucas.

He shook his head. "Man, this is awful. What now? Anybody got a secret stash of food hidden in your pockets?"

We stared at each other.

Strike threw his arms out wide. "Well, boys, I guess it's time for old Strike to avail you of the riches of my kingdom."

Lucas and I ignored him, speechless with discouragement.

Strike stood and donned his dry shirts one at a time, the rank smell now vanquished. He stood above us, an orator in his boxer shorts. "Like I told you, gentlemen, I can access a smorgasbord of riches that would rival any king." He punctuated his words with grand gestures. "All we do is cross the bridge down the river from here and head into town. I can treat you to a feast of food and adventure you never thought possible."

Lucas and I kept staring at him, shaking our heads in disbelief.

Strike shrugged, then bent to put on his pants. He grabbed a snaggle-toothed comb from the back pocket. The comb slicked his half-dried hair into place. Then, with open arms and a huge smile, he turned back to face us. "So, what's it going to be, boys? Who's with me? I'm offering you a once-in-a-lifetime adventure with the king of adventure. Are you gonna go for it or tuck tail and run home to mama?" Strike held his pose and waited for our answer. He had made his best offer with obvious pride.

Lucas and I glanced at each other and looked away. We picked up our clothes to get dressed. Strike, tired of waiting for an answer, sighed and sat on the rock to put on his shoes.

Questions collided in my mind. How did we know if we could trust this homeless guy? Could this be stranger danger? I sure didn't want to do something foolish. But I wasn't ready to go home. No doubt about that.

I looked at Lucas. He raised his head to return my look. Did I detect a smile? Were we two ill-fated fools, or on the cusp of a glorious adventure? Just one way to find out.

I gulped. "Okay, Strike, I'm in."

Lucas glared at Strike, then his look softened. "Yep, me too."

The three of us shoved our feet into our shoes, then jumped up to chest bump each other.

Strike clapped his hands. "Okay, my friends, let's do this. Just be careful to stay away from Officer Harold Jackson." He swaggered down the face of the boulder. Like an agile mountain climber scaling a cliff, he jumped from rock to rock.

We followed the leader.

I stopped and shouted, "Wait! Who's Officer Harold Jackson?"

Strike already stood on the shore. He pointed to his ear to indicate he couldn't hear me and shook his head. With a grin and a shrug, he sauntered into the forest.

CHAPTER TWENTY-EIGHT

Saturday noon, May 17, 1997

L ucas and I grabbed our sleeping bags from underneath a tree where we left them.

Strike leaned on the tree and watched. "Okay, gentlemen, let's mosey uptown. I need to stop at my place and grab my good shoes on the way."

Lucas raised his eyebrows. "Your place? I thought you didn't have a home."

Strike smirked. "Follow me and I'll show you my humble abode." He turned and strode into the forest with us close behind.

Craggy overhangs and steep washouts lay hidden in the woods. But Strike steered a path that would be the envy of any explorer. Lucas and I marched after him with boldness as our trust grew.

Our three-man parade approached a large rock that jutted from the bluff. Strike stopped and swept his arm in a grand arc. "Here we go, boys. This is my place. I told you it's humble, but it serves me well."

We squinted into the darkness of the rock overhang. In the shadows, we saw a hollow place with a dirt floor. A couple of old blankets and a dirty pillow lay thrown over a cushion of leaves and pine straw. Plastic milk crates stood to one side. Each contained a jumble of unidentifiable items.

I tried to make sense of what I saw. "Yep, this is a humble abode for sure, Strike." I glanced at Lucas.

We chuckled and stared back into the darkness.

Strike climbed into the dim space and rummaged through a pile of plastic grocery sacks in a milk crate. "Eureka. Found 'em." He held a worn jogging shoe in each hand. Sitting on the dirt floor, he changed out of his duct-tape shoes into the jogging shoes. "These babies got given to me last week at the church in Arradale. Nice." He crawled out of his cave, stood tall, and struck a pose.

"Okay, hotshot, let's go find some lunch," I said, wary of snakes hiding in a crevice.

Strike took off walking through the woods again. Lucas and I jogged to catch up.

After thirty minutes of trekking along the river bluff, we heard traffic in the distance. A little farther, we saw a bridge through the trees. The swoosh of cars and trucks bumping over the bridge joints provided a cadence for our march.

At the edge of the forest beside the bridge, we huddled together for Strike's instruction. "This bridge is my passageway to town. Now you guys stay close. We're gonna climb through that tall grass beside the bridge. Keep an eye out for snakes and critters."

Lucas looked at me and raised an eyebrow.

Fifty feet above, the bridge spanned the river. A shiver ran up my back as I gazed up at the bridge, then at the river far below.

Strike pointed to the top of the hill. "And don't dare look sideways as we walk across because those cars come flying by real close. The sidewalk is very narrow."

Lucas and I gave thumbs-up to show we could handle it.

My voice trembled. "Okay, here we go."

Strike took long strides up the bluff, cutting angles through the tall grass to keep from going straight uphill. My foot slipped on the slick grass several times, so I pressed my sleeping bag against the ground to steady myself. All the while, I expected to step on a snake or a giant lizard. Lucas struggled too.

I paused when we made it to the top of the hill. Strike never looked back. He stepped onto the narrow sidewalk and headed across the bridge. The constant flow of traffic on the four-lane highway terrified me. I ignored the temptation to look down at the river or at the traffic racing by. More than once, a panel truck zipped by with its side mirror inches from my head. My heart thudded and my legs shook. Swimming there, the river didn't look very wide. But walking across it now, the bridge seemed to go on forever.

At last, we neared the other side. My anxiety gave way to excitement. When our entourage took the last few steps on the bridge, Lucas and I shared a nervous laugh and nodded to each other. We stepped off the bridge onto the wide sidewalk leading into town. A celebratory cheer went up from the three of us.

Lucas smirked. "So, where we headed, Strike? You promised a lunch fit for a king, right?"

Strike stroked his face while his eyes darted about. "Right you are, Lucas. Let's figure this out. Too early to get in line at the homeless shelter uptown. And the restaurants are just finishing up their lunch hours."

My eyes widened. "You planning to take us to a restaurant?"

Strike laughed. "What? No. You think I'm an actual king or something? I'm homeless, as you might remember." His look turned serious. "See, the best food comes from the best restaurants, right? When those restaurants close, you get the best handouts from the back door of the kitchen. I might know somebody who can help us with some leftover scraps."

Lucas frowned. "Kitchen scraps? Are you kidding me? That's the royal smorgasbord you promised us?" His eyes flashed with frustration.

I jumped into the conversation to calm Lucas down. "That depends on how hungry you are, right? Hey, I say bring on the scraps. I just wanna eat."

Strike clapped his hands. "That's the ticket. Let's see what we can scrape up in the way of scraps." He grinned and walked toward town, and I followed. Lucas huffed after us.

The state highway narrowed from four lanes into two and became a city street. Our path to lunch took us along a cracked and crumbling sidewalk. The street led through an older urban area with run-down businesses. We walked past a car repair shop, a carpet store housed in an old drive-in restaurant, and an assortment of unusual specialty stores.

The sun came through the afternoon clouds. Sweat beads popped on my forehead as the temperature climbed. The coolness of the river seemed far behind.

Strike shouted over his shoulder, "Not too far now, boys! Several places are just ahead. Don't give up."

Three blocks later, we came to a small diner with a rusty sign hanging over the sidewalk. The sign read ED's—EAT CHEAP. Strike motioned us to follow him up the side driveway. A rotten-smelling dumpster sat at the end beside the rear parking lot. Strike made a right turn along the back wall and crossed the lot. A cook slumped on the back porch, smoking a cigarette. Strands of long hair hung from his hairnet and his face sagged with a blank expression.

Strike walked up to him with a big smile. "Hey, Johnny. Big lunch crowd today?"

The cook stared at the sleeping bags under our arms and ignored Strike. "Maybe. Whatcha want, Strike? You here for the usual handouts?" His face remained expressionless.

"Wanted to introduce Ed to my two young friends from

across the river. And maybe see if he would treat us to a little leftover lunch." Strike smiled again, trying to work his charm on the guy.

Johnny looked across the parking lot. "Ed's out sick today. I chunked all the leftovers about ten minutes ago. It's Saturday, you know, so we're closed tomorrow. Help yourself. It's all in the dumpster." He took a drag from his cigarette and exhaled a stream of gray smoke in my direction.

Strike threw his arms out sideways. "Okay, well . . . I guess we'll move on up the street. Thanks for your kindness there, Johnny. You're quite the host. Tell Ed hello for me, and I hope he feels better."

Johnny didn't answer or look at us.

Strike turned and mumbled something under his breath. I shook my head and followed him and Lucas around the building back to the street.

Strike called out over his shoulder, "Oh well . . . win a few, lose a few. Next stop coming right up."

Lucas turned mid-step and cut me an angry look. I felt frustration rise in my chest too. But no way I would turn back now. I gave him a shrug, and we kept walking.

CHAPTER TWENTY-NINE

Early afternoon, Saturday, May 17, 1997

My stomach rumbled, and I felt weak in the knees. I distracted myself by looking at the neighborhood we walked through.

The older commercial district gave way to renovated buildings and nicer businesses. Up ahead, a restaurant painted in bright colors occupied a renovated home. Walking toward it, I could see café tables along the sidewalk. A sandwich board read SISTER SARAH'S SOUL FOOD BISTRO.

A young couple sat at an outside table. They leaned close together and giggled. But they fell silent as we passed. The young lady scooted her chair close to the guy and watched us with suspicion.

Strike headed for the front door, and we followed. A large lady hustled through the door and almost knocked Strike down. She jerked backward, and we scattered. Tea from the pitcher she carried splashed on the sidewalk.

"Whoa!" she shouted. "Careful, please." She stepped back and a look of shock crossed her face. "Strike. Get outta my way.

I'm trying to care for that delightful couple over there." She stood a head taller than Strike and wore an African dress and turban featuring rich colors. Her golden-brown skin glowed in the sun.

Strike smiled up at her and took a bow. "Greetings, Sister Sarah, queen of soul food. I'm so happy I ran into you." He chuckled at his own joke.

Anticipating a confrontation, the couple didn't dare move, and neither did we.

Sarah frowned and wiped iced tea from her arm with a towel she carried. Her voice rose. "Strike, what are you doing here? You know the police want to talk to you? When are you going to come to your senses and quit running?" Sarah shifted her focus to me and Lucas. A warm smile replaced her glare. "And who are these two handsome young men tagging along behind you?"

Strike straightened his back and beamed. "Ms. Sarah, this here is Michael and Lucas." He motioned toward us, and we gave her a shy nod. Strike continued, "They're on an adventure, camping in my kingdom by the river. But their food and their money got washed away downstream. Probably done washed out to sea by now. Sad, very sad." He slumped pitifully and looked down.

Sarah smirked and tapped her foot on the concrete. "Well, I hope you aren't leading these young men astray."

Not to let the opportunity slip away for a handout, I piped up, "He's telling the truth, Ms. Sarah. We lost our backpack of food and money in the river. Strike promised he could get us something to eat in town. We followed him up here." I hoped she would take pity.

"Yeah, yeah, I hear you, baby. I guess I can help you out. Maybe I can scrounge up some dried cornbread or something for you adventurers." She stepped toward the customers. "Let me get these folks some tea and their check. I'll see what we got in the kitchen. You three scoot around the corner and sit at the table out back. I'll be out there with a little something for you in a minute or two."

Sarah headed toward her customers, and we took off around the restaurant to the backyard. The restaurant occupied a renovated wood frame house on a large lot. We stashed our sleeping bags on the back porch surrounded by a well-manicured yard. The neat lawn featured a lush flowerbed along the back fence. A picnic table painted purple sat in the middle of the yard. We took a seat and relived our day of adventure so far. A few minutes of laughter and smiles passed between us while we anticipated lunch. Strike and I exchanged happy memories of our brothers.

The screen door slammed against the wall when Sarah kicked it open. She emerged, arms loaded with paper plates of steaming food. "I got some fried chicken legs, collard greens, green beans, corn on the cob, and cornbread cakes for you boys. That's about all we got right now. That lunch crowd came like locusts on a pharaoh."

We received the plates with thanks tumbling from our lips.

Her smile washed over us. "I'll be right back with some iced tea. You boys dig in and enjoy the best soul food in town."

Generous helpings of mouth-watering food beckoned, and we answered the call by the forkful. I saw Lucas crumbling cornbread into his collards.

I stopped mid-bite. "What are you doing?"

Lucas frowned. "You don't know how to eat collard greens?"

Strike cut me a look. "Nobody's introduced you to the best delicacy known to man? Sad."

I shook my head.

Lucas stirred the crumbs and greens together. "We've grown collard greens on our farm for generations. Mom boils the leaves in a big pot. The juice is called pot liquor. The cornbread soaks it up so you can eat it by the spoonful. It's really good." He stuck his spoon in and took a big bite. The juice dribbled down his chin.

Feeling quite adventurous, I gave it a try. At first, the taste seemed too strong and vinegary. But as I chewed, brilliant flavors exploded in my mouth—sweet, spicy, salty, smooth, and grainy, all at the same time. I smiled and took another spoonful, bigger this time. I slid it into my mouth. Jacob would love this stuff. I glanced heavenward and smiled.

Sarah announced her return with a bang of the screen door. Grinning, she set cups of iced tea in front of us. "That's what I like to see, folks smiling as they eat my food. Good stuff, huh?"

Strike held up his Styrofoam cup. "A toast to Ms. Sarah and her soul food."

We tapped our cups together and settled into the rhythm of eating. I savored every bite. My stomach and my taste buds gave joyful thanks.

I wiped the juice off my mouth with my paper napkin. "Ms. Sarah, why do people call this soul food?"

"Well, Black folk in America have had it rough sometimes. What with slavery in the old days, then Jim Crow laws and discrimination, we needed some encouragement for our souls. Turns out the best food for the tongue is the best food for the body. And tasty, filling food also soothes our souls."

Her simple answer made sense.

Sarah looked me in the eye. "The most important thing in life is a sturdy soul, Michael. Nobody or nothing can give you what your soul needs most. Only my Lord Jesus can give me that." She winked. "So I serve up soul food to save the body and point people to Jesus to save their soul." Her smile shone as bright as the sunlight glittering through the oak trees.

I returned Ms. Sarah's smile. Her words proved as rich and filling as her food. It made me think of what Mr. Charlie and I talked about. For a fleeting moment, I missed him and hoped he was okay. And that made me think of Mom. I said a quick silent prayer for her and asked God to soothe her soul and let her know she wasn't alone.

CHAPTER THIRTY

Midafternoon, Saturday, May 17, 1997

We finished eating and sat back, satisfied. Nothing but a pile of chicken bones and a corn cob remained on each plate. We stretched our stiff legs and stood beside the table, ready for what might come next.

Ms. Sarah gathered the paper plates and cups and handed Strike a soapy cloth. He wiped off the picnic table. She surveyed the clean table and gave a nod of approval. "Hey, Strike, have you seen our friend Officer Harold Jackson? He ate lunch with me the other day."

Strike turned away and carried the trash to the metal can. When he turned and walked back to the table, he whistled a carefree tune.

She stood looking down at him. "I considered asking the officer if he had seen you around. But I knew better than to open that can of beans."

Strike smiled, swung the cleaning rag over his arm like a server in a fancy restaurant, and answered in a Londoner's accent, "Dear lady, you know the respect and affection I have for my friend Officer Jackson. So please, ma'am, when you see the officer again, give him my warmest regards. Now I'm going to take these young fellows to the park." He bowed low, danced across the yard and into the restaurant's back door with a flair.

Sarah stood with arms crossed, clucking and shaking her head. "That's my man Strike. Always trying to waltz around the trouble he stumbles into." She turned to me and Lucas. "Okay, gentlemen, time for this old gal to go home and put her feet up. It's been a long day. I enjoyed meeting you. Come see me anytime you wander this way." Her eyes twinkled. "Maybe you'll have a little folding money in your pockets next time." She chuckled and pointed. "Now run along and catch up with Strike. That man's always on the move." She swooped down to give us an engulfing hug.

I glimpsed Strike walking up the sidewalk toward town and pointed at him. Lucas scowled, and we switched into another gear. We caught up and came alongside him, striding uptown.

Strike looked at us with a haughty look as we walked. "Didn't believe me, did you, boys? I promised you a smorgasbord of good food, did I not?"

Lucas chuckled. "Yessir, you did. And, wow, did you ever deliver on that promise. That food tasted amazing. I'm sorry I doubted you."

"Then let that be a lesson to you. Trust me, boys, trust me. The king will not disappoint."

Strike led us across the street, and we detoured into an older neighborhood.

The sidewalk took us beside stately brick homes with distinctive arches and steep roofs. Some had picket fences around their tiny front yards for children and pets to play. The neighborhood intrigued me, so different from the cookie-cutter homes on my street.

After a few blocks, Strike led us down a side street with giant oak and elm trees overhanging. Stretched before us lay a city park in a valley. Azalea bushes in full bloom gave bursts of color. The trees shaded everything. We stopped and inhaled the fresh, warm breeze drifting through the park. Several moms watched their children play on the playground. A walking path circled the park, and senior adult couples strolled there.

Strike motioned us to gather around. In a dramatic whisper, he pointed into the park. "You boys see those swings way over there on the far edge of the park?"

We nodded and wondered what mystery he would reveal.

He motioned us closer, then shouted, "Last one there is a rotten egg!" He sprinted for the swings.

Lucas and I hesitated, then sprang into action as the challenge registered. We ran with every ounce of speed we had. Strike's running style resembled uncontrollable chaos, with flailing arms and legs churning like a wrecked windmill. He gasped for air, his mouth wide open and wild hair blowing straight out behind him.

We caught him at the three-quarter mark. Lucas and I touched the swing frame in a tie. Strike arrived two seconds behind us. With hands on knees and gasping for breath, we looked back across the park. Children, moms, and seniors stared at us.

"Come on, let's swing," Lucas said.

We climbed aboard the swings as the breeze cooled our sweating faces. Ms. Sarah had filled our bellies and lifted our spirits. We swung in that beautiful garden spot without a care. I hadn't swung like this since Jacob and I were little kids, soaring high with laughter. Mom and Dad always took us to a park on Sundays in our hometown. But now that memory seemed dim, faded, and far away.

The rhythm of the swing released the pain of the last month. Up and down, forward and backward, the recurring motion lulled me into a comfortable trance. I lost track of how long we swung.

Strike snapped me out of my reverie with a flying leap from his swing. He stuck an Olympic-quality landing on the soft sand below. Lucas and I bailed out of our swings and followed him. The senior walkers had headed home, and the moms and kids had packed it in. The quiet seemed eerie. Lucas and I sat on a park bench, and Strike sat on the curb of the walking path.

Lucas threw his arms across the back of the bench. "This has been a crazy-fun afternoon," Lucas said. "What now?"

Strike turned toward our bench. "Sounds like you guys feel satisfied with the experience so far."

A loud blast from a siren pierced the peaceful setting.

Lucas and I jerked upright. Strike jumped to his feet. We looked toward the sound. A city police car slowed at the entrance to the park up the hill.

A stern voice came from the car's loudspeaker. "Strike. What are you doing here in the park?"

From the passenger door, a dark mountain of a man emerged, still holding the loudspeaker mic. A second officer appeared from the driver's side, ripped off his sunglasses, and smashed his hat onto his head.

I recognized his slender build and wide shoulders—the investigating officer from the day of the snake.

Strike whispered, "It's Officer Harold Jackson. And his partner, Officer Parker."

Jackson's voice boomed again from the speaker. "We've been looking for you. Why do you have those two kids with you?"

Lucas and I gasped and jumped to our feet.

Jackson continued to talk into the mic. "Stay where you are." His voice sounded edgy. "Officer Parker and I need to have a chat with you three. Do. Not. Run."

Parker walked a few steps into the park. His hands rested on his gun belt. Could the police be looking for me?

Strike thrust both hands in the air and faked a grin. Through the grin, he whispered, "When I drop my hands, take off running for the woods behind us. Jump the fence. If we need to separate, let's meet on the street behind the park. I know a hiding place."

Strike dropped his hands. We took off in different directions, running helter-skelter across the park. This time, our running wasn't for fun.

The officers gave chase, but we had a big head start.

We kept running and made it to the woods. I jumped over fallen trees and avoided rocks that might break an ankle. An old fence loomed ahead. I scrambled over just behind Lucas and Strike.

The three of us emerged from the forest onto the back street. But the police car screeched around the corner and headed straight for us. They had anticipated our escape route and driven around to cut us off.

Strike shouted, "Back into the woods! At the fence, turn left and run to the canyon."

We took off running again. I heard the police car skid to a stop behind us. Car doors slammed and the officers gave chase. They crashed through underbrush and saplings, closer with each step. We ran in desperation to maintain our lead.

Officer Jackson's voice carried through the trees like a roaring lion tracking prey. "You can run, but we will find you. That's a promise." They kept coming, relentless.

The fence appeared in the underbrush ahead. We made a quick left turn and scrambled downhill. The fence ended at the opening of a small canyon. Lucas and Strike headed toward the mouth of the canyon.

I stopped and gasped for air. I rested my hands on my knees and peered back up the hill at our pursuers. Through the trees, I saw Jackson and Parker stop running. They slumped against the fence, huffing for air. Parker shook his fist in the air and shouted, "We will find you."

Satisfied they had given up, I jogged ahead and caught up with Lucas and Strike waiting at the end of the fence. I said quietly, "They stopped chasing halfway down the hill. They're slumped over, looking defeated." I gave them a thumbs-up. We resumed our walk toward the canyon.

Stopping at the canyon's mouth, we tuned our ears to hear any sound. Silence. Strike motioned us forward. We stepped quietly a few yards into the canyon to hide and wait. Strike sat on a fallen tree beside a spring. We joined him, our breathing returning to normal.

Lucas and I glanced sideways at each other. Who knew our adventure would include being chased by police officers? No way we bargained for that. If they had caught us, how could we explain that to our parents?

Despite the close call, Strike giggled like a little kid who had just won a race. I couldn't help it. I snickered right along with him. Maybe from the release of tension. I tried to stifle it with my hands over my mouth.

Lucas shushed us with a frown. He whispered, "We are hiding in the woods from two cops. We're being chased like criminals. And you two are giggling like little girls. Stop it. Now."

Lucas's glare doused my laughter like water on the campfire. I regained my composure and turned toward Strike. "Okay. So why are the police chasing you, man?" I tried to sound intimidating. "We deserve to know the truth. Those guys looked serious."

Strike turned away. "Nothing serious. I'm just a small-timer. Officer Jackson enjoys chasing me for sport when he has nothing else to do."

Lucas sighed. "Come on, dude. There's gotta be more to it. Give it to us straight."

Strike leaned forward and smirked. "Well, I do have a pretty long record of small stuff."

I squinted at Strike. "Hey, you tell us what stuff. We'll decide how small it is."

"Well, basic stuff . . . assault on another homeless guy, breaking and entering, panhandling, trespassing . . . minor annoyances like those."

Lucas whistled and looked at the sky.

I threw my hands out. "Strike, that's a lot of small stuff."

He shrugged. "Okay, so here's the truth. Homelessness is survival of the fittest. Those misdemeanors happened when someone tried to hurt me or my friends. Just necessary actions to survive in my world. I'm not some vicious meanie. I gotta protect myself, you know."

Lucas sat forward. "Can't you stay away from trouble somehow? My dad always told me to turn and walk away."

Strike nodded. "Maybe a smarter man would stay away from town and keep to himself on the river. But it's plum boring over there. I like the lights and the excitement of the city." He grinned. "And old Strike here kinda enjoys playing chase with the officers. That's my favorite sport. And, as you may have noticed, I'm winning."

We frowned and shook our heads.

His grin faded. "Besides, there ain't no warrant out for my arrest. Just a fun little game of chase when the three of us get bored."

Lucas and I looked at each other. I turned back to Strike. "And there's nothing major on your record? Tell us now or we're outta here. I mean it."

"Nope, nothing major. I swear. Just some petty charges. Mostly dismissed. Believe me, I'm not the bad guy." He stood and thrust his hands out. "You gonna put me in cuffs and turn me in, or we gonna continue this little adventure?" A stubborn look of defiance crossed his tanned face.

For just a moment, I considered turning toward home, then

banished that thought. "Okay, let's keep going. You satisfied my doubts. I'm good with it."

"No. No way," Lucas hissed. "Are you crazy?"

I stared at him, my mouth hanging open. Strike stood frozen in shock.

"If my mom and dad find out we've been hanging out with a convicted criminal . . ."—Lucas struggled to find the words—"they will string me up. No matter if the offenses are petty, I'm outta here." He stood and headed out of the canyon.

I gasped. "But . . ."

His stride matched the determination in his voice. "No. I said no. Not gonna happen. Come on, we're going home." Lucas didn't look back, just kept walking.

Strike and I hurried to catch up. We followed in silence.

The stream led us back toward the park. A heavy blanket of frustration hung over the three of us stomping along the creek bank. Strike regained his composure and hustled to catch Lucas. With a deft move, he scooted around Lucas to regain the lead.

We walked and he talked. "This here creek runs through the lower end of the park. When we get to the park, we'll survey the situation. If the officers are gone, we'll walk the tree line back to the main road. We'll stop at Sarah's, grab the sleeping bags, then . . ." His voice trailed away as he left the words unsaid.

Our little parade trekked through the woods toward the park.

Twenty-four hours ago, Lucas and I left home on this little getaway. So far, the adventure exceeded all my expectations. Was this the end? We would see.

CHAPTER THIRTY-ONE

Mom's Journal: Entry Seven- Saturday, May 17, 1997

Hello, God. It's me, Susan Judson. Do you remember me? I sure hope so. We used to hang out together a long time ago. My son Jacob is telling me I need to bring my issues to you, face-to-face, one-on-one.

But you already know that. Of course you do. You know everything.

How should I address you? Your Majesty? Creator of the universe? Lord? In my church days growing up, I always loved calling you Lord. So personal, yet so holy.

Now so many years have come and gone. I'm afraid I haven't talked to you much during my adult years. Please accept my apology. That's my fault. Like Mr. Charlie's song says, you are always here for me. I remember you telling me this yourself during my younger years. But sadly, adulthood blurred your promise. Some-how, in the challenges of daily life, I forgot what you told me. Jacob reminded me of your promise last night. I needed that reminder.

Tonight, my other son, Michael, is out on a camping trip. I've been alone since yesterday when he left. These lonely hours brought excruciating pain. So please protect Michael. If he doesn't come home, I will never survive. That's not a threat, just a confession. So please don't even think about taking him too, okay? Please say you'll protect him.

You commanded us to confess to you, right? Well, I must confess, I'm taking medication. The doctor prescribed the drug—an anti-anxiety pill. So my conversation might be a little fuzzy around the edges. Please don't think I'm disrespecting you. I'm not. In fact, I believe you provided this medication to help me survive. After all, I remember from childhood reading in my little pink Bible that you are the giver of all good gifts. And my little pill has been such a good gift. Thank you.

My problem is I've become dependent on those meds. That's embarrassing, but there it is. And with Michael away from home and my anxiety on high alert, I've lost track of my dosage schedule. Yeah, I know . . . stupid. And very scary. I started taking one pill daily to calm the war of questions raging in my heart and mind. But then the meds took me to a place of silence and darkness. Please don't allow them to overtake me. Can you hear me, God?

So, that's my first area of concern. Can you keep me from becoming a despicable addict? I've always despised people who get hooked on drugs. I mean, you gave me the ability to take control of my situation and engineer my circumstances. Who needs drugs, right? I can take care of everything. At least, that's what I always thought.

And now, look at me. Confused. And addicted? I hope not, but hey, maybe I am. God help me. I don't want addiction to be my destiny. Michael deserves better. And so do I.

So let's work through my list of questions. I'm trying to stay focused. The challenge is more difficult by the minute. I think I took a leftover half pill after Michael called today. But I'm not sure. I should have made a list. Oh well, too late now. So here we go with my questions.

Why did you have to take Jacob? You're God. You could have plugged the pistol with your finger. You could have locked the trigger so it wouldn't fire. Why did you let this happen? Michael says the answer is because you allow us to live in freedom. Okay, we all want freedom. But does freedom have to end with tragedy? Can't you be more discerning about what you allow?

So, there it is. That's the crucial question I've been wanting to ask you. But I've got more questions too.

Second . . . oops, I forgot the second question. Wait a minute, let me think. Oh shoot, it's not coming to me. Must be the pill taking effect. I can really feel it now. It creeps up on me and then lowers the boom. So . . . where am I? I meant to make a list of my questions. You know . . . the little engineer. Me and my lists. Haha.

Aside from that, just to let you know, I'm keeping this journal. When it's all said and done, I plan to hide it away somewhere. Not sure where. Someday I'll share it with Michael. Or maybe he'll find it among my possessions when I'm dead and gone. Who knows? Dead and gone. Death doesn't sound like a bad alternative to my messy, frustrating life, ya know? At least I would be with Jacob. Can you protect this journal and get it to Michael someday? I would appreciate that.

Sorry, God. Floating, lost at sea. Can't find my compass. Come on, Susan. Focus.

So, God, where were we? Oh yeah, can you give me some hope? Is there any hope in the world anywhere anymore? I'm not sure. Who knows? But hey, God, I really need some hope. I really do. The minister at Mr. Charlie's church says hope can only come from you. Nowhere else. For real? First you take my Jacob and now I'm supposed to come to you for hope. Strange. Doesn't compute.

Has it been five weeks since Jacob left? Seems like eternity. Sunday school teachers always told us you sent Jesus to show love. To give hope. You got any? I need both. I'm lost. Lost as a bullet fired by accident, ripping through life with no target in mind.

Please find me, God. Take me back. Embrace me in a big God hug. I haven't had a hug from anyone in so long. Maybe Michael hugged me before he left for the weekend, but I can't remember. Help me. Hold me. I'm crying out to you. Something has to give. Even if it's something tough, painful, hard to endure . . . whatever it takes, come find me.

I need you. The darkness and silence are closing in.

I see a light in the distance. I sure hope the light is you. But I don't know how to find you.

Find me, God. I need you. Please find me.

I love you, Lord.

CHAPTER THIRTY-TWO

Late afternoon and evening, Saturday, May 17, 1997

We saw no sign of the police officers or their car in the park. But we couldn't assume they weren't watching from a hidden location. So we moved from tree to tree, ready to run back to the woods.

When we arrived on the street, Strike motioned us to stop. The three of us scanned the area in all directions. Seeing nothing, we hurried toward the main road. We cut through an alley and paused at the corner behind an ancient oak. Nothing in sight. The cops had left the scene.

I faced the reality that our adventure was over. Dejection laced my voice. "Nothing left to do now but hustle over to Ms. Sarah's and grab the sleeping bags. Then we'll head home, I guess." I frowned at Lucas.

He turned his back and headed across the street.

We jogged to Sarah's place and around to the back porch. Our sleeping bags lay where we left them. A big hunk of cornbread wrapped in cellophane sat on top of each.

Strike grinned despite his frustration with Lucas. "That Sarah is a special lady, isn't she?"

Lucas and I gave a solemn nod. I kneeled and shoved the cornbread into my bag alongside the other lumps poking out.

Strike stared at us, then shrugged. "I guess the cornbread will be our going-away gift since y'all decided to tuck tail and run." He raised his eyebrows and looked back and forth at us, waiting.

The breeze stirring the backyard trees provided the only sound while we delayed our inevitable goodbyes.

Without warning, Lucas sprang to his feet. "I can't do it." His voice rose in an uncharacteristic shout. "I can't force Michael to go home yet. Not to that mess." He stared at me, confusion written across his face and pulling his shoulders into a slump.

Strike and I sat stunned, staring at him.

Lucas turned away for a moment. When he faced us again, his words poured out like syrup. "I ain't ready for this to end. And irregardless of the criminal record, we'll be home tomorrow. So I guess I'm okay to keep going."

I gasped and shouted, "Yes! Thank you, Lucas. Please . . . don't let this end yet." I stood, pumped my fist, and grinned at my friend.

He wouldn't return my grin. Instead, he crossed his arms in defiance. With a stern look, he pointed to Strike. "But if this goofball gets us in trouble, I'm blaming you, Michael."

Before I could respond, Strike stepped over. He shook Lucas's shoulders until his crossed arms fell free, then grabbed and pumped Lucas's hand, laughing. I stood, and he shook mine too. "I give you my word, gentlemen. You shall not regret your decision. I hope today's events prove my mastery of adventure on demand. And you can trust me to keep you safe."

A relieved laugh tumbled out of me. "Well, yeah, the past twelve hours go way beyond anything I ever imagined." I snorted, amused by my sudden turn from sadness to joy.

Lucas gave me a slow, weary smile.

Strike motioned for us to huddle up. His energy and enthusiasm had returned full force. "Okay, boys, y'all ready to head uptown?" We nodded. "I've got several ideas in mind. Follow me into the next chapter of this here adventure."

And away we went into the great unknown.

The sunset cast shadows around the homes and businesses along the street. Cars ambled into the city in search of whatever this Saturday night might offer. Our legs felt stiff, aching from the chase with the police. We took our time.

"Whatcha got in mind for the evening, Strike?" Lucas asked.

Strike talked over his shoulder while he walked. "Well, my friends, you think you can handle any more excitement after a day like today?"

I picked up my pace. "I'm up for whatever you got in mind."

Strike smiled and gave us a thumbs-up. "Excellent. Here's what I'm thinking." He stopped walking and turned toward us. "We can't sleep in a homeless shelter because they'll call the cops. So, hey, let's take a little tour of the town and see what's happening. I got another friend who'll give us some dinner. And I know a place where we can bed down safe for the night." He paused with raised eyebrows. "Sound like a plan?"

I nodded. My trust in Strike had grown throughout the day. "Sounds okay to me," I said. "Lucas, you okay with that plan?"

Lucas dropped his sleeping bag on the sidewalk, sat on the curb, and looked up. "This has been a fun day, but I'm wearing out. Can we hang out somewhere for a while?"

I sat beside Lucas. "Yep, come to think of it, I'm running out of steam too." I looked at Strike. "Got an idea to give us a little rest?"

"Sure. Old Strike is an endless fountain of enchanting ideas —even ideas that involve hanging out and cooling our heels. I got just the place in mind, two blocks away."

We helped each other stand, hoisted our sleeping bags, and resumed our slow walk toward town. In the next block, we entered a warehouse district with trendy shops, a coffeehouse, a bakery, and apartments. Just ahead, I saw a two-story brick building with a tin roof and a large, paved parking lot. The elegant carved wood sign hanging over the sidewalk read BAUSCHATZ BREWERY AND JAZZ CLUB.

Bare lightbulbs hung along the outside wall and illuminated our way as we came alongside the club. We stopped and listened. A live band played cool jazz inside. Laughter and conversation flowed over a courtyard fence out onto the sidewalk.

"Why don't we stop and listen for a while?" I asked, feeling the music soothe my tired body.

Strike stopped and stretched. "You read my mind. This is our next destination. Thought you might favor a little Saturday night entertainment." He pointed to a dark corner of the building. "Let's sit over there in the shadow beyond the streetlight, just in case the cops ride by."

We agreed and headed over.

I checked the digital wristwatch Mom gave me for Christmas —a little before eight o'clock. The crowd inside sounded small. But as cars trickled into the parking lot, the noise level grew.

"What time is dinner?" Lucas asked, taking a seat in the shadows.

Strike looked up the street toward town. "Oh, we'll rest here about an hour. Then we'll walk into town and meet my buddy Jiménez for dinner. He'll be at the place where we'll sleep tonight."

Lucas yawned. "Okay, dude. Whatever." He shook his head. "I'm not even going to ask who Jiménez is, or what he's got to do with dinner or a place to sleep." I laughed.

Our sleeping bags became cushions as we leaned our backs against the wall. I stretched my stiff legs and sore feet. "Why don't we play that game where we count cars by color?"

Lucas nodded. "Our family calls it the Color Car Counting Game."

Strike pointed at a passing car. "I'll take white cars."

I chose red and Lucas chose blue. We agreed to play until the digital clock on the bakery sign read nine o'clock. The lead kept changing as cars streamed by. The minutes ticked by and Strike's points mounted. At nine o'clock sharp, he proclaimed himself the winner and danced a victory jig on the sidewalk.

When Strike finished tripping over himself, we grabbed our sleeping bags and headed uptown. The buildings stood taller and sat closer together. City lights cast a fascinating sparkle all around us. We entered the city in wonder. I had only ridden through the city with Mom driving, so walking up a city street at night proved to be a novel experience.

I looked in the store and office windows we passed. A two-story white office with landscaped shrubbery and a manicured lawn loomed ahead. The attractive building sat perched between two taller structures standing guard on either side. Over the office door, gleaming metal letters read LAW OFFICE. Above that was a fancy sign with the law partners' names.

Strike stopped, looked up at the sign, and threw his arms out wide. "This is the place, boys."

"The place for what?" Lucas asked.

"The place where Mexican manna from heaven shall fall upon one old guy and two young boys. But you gotta have faith, my friends." Strike assumed the role of a preacher at the pulpit. His eyes flashed. "We must have the faith to believe God will provide the blessed manna we need right now." He pointed at us. "Do you believe?"

I nodded. What would falling manna sound like? I heard the breeze in the trees, the distant sound of a garbage truck, and the hum of a lone car wandering up the street. But no manna falling.

Lucas, sleepy-eyed, stared at Strike. He walked a few steps away and sat on the curb of the parking lot. Strike and I shrugged and joined him. The three of us sat in the quiet and waited for our manna to fall.

Another sound in the distance caught my attention. A truck huffed and puffed a few blocks away. It rattled like a pioneer wagon and chugged up the street toward us. I squinted into the darkness, curious to see what this could be.

Strike put his hand to his ear and whispered, "You gotta believe, my friends. You gotta believe."

A few seconds later, the rattletrap emerged from the shadows and turned into the law office parking lot. The odd contraption rumbled past and pulled into the last spot on the other end.

Spike proclaimed triumphantly, "Manna from heaven, my boys. You're seeing the future before your eyes. A Mexican food truck."

Lucas and I stood, looking in amazement. A Mexican sombrero, hand-painted in bold colors, adorned the side of the rusty panel truck. Under the sombrero, a flourish of capital letters proclaimed, NEZ DOES MEXICAN, GET YOU SOME. Over a giant sliding window on the side of the truck, the words FOOD TRUCK LICENSE #0003 had been stenciled.

"Hey," Strike crowed, "don't just stand there with your mouths open. Let's see what's for dinner."

The driver's door swung open, so we made our way to the truck. A short, stocky guy hopped out and stretched his arms over his head. He sported curly black hair and a full mustache. His eyes flashed with recognition. "Ay caramba, look who is walking across my parking lot. Nobody but the infamous Strike, the king of the world."

The man laughed and fist-bumped Strike as they met under the streetlight. Strike grinned as wide as the half moon hanging overhead. "My man Nez. How's the world treating you?" They embraced in a bear hug and took a step back to look at each other.

The smile on Nez's face matched Strike's grin. "Doing good, my friend. Been serving Mexican food to hungry customers all over town. What brings you into the city on a Saturday night?"

"Just giving these two suburbanites a quick tour of the place." Strike gestured toward us. "Met them yesterday at the county campground in my kingdom. They're mighty hungry. But I'm afraid they ain't got no money for you."

"S'okay. Any friends of Strike are friends of mine." Nez laughed and stepped forward with a hand extended. "Greetings, gentlemen. My name is Jiménez. Nez for short." He shook our hands and flashed us each a big smile.

I returned his smile. "I'm Michael, and this is my best friend, Lucas. Pleased to meet you, Mr. Jiménez."

Strike stepped beside his friend and laid a bony hand on his thick shoulder. "Me and Nez met three years ago when I moved to town. Both of us had Mexican fathers, so we grew up being cussed at in Spanish."

Jiménez took up the story. "Yep. Me and Strike, we are buddies for life. He helped me get my taco truck going. With his expertise installing kitchen equipment, he and I put everything in my truck I needed to cook."

I exchanged a glance with Lucas and said, "Wow, Strike. You knew how to do all that? Amazing."

Lucas nodded. "Total surprise, bro."

Strike stuck out his chest and beamed. "I cooked in restaurants all my life. I had to troubleshoot kitchen equipment a lot, ya know? No big deal to retrofit a kitchen into an old panel truck."

Nez rocked back on his heels with arms across his barrel-size chest. "So, you boys, you are hungry, eh?" A smile curled his mustache.

Lucas and I answered in unison, "Yessir."

Nez sprang into action. He uncoiled a heavy extension cord from his truck and plugged it into an electrical outlet on the office wall. "Okay gentlemen, I've powered up my kitchen. We got chicken, beef, lettuce, cheese, and wraps. I'll open my window, and you tell me what you want."

Nez bounded back inside the truck and slid open the large serving window on the side of the truck. "Order, anyone?"

"I'll have a chicken burrito with chips," Lucas said.

"Me too!" I shouted.

"Me three," Spike agreed.

Jiménez threw the chicken on the grill. "I've got just enough to fill those orders. Gotta run by the store in the morning and stock up for my Sunday run." He chopped fresh lettuce, tomato, and cheese to spread atop the chicken. The burritos he handed us sat on cheap paper plates with chips piled high. Soft drinks in paper cups came next. We accepted his generous offering with gratitude and headed to the curb to enjoy our manna from heaven. Nez closed the serving window and stepped outside to sit on the lower step of his truck. "Good day for me today. A good day's wage for our dream account at the bank. One day soon, my loved ones will join me here."

Between bites, Lucas asked, "Where are they now?"

"My wife and two daughters are in Guadalajara. My wife, she is a teacher. I came here four years ago. I go home to visit twice a year. But America is our dream destination. By God's grace, I hope to reunite my family here this fall. I'll open a small restaurant where we can work together. And then the American dream will be ours." His laughter rang from building to building, and his stocky frame bounced up and down. How could he be so joyful with his family living more than a thousand miles away? Such determination to pursue a dream inspired me.

Lucas finished chewing and asked, "Why do you park here at the law office?"

Nez smiled. "This lawyer, he helps immigrants and their families get visas. The legal work to bring my family here has already begun. My lawyer friend loves God and people. He is a great man." Nez gestured toward his truck. "Last year, when he discovered I needed a place to park, he offered his parking lot. I sleep in my truck above the cab in a bunk. Strike and I installed a water tank. And, of course, I have my kitchen. Behold, my little home on wheels." Nez swept his hand toward his food truck. "I keep walking close to God and trusting him, and he keeps providing." He stood and yawned. "And where you guys sleeping tonight?"

Strike scratched his head. "Well, we're too tired to walk any more. Can we have some of your used cardboard boxes? We can sleep on the back veranda here at the law office. We'll use the boxes to keep the dew off and give us a little cushion."

"Sure, the boxes are next on my list for the dumpster. Might as well use them first." He motioned us to follow.

I gathered up our dinner trash, and the three of us followed him to get the cardboard. I handed Nez the trash, and he dumped it in a large trash bag destined for the law office dumpster. We bid Nez good night and went to arrange our outdoor sleeping quarters. The cardboard boxes provided each of us a pallet under our sleeping bags and a folded shelter overhead. The ceiling lights lit the veranda, but Strike assured us the dimmer would switch them off at eleven o'clock.

Today had been a great day of adventure, far beyond anything I expected. We settled into our sleeping bags, our bodies worn out from swimming, walking, and running. For a moment, I thought again of Jacob. Deep inside, I longed for him to be with me right now. I looked into the night sky, hoping to see his eyes. But the city lights and bright moonlight obscured the stars.

When the lights went out, so did we. But an hour later, I found myself in another chase.

CHAPTER THIRTY-THREE

Just before Midnight, Saturday, May 17, 1997

A spasm shot through my shoulder muscle. I awoke in pain. Massaging the hard knot gave some relief, but not much. I sat up and stretched both shoulders, then swiveled my head to loosen my neck. My watch read 11:52 p.m.

The cardboard didn't provide enough cushioning. And after sleeping on the ground the night before, my shoulder could take no more. I shrugged off the sleeping bag and slid into a sitting position. Just as Strike promised, the porch lights had shut off at 11:00 p.m. Strike and Lucas snored alternately. Beyond the veranda, an eerie quiet had fallen on the city. The glow from nearby streetlights cast intriguing shadows beyond the law office.

The ache in my shoulder eased some while my mind wandered across the past weeks. The image of Jacob's eyes invaded my thoughts again. Most of the time, I pushed that thought away. But now I allowed his eyes to come alive in my imagination. I wondered what the adventure of the last two days would have been with Jacob here. He would have had a blast.

And so would I, experiencing all this together. Then the emotion hit me, as always. I missed him so much. But I didn't want to give in to the grief.

I slipped out of my sleeping bag and stood up to stretch my stiff legs. Grabbing my jeans, I put them on, then wedged my feet into my shoes. They ached from yesterday's chase. My whole body felt sore. I didn't care. There might be regret tomorrow, but the urge to wander with only my thoughts as company pulled me into the city.

Making my way around the front of the law office, I walked alongside the taco truck. The bright colors glowed in the dark. The sound of Nez's snoring rumbled from the open truck window. I strolled across the parking lot and looked up and down the street. Nothing in sight and not a sound to be heard. I headed back the way we walked earlier that evening.

Mom came to mind. I felt my gut wrench at the thought of her depression. Why couldn't she understand God is here for us? She obviously loved Mr. Charlie's song. If only she could accept how much God loves her. Such a hard thing to realize while going through anger and grief. Hey, I should know. But my state of mind improved when I realized God is here beside me. What a comfort that has become. Of course, I'm sure there will be many more difficult times. But for now God's presence is enough.

Lost in thought, I had walked two blocks. The quiet of the city at night scared me a little, so I whistled as I strolled along. I turned the corner, ready to circle back to the law office. From behind, something bumped against my leg. Shocked, I let out a muffled cry and jumped sideways.

Oh, a black Labrador retriever. Maybe my whistling attracted him. I stepped back, hands drawn tight against my chest, to make sure he wouldn't bite. His face lifted toward mine, and I could have sworn he smiled at me. The dog's wagging tail shook his whole body. What a friendly pup. Before I could stop myself, I reached to scratch him between the ears. I always wanted a pet dog, but Dad wouldn't go for it. He said work kept them too busy to care for a pet.

My newfound friend could not be a stray. He had a collar and a shiny coat. When I stopped petting his head, he whimpered for more. Maybe he lived nearby and wanted a friend who would take him on a walk. That reasoning worked for me.

"Hey there, boy. What's your name?"

Of course, he didn't answer. That would have been real freaky. We fell in step together and I whistled another made-up tune as we walked along. His presence comforted me.

When we turned the next corner, my canine friend suddenly drew back, crouching and growling. I stopped. Nothing appeared out of the ordinary on the street. All quiet and still. "Come on, boy," I said. "I gotta get back . . . before my buddies wake up and find me missing. Let's go."

But he wouldn't budge, continuing to growl and stare up the dark street.

A woman stepped out of the shadow, sneering at me. Her matted hair, face, and clothes looked filthy. "Hey, kid, you got the goods you promised me."

I gulped but found my voice and attempted to sound forceful. "Ma'am, you've got the wrong person. My dog and I are just taking a late-night walk. Whatever you're looking for, I don't have." A shudder ran up my back at the horrifying sight of her.

A strange, toothless smile crossed her face, and she glanced into the alley beside her. I followed her look. A man stumbled from the shadows. I recognized the man. Johnny from Ed's Place. He swayed and leered at me. The dog let out a violent bark and lunged forward one step. The woman laughed with a pitiful moan in her voice and moved closer to Johnny.

He snarled, "Shut up, you mongrel. One more sound out of you and I'll turn you into dog food." He drew something from his pocket, and with a shaky hand flipped open a switchblade knife.

The dog whined and sat beside me.

Johnny turned toward me and continued to tilt side to side in a stupor. "Enough small talk, kid. We're not playing with you. You wouldn't be out here on the street unless you had a little something to sell. So where is it? Hand it over." With a shaky step, he lurched toward me, pointing the knife at my chest.

"Run!" I shouted to the dog.

I ran with all the speed my sore body could summon. My dog friend sprinted alongside me as the crazed couple gave chase. Pounding the pavement of the sidewalk, my tired legs carried me down the dark street toward the law office. My imagination went wild with fear of what might happen if that dangerous duo caught us.

While I ran, I dared to glance over my shoulder. The ragged twosome giving chase reminded me of a scene from a zombie movie. I tripped on the dog and fell flat on the sidewalk.

Ouch. I rolled to avoid the two pursuers lunging toward me. My newfound friend came to my rescue. With a menacing growl, he charged at them, nipping and biting. Johnny and the hag backed off several steps.

I took advantage of their retreat, jumped to my feet, and continued running. I heard Johnny cursing and feared he would attack the dog with his knife. But after a few steps, the black Lab caught up. The groans from behind told me the zombies had continued the chase. But now we had a more comfortable lead.

The dog and I sprinted side by side until the law office came into sight. What if they attacked Strike and Lucas? *Please, God, don't let this evil force chasing me bring more tragedy.*

At full speed, the dog and I rounded the corner of the law office. I saw Strike standing in the shadows. I pulled up beside him, breathless. He sprang from the shadow and stepped in front of the onrushing pursuers. They crashed into Strike and barely caught themselves before falling.

Strike put his hands on his hips. His voice took on a parental tone. "Well, Johnny, fancy meeting you here. Put up that knife right now. You and your lady friend can just turn around and head back to the den of iniquity you came from."

Johnny frowned and leaned forward precariously. The woman slumped on him, panting. He pushed her away. "Strike, get out of my face. Somebody owes us some goods."

Strike took a slow step toward the two. "Okay, you put up the knife. Then . . . we'll talk. You know I can take you down, so don't threaten me. I've done it before and I'll do it again." He stared Johnny down.

Johnny snorted, closed the knife, and stuck it in his pocket.

Strike smiled casually. "Excellent decision, my friend. Now listen carefully. You are obviously drunk or high, or both." He pointed at me. "This young man is not the person you think he is. He's a nice kid from across the river. In fact, I introduced him to you this afternoon at Ed's. So cool your jets and go home. He ain't got nothing for you. Got it? Get out of here. Now." He pointed up the street we had raced down.

The hag leaned on Johnny again and whispered to him, "You gonna let that man talk to you like that?" She swayed, on the verge of a face plant.

"Shut up," Johnny muttered to her. He turned, motioned her to follow, and walked haltingly across the street. She scurried behind, and they headed back the way they had come.

Strike and I watched in victory, my rescuer standing between us. I let out a relieved whistle, and Strike clapped me on the back.

Breathless, I muttered, "Thank you, sir." Then I petted the dog. "And thank you too, sir."

The dog smiled and relief flooded my whole being.

Lucas stumbled around the corner, his hair poking out in all directions. With a groggy voice he mumbled, "What, umm . . . what are y'all doing out here . . . in the middle of the night? And where the devil did that dog come from?"

I laughed. "Not from the devil. Never mind, dude. I'll fill you in tomorrow. Let's all go back to sleep."

The black Lab nosed my leg, so I petted him between the ears. "Come on, fellow, you can watch over us tonight." I looked at Strike. "And hey, man, thank you for watching over me too."

He gave me a thumbs-up.

We shuffled toward our makeshift bedroom, with the dog following. I slipped off my jeans and shoes and slid into my sleeping bag. My canine friend sat a few feet away. I yawned and patted the cardboard beside me. "Come on, boy." He slunk over and settled next to me under my folded tent. I rolled onto my side and looked into his eyes. He stared back with his head resting on my sleeping bag.

Fatigue engulfed me, but a thought came to mind. Maybe God sent this dog to be my protector. I pursed my lips. Did God provide protection from unexpected sources? Sure, why not? I wondered how many other protectors God had provided me during the five weeks since Jacob died.

Would there be more?

CHAPTER THIRTY-FOUR

Morning, Sunday, May 18, 1997

The morning light shimmered between the tall buildings of the city. Sleep faded. A whisper of sound repeated a continuous rhythm. Through sleepy eyes, I saw sprinklers sweeping back and forth across the lawn. The cool mist drifted under my cardboard tent and cooled my face. The fresh mist woke me little by little.

My body ached. My midnight chase came back to mind. I looked for my dog friend, but intuition told me he had moved on. Maybe he found someone else to rescue. Such a godsend.

Despite the soreness, I felt well-rested because my canine friend provided extra security through the night. I rolled over onto my back and stretched my legs and arms. My mind wandered toward home. Mr. Charlie would be in church. And Mom—was she holding on? I pushed thoughts of her from my mind.

What would this Sunday morning hold in store?

A church bell rang in the distance. The deep chimes served

notice throughout the city, announcing this as God's day. The melody sounded ancient, yet familiar. I counted the low bongs that struck the hour. Nine o'clock.

I sat up. Strike kneeled over a sprinkler head, rinsing his face and hair. He saw me watching and motioned me to join him. Lucas remained deep asleep.

I crawled out of my sleeping bag, walked to the sprinkler, and joined Strike. After my makeshift shower, I shook my hair dry and wiped my face. My stiff muscles began to stretch and relax. I felt excited for our last day of adventure.

Strike reached over and tousled the water from my hair. "Happy Lord's Day, Michael. No telling what Almighty God has in store for us this beautiful Sunday."

"Yep, no telling. But I don't see how today could be as memorable as yesterday."

We shared a laugh.

Strike reached into his pocket and pulled out a package wrapped in aluminum foil. He held it high like an offering on the altar. "And now it's time to eat some of Ms. Sarah's cornbread for breakfast."

I smiled at the thought. "Let's do it. I'll wake up Lucas so he can join us."

"Good idea. When Nez is up and around, we'll ask him for a drink to wash it down."

"Too bad we don't have any collards to go with it," I said, grinning. Then I trotted over and lifted the cardboard tent over Lucas. "Wake up, farm boy. Time to eat some of Ms. Sarah's cornbread for breakfast."

Strike strolled over to watch. "Yeah," he said through a mouthful of crumbs. "We done washed in the lawn sprinklers. So the two of us are ready to go to church this morning."

Lucas stuck his head out of the sleeping bag. His hair stood straight up. "Church?"

"Sure, why not?" Strike said. "They got good preaching and singing at the Triune Mission Center just up the street. And best of all, they got a lunch to beat all Sunday lunches."

"Yep, one thing we've learned so far," I said. "This man knows where to eat."

We heard the sliding window of Nez's truck fly open. Nez stepped through the door of his truck in his T-shirt, looking mad. "What are you three doing out here raising such a ruckus on a Sunday morning?" He stared. Then his face dissolved into a wide grin. We laughed.

Strike took a bite. "Sir, do you have anything to drink we might beg from you?" With each word came a shower of cornbread crumbs.

"Sure, come on over."

The three of us hustled to the truck, desperate for something to quench the cornbread desert in our mouths. After a long minute, Nez handed each of us a cup of cola through the serving window. Strike grabbed his cup and took a large swallow, wiping his mouth on his sleeve. Lucas and I sipped the cool, fizzy liquid for as long as we could make it last.

Nez, already dressed in his work pants, stepped out the door and slid his arms into a colorful shirt. He buttoned it up and watched us. Lucas and I sat on the curb and finished the last of our cornbread and cola. A simple soda in a Styrofoam cup never tasted so good.

"Nez, you coming to church with us at Triune Mission today?" I asked.

"Nope, sorry. Can't make it, Michael. I'd love to join you, but I gotta get going." He gestured toward town. "I'm heading to the City Center to catch the Sunday lunch crowd. They come to the museums and parks with their families and their pets. Gotta make that money for my American dream." He smiled. "But hey, you'll like Triune. God's presence is all over that place. They got powerful preaching and singing, and the free lunch is outstanding."

We stood and brushed the crumbs from our clothes. Nez smoothed the front of his shirt and slicked his hair back.

Strike stepped over to his buddy. "Nez, the manna-from-heaven-man. I appreciate you, my friend." They exchanged a hearty hug, then stepped back and grinned at each other.

"Be safe and strong in your river kingdom, Strike." Nez turned to me and Lucas. "And God bless you boys. I pray you have a great day and a safe return home. Don't let Strike get you in trouble. Godspeed." He chuckled, bowed to us, and mounted the steps into his truck.

Nez settled in the driver's seat and started it with a roar. With a wave, he drove out of the parking lot and rattled down the street, headed out to raise money for his American dream.

A light breeze stirred the treetops, and the sun lit the streets with a golden glow befitting a Sunday morning. A rumble of thunder stopped us in our tracks. We turned and saw dark storm clouds gathering on the horizon across the river near Arradale. The sound of the thunder motivated us to get moving.

Strike gathered our cardboard and put it in the dumpster. Lucas and I hurried to a gas station a block away to clean up in their public bathroom and change clothes. On our way, I told Lucas every detail of the zombie pursuit from last night. He couldn't believe he slept through it.

When we returned, the thunder rolling across the river sounded closer. An outside staircase leading to the second floor of the building sat along the far back wall. Lucas and I stashed our sleeping bags under the stairs, then hurried around to the front.

Strike paced in the parking lot. "We better get going. Don't wanna get caught by that storm. It's coming our way."

Lucas and I agreed. We headed uptown in the same direction

as yesterday. Strike took the lead as usual, and the three of us jogged up the street.

Along the way, we watched the storm clouds cover the bright sun across the river. The weather reminded me of my life—the bright hope of moving to Arradale now covered by the dark grief of Jacob's death. I turned my thoughts away from the storm and focused on the light of hope.

CHAPTER THIRTY-FIVE

Late Morning, Sunday, May 18, 1997

Eight blocks up the street, Strike, Lucas, and I arrived at the Triune Mission Center. High-rise office buildings surrounded the church. The red-brick sanctuary looked like a sedate grandma sitting between the youthful skyscrapers. A steeple rose square and solid beside the church. Her red terracotta roof and arches reminded me of the older homes we had passed the previous day.

We slowed our pace and approached the classic building in awe. The sight of so many people approaching from all directions surprised me. Homeless people walked toward the church from throughout the city. In contrast, well-dressed folks parked their nice cars along the street and strolled toward the front door. But most of the crowd wore everyday clothes, unlike the folks at Mr. Charlie's church who always wore their Sunday best. Plus, the people came in a variety of skin colors. Also unlike Mr. Charlie's church.

We continued our quick step right up to the front door of the church.

"Welcome to Triune," said a smiling lady standing beside the large wooden double doors.

The man beside her gestured and said, "Come on in."

Continuing through the arched entrance, we walked slower into the worship center. The coolness of the inside air jolted our bodies after being outside for two days. Ushers at the back gave a warm greeting to regular attendees and helped visitors find seats.

One usher motioned us forward down the aisle. "Can I help you fellows find some seats?"

"Yes, sir," I said, "but not too close to the front."

We followed him down the aisle, looking at the majestic worship space. I gazed in wonder at the high wooden beams crisscrossing the vaulted ceiling. The expansive ceiling height and beautiful stained-glass windows lifted my spirit. I felt certain we could meet God in this awe-inspiring space. I wondered how many generations had found hope and promise in God's presence here.

The usher pointed to three empty seats in the middle of a bench. I felt pleased to see seats available because the place seemed packed. Strike led us to the vacant seats and sat. Lucas and I squeezed down the row into the remaining two spaces. The seat cushions felt far more comfortable than the curbs and sidewalks of the last two days. While we settled in, I heard a rumble of thunder. The sunlight streaming through the large stained-glass windows dimmed. The thunderstorm we saw across the river had arrived uptown.

Looking around at the people sitting near us, I whispered to Strike and Lucas, "There are so many kinds of people here. Some look homeless. But others look like folks from Arradale, or maybe even the rich side of town. This is cool. People of every kind, all here to worship together. Wow."

Lucas agreed, but before he could answer, the chatter of the audience fell quiet. We turned our attention to the stage.

A young man walked onto the platform and picked up a

microphone at center stage. He welcomed everyone and introduced himself as the pastor, then invited us to pray with him. "Heavenly Father, thank you for these wonderful people here today. Each of us is your child through Jesus Christ. We celebrate our differences because you created us different from each other. Draw us close to your heart. In Jesus's name. Amen." During his prayer, I heard raindrops on the roof. When his prayer concluded, the rain became a shower.

A thunderclap rolled through the silent building. I turned to watch a commotion at the back of the worship center, where the front door slammed behind someone hurrying from the storm. An usher stepped toward the lady while she shook rain from her umbrella. Dressed in white, she huffed and puffed at the downpour that dampened her nice clothes.

When I saw her face, my heart jumped. Ms. Sarah from the Soul Food Bistro. I nudged Lucas and nodded toward her. He glanced back to see her and shot me a big smile.

Strike turned to look too. He grinned and whispered, "Ah, the queen has arrived. And looking spectacular in her royal wardrobe, I might add. We'll find her when church is done."

Lucas and I elbowed each other with joy. We turned back toward the front.

A young couple carrying musical instruments walked onto the platform. The pastor introduced them as folk singers who wrote songs about spiritual things. The husband played guitar and mandolin. His wife played percussion instruments and a small accordion. Their voices blended with cool harmonies. The opening song expressed hope found in a bird that sang through a raging storm. How appropriate for a stormy day like today.

I enjoyed the four songs they sang because they spoke about real life—different from Mr. Charlie's more historic church songs. On two of the songs, the audience sang along with the duo. I guessed they sang here often because everyone seemed to know their songs.

After the musicians left the stage, the pastor invited us to pray our own prayers while he led. We stayed seated and bowed our heads. Lucas and I opened our eyes and exchanged a look when people around us began talking aloud to God. A few prayed in silence, but most of them talked like God sat right beside them. I heard Spanish, English, and several other languages lifted to God, all at the same time. The rainstorm pounded the old tile roof and added to the symphony of sound from the verbal prayers. To my surprise, I heard Strike praying too.

Since no one paid attention to anyone else, I joined right in, talking out loud to God. My anxiety over Mom's state of mind poured out first. The agony of missing Jacob and the pain stabbing my heart came next. Tears welled behind my eyes, but I held them back. I tried to close on a positive note by thanking God for Lucas and all the food Strike found for us in the city. And for the dog that rescued me last night. After my prayer, I glanced at Lucas and Strike. They seemed unfazed by the unusual prayer time, having their own audible conversations with God. At last, the pastor closed with an energetic "Amen." We echoed with our own boisterous "Amen."

The pastor then introduced today's speaker, Marcus Jones, a former football star who played at the university here in town. Lucas bolted upright, grabbed my forearm, and shook me with excitement. He whispered, "Dude, Marcus is my hero. I can't believe he's the speaker today. I've wanted to see him in person since I was a little kid." Dropping my arm and scooting to the edge of his seat, Lucas focused on the man walking onstage. The crowd applauded, but Lucas whistled, clapped, and cheered louder than anyone. I couldn't remember ever seeing my slow-moving, soft-spoken friend go over-the-top about anything like this Marcus guy.

When the applause and cheering died down, the pastor described Marcus's college days and successful career in the NFL before he suffered an injury. Now he served as a chaplain for a prominent college team a few states away. The pastor gestured to him, and Marcus took center stage, his muscular frame poised in game time mode.

He thanked everyone for coming and invited us to pick up a Bible from the book rack in front of us. Lucas helped me find the verse in the Old Testament part of the Bible. We all stood and read aloud Jeremiah 29:11. In this verse, God told us he has a plan and a future for his children.

After reading the scripture, we sat again. Jones pointed at different people in the crowd and asked why we came today. I blushed when he seemed to point straight at me. "Some of you are running away from something," he said. "Others are chasing after something you cannot find. Many of you don't even know what you are searching for. But God knows. You are running away from hurt and pain and running toward hope. Know this, only God himself can you give you the hope you need."

His deep voice rose and fell above the sound of the rain on the roof. "No matter what's happened to you, God still has a plan for your life. And that plan will give you hope and prosper you in the future." He used a very direct speaking style, and I felt like he knew me. "God sent His Son, Jesus, to seal the deal. Jesus died for our sin, then rose again to sit right beside God and plead our case. In fact, he's talking to God this minute about you."

His words mesmerized me. *Yes*, I thought, *I'm running away, searching for healing, and desperate for hope.* I slid forward to the edge of my seat, eyes fixed on his every movement, ears tuned to every word.

He shared how his life went sour when an unexpected injury forced him to retire from pro football. Then he shared stories of friends and family who also endured hard things. But in every case, God showed up to heal their hurt and supply the hope they needed. His powerful voice sounded impressive. But the power of Marcus's message made a much deeper impression.

I thought about the last several weeks. The familiar ache still stirred in the depths of my soul. But something else stirred there too, alongside the pain. I realized that when Jacob died, Mom and I lost hope. Any future happiness seemed very far away. Especially when we thought we might have caused his death. But Marcus Jones told how God is bigger than tragedy—big enough to give us hope and a future. Oh, how I needed that hope.

The Bible verse he quoted went right along with the message of Mr. Charlie's song. Both the scripture and the song assured me God was with me every day. That powerful truth planted a seed of hope in my spirit. Now I knew. The feeling stirring in my heart gave real evidence this seed has grown. I welcomed my newfound hope like manna offered to a hungry wanderer.

Marcus finished his message and led in prayer, then walked offstage without acknowledging our spontaneous applause. Lucas and I still sat on the edge of our seats. The pastor returned, invited everyone to stay for lunch in the fellowship hall downstairs, and dismissed us with a prayer.

We stood, nodding in agreement with all we had heard.

Lucas turned to me, beaming. "Man, who knew that Marcus Jones would be the speaker today? That is so awesome." In a wistful voice, he added, "I wish your brother could have heard what he said. Jacob would have liked that message."

"Yeah, Jacob would have loved this place. But, wow, Marcus's message sure hit home with me." I sighed, then perked up and looked across the crowd. "Hey, let's go see Ms. Sarah."

Strike chuckled. "At present, she's standing at the back, surrounded by a gaggle of admirers. The queen and her court."

Lucas nodded. "Okay, but first, I gotta go meet Marcus. This is my big chance. I don't want to mess it up." He slid down the row and cut a path through the crowd with uncharacteristic speed. Marcus stood floor level at the edge of the stage, chatting with folks from the audience.

"I'll wait here," Strike said.

I hurried to catch up with Lucas.

Lucas and I waited behind a young couple who complimented Marcus on his message. When the couple moved away, we stepped up and shook his hand. What a powerful grip he had. I stepped back so Lucas could speak to his idol. But his mouth hung open, speechless. Marcus smiled at him and waited. Seeing Lucas dumbfounded, I swallowed and spoke. "Good morning, Mr. Jones. Thank you for that outstanding speech. My name is Michael, and this is my best friend, Lucas." I nodded toward Lucas. "He's a huge fan of yours. You're still his favorite to ever play here. He really wanted to meet you."

Marcus chuckled and put his big hand on Lucas's shoulder. "Well, Lucas, the pleasure is all mine. I'm thrilled to meet such a great fan. And I pray you boys have found some hope in my message today."

Lucas blurted out, "Michael's little brother died a few weeks ago. It was an accident." Then a horrified look crossed his face. He looked at me, embarrassed.

I assured him it was okay to tell and met Marcus's gaze. "Yes, sir, it's been very tough. But God has helped me know he's here for me."

Marcus put his other hand on my shoulder. "Michael, I'm so sorry. That's heartbreaking. Please know that God is with you, son." He patted both our shoulders with his muscular hands. "God will carry you through and give you hope. He's done it for me, and he will do it for you. You're never alone."

Wow. I didn't expect to hear those familiar words. "Thank you, sir."

A group of teens walked up to speak to Marcus, and we stepped away.

Walking up the aisle, Lucas whispered, "I'm sorry, man. It just came out. I didn't mean to say that."

"It's okay. I'm glad we talked to Marcus about it. Did you

hear what he said? You're never alone . . . the same words as Mr. Charlie's song."

Lucas smiled.

God had planted his seed of hope. Now hope was growing— in both of us.

CHAPTER THIRTY-SIX

Noon, Sunday, May 18, 1997

Ms. Sarah waved when she saw us weaving through the crowd toward her. She resembled a queen in her white dress, white hat, and white high heels. Her outfit presented a perfect palette for her golden-brown skin. I broke into a trot and dove into her arms. The warmth of her hug engulfed me. I wished I could feel a hug like that from Mom.

Sarah laughed. "Look who came to Triune this morning. I thought you boys woulda high-tailed it back across the river by now. Where did you sleep last night?"

Strike stepped forward. "Well, milady, the city provided our every need. First, my buddy Jiménez cooked us a wonderful dinner. Then we slept like royalty under the portico of my favorite law firm. Accommodations fit for the king and his two attendants." I noticed he failed to mention the chases with the police and the zombies.

Sarah's skeptical look showed she wasn't buying Strike's hype.

Strike dropped his voice. "We even showered this morning in the sprinkler system of said law firm."

Sarah laughed and pushed him aside.

Undeterred, Strike scooted back in front of her. "So here we are, clean before the Lord and ready to partake of a sumptuous Sunday dinner. May we escort you, Your Highness?"

She raised a gloved hand with a flourish. "Yes, gentlemen, you may. Lead on."

Our entourage headed to the stairs and joined the lunch line.

At the top of the stairs, Lucas leaned close to Sarah and whispered, "We got chased by two policemen."

Strike shushed Lucas with a finger across his lips.

Sarah stopped, looking indignant. "You did?" She tapped her cheek with a forefinger. "I wonder why Strike failed to share that information? Okay, boys, talk to me."

Strike turned his back but continued to lead us down the stairs to the food line.

Lucas and I took turns recapping our play-by-play chase with the police officers. Sarah gave us her total attention while we progressed in the slow line.

When we finished our story, she raised her eyebrows and lifted her hands. "This Officer Jackson fellow must be a little slow of foot . . . and mind. You're telling me you three track stars left him in the dust?"

We had a good laugh at that. Strike turned to join in too.

Our foursome arrived on the lower floor. Since we still had a way to go before the serving window, we told Ms. Sarah about the manna from heaven provided by Jiminez's food truck.

She frowned. "Stop right there. I know you're not saying Mr. Jiménez is a better cook than me?"

Lucas jumped in. "No, ma'am. Nobody cooks as good as you, Ms. Sarah. Not even my mom." He covered his mouth with his hand and looked away.

I elbowed him and snickered, "Don't worry, I won't tell her you said that."

When we reached the serving window, we picked up a plastic cup and utensils. A sign said several neighborhood churches provided the food today. The servers dished up baked ham, pineapple casserole, hash brown potatoes, green beans, and a golden-brown yeast roll. We thanked them and weaved through an obstacle course of folding chairs and moving people. We found four seats together, sat, and attacked our plates piled high with food.

For such a skinny guy, Strike sure had an affection for food. I guess he didn't get to eat a feast like this very often. Probably because the police officers had banished him across the river.

Sarah wiped her mouth and looked at me. "When are you boys headed home?"

I stared at her. Going home had to be the furthest thing from my mind at that moment. Lucas and I exchanged a nervous glance and looked away. I didn't want to think about that yet. Home felt like a faraway place in a dream. Meanwhile, our adventure had become our reality.

Silence hung between us while Ms. Sarah waited for an answer. I swallowed. "This adventure in the city has been so much fun. I guess we kinda put home out of our minds."

She shook her head. "No way, not buying it. Somebody better wake up and put a plan together right now." She glared at Strike. "You're the one who brought these two young men across the bridge. So how are you going to get them home? These boys have school tomorrow."

A knot clenched in my stomach. I shot Lucas a stunned look. To avoid her question, I stood and headed to the dessert table. Lucas followed. We glanced back and saw Ms. Sarah leaning close to Strike. She talked. He listened and nodded, solemn and downcast.

I nudged Lucas with my elbow. "I feel like somebody just hit me in the face with a bucket of ice water."

"Yeah, we gotta get home. It's a long way from here. We need to get going as soon as we finish dessert."

I agreed, and we returned to the table.

Ms. Sarah leaned back in her chair and stared at Strike. To distract her, Strike stood and applauded when we handed him his dessert. "Before we talk about going home, friends, we're gonna have us a little pie celebration right here. Dig in."

We sat and plunged our forks into our luscious dessert. Oh my, that pie—the crowning glory of a wonderful Sunday dinner. We savored every bite.

Ms. Sarah watched until her patience ran out. She stood when we pushed back from our empty pie plates. "Well, gentlemen, it's time for y'all to hit the road. I guess you'll head over to the law office and get those sleeping bags, right? Then you better hustle home for dinner." With arms crossed and her high heel tapping the floor, she waited for our answer.

Frowning, Lucas and I looked at each other, then at Strike. Our adventure fast approached its end. We faced a long walk home.

Strike shrugged. "Okay, Your Highness, I give you my word. I'll get these fellows back home right away. Let's hit the road, boys."

We stood reluctantly and gathered our trash.

Ms. Sarah's skeptical look gave way to a smile that warmed our little circle. I think she felt the same affection for us we felt for her. "When you boys get back home and confess the truth about your weekend, tell your parents about me. Then bring them over to see me. I can cook up something special for y'all. Maybe some collards for Michael." She winked at me. "Y'all get on home now. I'll see ya soon."

Without another word, Ms. Sarah paraded like a queen to the back staircase. Her white dress swirled around her swagger. She waved a regal goodbye without looking back. We watched in awe. She seemed to float up the stairs.

"Now that's a proper lady, my boys," Strike said in quiet reverence. "A verified queen of a person." Lucas and I stared at the emptiness she left behind.

The time had come to go home. I forced myself to grasp this reality. The realization brought a boatload of questions. Would our parents be angry we came into town without their permission? Would the bullies be waiting for us at school tomorrow? Would Mom be better when I got home?

Only one way to answer those questions—head home and face whatever waited.

CHAPTER THIRTY-SEVEN

Mom's Journal: Entry Eight- Sunday, May 18, 1997

Is anyone there? Jacob? Michael? God? I'm lost, overwhelmed, overcome. Where are you? Where am I?

I've been trying to avoid the truth. Not anymore.

Early this morning, I ventured into your room. That's when I knew, Jacob. Yes, I knew. The emptiness in your room reflected the emptiness in my soul. Laying across your bed, I cried uncontrollably. Couldn't stop.

Yes, you are gone. But one day soon, I will see you and hold you again. I'll cling to that knowledge.

After crying, I took an extra pill, dressed, and walked out to sit beside the Jacob tree. The pine straw drew me down to the place where your life poured into the ground. I lay beneath your tree. Time stopped. I must have been in a trance. I stayed there an hour. The neighbors didn't notice. A storm chased me inside.

I sat on the den sofa, watching the rain wash

away the last traces of my son. Did I take another pill? Lost count.

The storm raged. I curled up under a blanket and fell asleep. Deep asleep.

That's when I saw you, God. You stood there with your arms outstretched, smiling. I felt your touch. You leaned forward and kissed me on the forehead. Your presence sparkled and lit up the room. But best of all, you hugged me. Wrapped your powerful arms around me and gave me a hug. You remember me. Thank you, Lord. I slept again while you held me tight. The rain stopped.

I'm writing in my journal now, scared I might pass out soon. No words can express. Only, "Forgive me. I'm so sorry."

I'll hide this journal in my nightstand. The night-stand where I should have locked my gun. Don't cry, Susan. Hide the journal, then go talk to God's birds. The storm is passing.

I'm in a slow fade. But I love you, Lord.

Hold my boys in your loving arms, like you held me.

CHAPTER THIRTY-EIGHT

Early afternoon, Sunday, May 18, 1997

S trike led Lucas and me out the door of Triune Church. Time to return and face my world.

While we walked, I savored worshiping with so many kinds of people. The thought hit me how people are all alike on the inside, despite our outer differences. We all experience tough times, like Mom and I have. No one wants to crawl out of bed each morning and face a life of turmoil and tragedy. But we do it and keep going. And every day, God offers us hope and a future.

Our pace quickened toward the law office, with us aiming to arrive home by late afternoon. The morning rainstorm had passed. Water glistened on the grass and trees with a bright sheen of fresh color. A renewed sense of hope sparkled in my spirit too.

Strike whistled and took long strides up the street. Lucas and I hustled to keep up. He shouted over his shoulder from a few feet in front of us, "I just want to remind you boys that old Strike promised you an adventure fit for a king. Did I not?"

True enough. The man had delivered on his promise. "Yep,

this has been two exciting days, for sure," I said. "The scary walk across the bridge with traffic speeding all around felt like an amusement park ride. But Ms. Sarah and her soul food took the prize. And of course, my first taste of collards."

We laughed.

Lucas chimed in, "And I'll never forget the chase with the officers. But hearing my hero, Marcus Jones, was the best."

We high-fived without losing our pace.

With a bounce in our step, we headed up the street to retrieve our sleeping bags. The law office came into view. Our pace slowed approaching the building. We strolled across the front and headed along the sidewalk toward the back. This same concrete walkway had provided sleeping quarters for the three of us last night. What a great day so far. Strike led us around the back corner of the building.

Rounding the corner, Strike gasped and stopped in his tracks. Lucas ran smack into him with a grunt. I sidestepped Lucas and looked into the shadow of the stairs. Squinting, I saw what had commanded Strike's attention.

Officer Parker sat on the third step, holding my sleeping bag. He had Lucas's bag tucked tight between his ankles. "Hello, boys. We thought we might find you here." A grin curled his lips.

Strike moaned and turned to make a quick retreat. He bumped into me and knocked me into Lucas. Like dominoes falling, we sprawled backward onto the sidewalk. Strike stumbled and fell in slow motion on top of us. All three of us scrambled to regain our footing.

Parker tossed my sleeping bag onto the step behind him and sprang to his feet. He lunged to get a hold of me. Shocked by this sudden change of events, Lucas and Strike scooted backward like two crabs to avoid the melee. With my best shake and bake move, I tried to dodge the charging officer.

But I wasn't fast enough. Parker grabbed my shoulders when I tried to run around him. We wrestled for a few seconds, but he got the better of me. He grabbed my wrist and spun me around with my arm behind me. His other arm locked over my shoulder and across my chest. He had me.

I screamed to Strike and Lucas, "Get out of here! Save yourselves."

They jumped to their feet to make a break for freedom.

A voice boomed behind them, "Stay where you are! Do not run. We must talk."

Parker maintained his tight grip on me. I swiveled my head to see who had spoken. Lucas and Strike stopped on a dime. They twisted sideways to look toward the voice.

Officer Harold Jackson stepped around the corner of the building. His muscular body loomed, framed by the bright afternoon sun behind him. Chiseled arm muscles flexed and bulged under his short-sleeve uniform shirt. His face appeared to be carved from stone.

He kept his voice low and calm. "Strike, you have done nothing wrong. We will not arrest you." He took one step toward him and held his hands out, palms up. "Work with me, man. I have a proposal for you. Let's talk. Then we'll return these boys to their homes for you."

Lucas pivoted toward me. He shot me a terrified look and shouted, "No way! I'm not going home in a police car. My parents will kill me. No way." He glared at Officer Parker, holding me captive in his grasp. Then he panicked and made a break for it.

Jackson moved in fast. Lucas ran right into him with a thud. The officer squeezed him in a bear hug, picked him up with one arm, and held him across his shoulder. Lucas stared wide-eyed, draped across Jackson's shoulder, held firm by the officer's arm encircling his midsection.

Jackson spoke with constrained intensity. "Strike, do not run. Let's talk about our options. We're here to help you. Give us a break."

Lucas and I stopped squirming against our captors. All eyes fell on Strike.

He relaxed and backed away a few steps, then a pleasant smile crossed his face. "Well now, Officer Harold Jackson wants to sit down with little old me. Don't that sound cozy? Two old friends having a nice little chat." His voice turned serious. "Except the two old friends are a homeless vagrant and the dang police dog chasing him here and yon. So tell me why I shouldn't run as fast as these skinny legs can carry me."

Officer Jackson slid Lucas off his shoulder and kept one massive arm locked around his chest. With his other hand, he pointed a powerful finger at Strike. His negotiation tone gave way to anger. "Strike, I'm finished playing with you. I have a verified offer for you. It's a plan that will help you. Don't be a fool. I'm going to count down from five. When I get to one, I expect you to surrender." He glared, hand on hip. "If you cooperate, we'll all walk calmly to the car, then drive to the station to sit down and talk. Parker will return the boys to their homes. You and I will discuss my proposal to get you off the streets. You got it?"

Strike met Jackson's glare eye to eye. A sneer crept across his lined face. "Sure, I'll bet you have me a nice little room somewhere. And a nice little recovery program. And a nice little job." The sneer turned into a frown and he shouted, "Most likely at the county jail! Probably for many years to come."

Officer Jackson snorted and threw his hands out, palms forward. "No. You're not listening. This is a bona fide offer. You have my word. Just come to the station and we'll lay it on the table. You can walk away if you don't like the plan."

Lucas and I shot each other a look. I gave him a quick nod. On cue, we pushed with all our strength to break free. No luck. Two scrawny sixteen-year-olds could never overpower these two grown men.

Parker barked, "Give it up, boys. You're not going anywhere until Strike surrenders."

Jackson focused on Strike. "I'm going to start the countdown. All you have to do is allow us to escort you to the car."

"Five . . . " He stared at Strike.

Strike stared right back with a wry smile.

"Four . . ."

Strike paced back and forth on the sidewalk, stroking his chin and looking thoughtful.

"Three . . ."

Strike glanced at Lucas, then back at me.

"Two . . ."

Strike stopped pacing. "So if I come in and talk this out, you'll make me an offer?" He raised his arms to his sides. "But you won't tell me what the offer is. So how do I know if it's a good or bad offer?"

Officer Jackson never shifted his glare from Strike, nor loosened his grip on Lucas. "I already told you. It's an excellent offer, an offer for a job and a fresh start. I'm on my last number, Strike. What's it gonna be?" He took a deep breath and grunted, "One . . ."

A low growl started in Strike's throat. The growl rose into a cackling laugh. The officer released Lucas and shoved him aside. Lucas stumbled sideways and fell backward on the grass. He sat stunned, too surprised to run.

Jackson circled onto the grass, attempting to cut off Strike's path of escape. In a flash, Strike jumped up and ran straight at Officer Jackson. The officer took a quick step backward.

Strike and Jackson juked each other back and forth like a running back and a linebacker. Strike lunged toward the mountain of a man.

Lucas squeezed his eyes shut. I gasped.

With no hesitation, Strike charged straight ahead. He reached Jackson at full speed. Just before contact, Strike veered and dove into a full body slide on the damp grass, just beyond the officer's grasp. Lucas jumped to his feet, eyes wide open, as Strike flew past. The officer's huge hands grabbed for Strike, scrambling to snag him and snatch him up as he slid by.

But the officer came up empty. Strike emerged behind him and popped to his feet.

Silence. Every eye on Strike. He whooped in victory and sprinted to the shrubbery hedge. Jackson grabbed Lucas by the arm before he could chase after Strike.

At the edge of the yard, Strike turned toward us with a flourish. In one smooth motion, he swept a flowing hand from head to foot in a full stage bow, a crazy grin on his face. Then he crossed his arms and assumed the smug pose of a star performer before an adoring audience.

Officer Parker relaxed his grip on me and swore.

I applauded and hollered, "Thank you, Strike, for the greatest adventure ever!"

Parker snarled and locked me into the constraining hold again. Lucas laughed and cheered too, until Jackson locked him down with a powerful arm.

Strike shouted and waved from the other side of the yard, "Best wishes to ya, Michael, and Lucas. Salutations, Officers Jackson and Parker. Maybe one day we'll sit down and talk about that offer. Not today, though. Not today." He pointed a bony finger at me and Lucas. "Okay, boys, don't be strangers. You know where to find me." He waved, and we waved back as best we could under constraint.

Strike pranced across the parking lot, swinging his arms like a circus clown and grinning. He broke into a gallop when he reached the road. His head swung from side to side, his laughter ringing up and down the street. He zigzagged from sidewalk to street and back again, dodging honking cars and rainwater puddles.

His crazy cackle faded away when he disappeared from view.

CHAPTER THIRTY-NINE

Midafternoon, Sunday, May 18, 1997

L ucas and I pouted in the back seat of the police car while Officer Parker drove. A thick metal screen separated the back and front seats. Jackson watched us from the front passenger seat in the visor mirror. We avoided his eyes.

Parker exited the parking lot in no hurry. Nonchalant, he pulled the car onto the street and headed toward the river. With one hand relaxed on the steering wheel, he drove down the street we walked up last night. The difference in our current circumstances blew me away.

I stared out the window beside me, my mind a whirlwind of troubling thoughts. After the tension and excitement of the law office encounter, I needed to figure out this predicament.

Parker broke the silence. "We'll head over to the substation to write up our report. Then we'll call your parents and let them know we're bringing you home." He sniffed and slung his right arm across the back of their seats. "So what's the story? Why did you guys run away?"

Lucas crossed his arms and spoke in a slow, defiant voice. "We didn't run away. We just went camping in the woods."

"So your parents know you went camping for the weekend?"

I nodded. "They know we camped at the county park by the river. But they don't know we went into town with Strike." I looked into the visor mirror again and met Jackson's eyes.

His forehead wrinkled. "How did you guys meet Strike?" For just a moment, he looked like a real person, not a talking mountain.

The car stopped when the traffic light ahead turned red.

Lucas shifted forward in his seat and explained how Strike invaded our campsite and earned our trust when we lost our food and cash. When Lucas said he knew Strike from working on his family farm, the officers sighed and glanced at each other, shaking their heads.

I hurried to explain, "We were desperate. Our food and money had washed away. So we agreed to follow Strike into town. If we didn't find food, we would have to go home. No food, no adventure. We weren't about to let that happen."

Parker accelerated when the light turned green.

Officer Jackson let out a low whistle. Lucas glanced up, saw his look, and refocused his attention outside. I leaned sideways to look in the visor mirror but quickly turned away when I saw his forehead furrowed and face drawn tight.

With a stern voice, Jackson said, "Listen to me, boys. For all you knew, Strike could have been a serial killer. Didn't your parents teach you about stranger danger?" He turned in his seat and looked at us over his shoulder. His voice intensified. "Officer Parker and I could just as well be cruising to the morgue to identify your bodies. That's not adventure, that's catastrophe." He turned back to face the front and flipped the visor up in a huff.

Jackson's words exploded in my brain. Tears welled in my eyes. I struggled to catch my breath. Lucas wouldn't look at me. How could we have been so naïve? We trusted Strike without knowing enough about him. And the officer spoke the truth. This could have ended in a catastrophe.

Officer Parker changed the subject. "Where did the wild man take you to get food?"

A lump rose in my throat. I did not want to tell them anything more. "Just some places along the street that he knew about." I sat back and crossed my arms.

Parker snickered. "Oh, come on. It's no big deal. I'm just curious. No harm in telling us."

Lucas turned and spoke with an edge in his voice. "If you gotta know, Strike took us to this place called Ms. Sarah's Soul Food Bistro."

Officer Parker laughed. "Did you meet the amazing Ms. Sarah? I hear she's quite a lady." He looked at Jackson, who ignored him.

So did we. Silence.

Parker snorted under his breath. "What gives here? Why aren't you guys talking?"

In a flat voice, Lucas answered. "Maybe we don't want you to know everything we did. Are we on the witness stand or something?" Lucas glanced at me, and we shared a subtle smile.

Officer Jackson shifted his huge shoulders toward us and snapped, "Okay, boys, stop this little game of cat-and-mouse right now. The fact is, Parker and I have been tracking your every move." He twisted to look directly at us. "And Ms. Sarah told us where you were." He held our shocked eyes in his glare for a few seconds, then faced forward again.

"What are you talking about?" Lucas exclaimed at the back of Jackson's head.

Officer Parker clicked his tongue. "Well, boys . . . Ms. Sarah is Officer Jackson's sister."

Lucas and I gasped at the same time. We both said, "Your sister?"

Jackson's voice remained matter of fact. "Yes, my sister."

Parker stopped at another traffic light and glanced over his shoulder as while he waited for the light to change. "Yesterday, when you guys left Sarah's restaurant, she called and told us you had walked into town with Strike. Then she notified us when you headed to the park. That's how we found you. We suspected you might be runaways."

The light turned green, and the vehicle turned a corner and headed down a side street lined with older businesses. I stared at the floor. The visor flipped down again, but I didn't look up.

Jackson picked up the story. "Today after lunch, when you left Triune, she called me again. She told us you had left the church and headed to the law office. Sarah tracked your journey every step and reported your locations."

The car stopped and the front door opened. "Okay, guys, let's go."

The revelation about Ms. Sarah overwhelmed us. We didn't even notice our arrival at the police station. Were we supposed to feel betrayed or protected? I didn't know what to think. I sat in the parked car and tried to absorb this stunning development. Why would such a caring person as Ms. Sarah give us away, even if she was Harold Jackson's sister?

The officers opened their doors and stood to stretch. Parker stepped over and opened the back door beside Lucas. He bent and spoke quietly, "You didn't stand a chance, guys, even when you outran us in the park. Sister Queen and Brother Cop tracked you every step of the way. Ultimately, the three of us are caring people and are very concerned for your safety." He extended a hand to Lucas to exit the car.

Jackson opened the door beside me and motioned. "Let's go, kid. Time to get that report done and phone calls made."

The policemen escorted us into the substation, nodded to the receptionist at the front desk, and ushered us through a door to a back room. They directed us to sit on hard plastic chairs facing one of four gray metal desks in the room. Jackson sat behind the desk, and Parker sat on the corner facing us. Officer Jackson opened a desk drawer, pulled out a couple of forms, and grabbed a pen. He talked us through the report, getting our names, addresses, parents' names, and phone numbers.

A sick feeling rose in my stomach. Sitting in a police station questioned by officers? No way we included this in the plan. And waiting for the police to call our parents and report us like delinquents scared me even me more. My pulse raced and my head pounded.

Jackson stopped writing and looked at us. "Okay, we won't charge you boys with anything, so don't worry about that. After all, you camped in the county park and wandered into the city. No real problem there."

Relief swept over me, and I hoped for more good news.

Jackson pointed the pen at Lucas, then at me. "The problem is . . . you came across the river into town without your parents' permission. You're not old enough to do that. Plus, you were in the company of a vagrant with multiple minor offenses." Jackson gave each of us a stern look, then continued filling out the form.

I sat up straight in my chair. "We tried to call our parents from the park's pay phone. But my mother wasn't in a mood to talk and Lucas's parents didn't answer." I stared straight ahead, knowing I had just lied about calling Lucas's parents.

Jackson kept writing. He spoke without looking up. "Then you should have gone home."

Lucas and I sat and stared at the floor, trying to ignore that statement. We would have done most anything to avoid going home just a few hours into our getaway.

Parker spoke in a level voice. "So, no charges filed against you. But we need to call and tell your parents what happened. Then we'll take you both home. Arradale is in our jurisdiction, so we'll escort you to your front doorstep and hand you over to your parents."

Lucas jumped to his feet. "No, no, no. That can't happen.

Can't you skip calling our folks? Please, just let us out of the car at the end of our street." His voice rose with each sentence. "If my parents find out I went to town without their permission, I'll be in really big trouble. I may never see the light of day again."

I dropped my head and mumbled, "Like you said yesterday, if we get caught, it will be my fault. This is on me. I'm the one to blame."

Officer Jackson shook his head, picked up the desk phone receiver, and dialed. When the phone rang, he looked at us. "It's the law, guys. I'm required to follow procedure."

Lucas continued to stand, staring at the officer.

Someone answered, and Officer Jackson introduced himself. We could tell by the conversation that Lucas's mom had picked up the phone. Jackson methodically explained the situation to her.

Lucas slumped back into his chair and sniffled. A tear ran down his cheek. I tried to catch his eye, but he wouldn't look at me.

"We'll deliver him to your front door in fifteen to twenty minutes," Jackson said and ended the conversation. He replaced the receiver on its base, then looked at me casually. "Next."

I scooted to the edge of my chair. My voice trembled. "Officer Jackson, I need to tell you something about my mom. My little brother died last month in a handgun accident at our house." The whole sad story came spilling out in a torrent.

The officers listened, motionless. Then Jackson grabbed a folder from the desk and thumbed through some papers in it, nodding.

I hesitated. "Mom has been zoning out most afternoons and evenings for the last few weeks. I think she's hooked on her prescription drug. It's gut-wrenching to watch." Jackson looked up from the folder with concern. I continued. "That's the main reason Lucas and I went on our adventure this weekend. I couldn't take it anymore. If you call her, it might push her over the edge." I looked down at my hands folded in my lap.

Officer Jackson cleared his throat and sighed. "I'm so sorry, Michael. I know that's heartbreaking."

Parker inhaled slowly. "I remember covering the scene of the accident. Terrible tragedy. I hate that you've had to endure such a thing." He looked away.

Jackson dropped his voice. "But if we don't call your mom and she finds out on her own, it will be far worse." He tapped the folder. "This report says she's barred from gun ownership already. We'll talk with her when we take you home. Based on that interview, we'll decide what to do about the drug usage."

Panic seized me in a vise grip. I had made Mom's drug abuse an excuse for my own actions. And by doing so, I had dragged her into deeper trouble—the possibility of an investigation. I should have kept quiet about her drug use. I hadn't felt the ropes of grief tying me up all weekend, but now they were back. I struggled to calm my breathing and get myself under control.

I sat back in my chair and tears dripped down my face. The room remained silent while Jackson continued writing. My breath came in gasps and I hyperventilated. Sure, Dad always said guys don't cry. I didn't care, because I couldn't hold this pain any longer. The dam broke, and I dropped my head in my hands to hide the tears.

After half a minute, I heard Officer Jackson stop writing. I looked up to see him waiting. I dried my tears on my sleeve and his eyes met mine. He lifted the receiver on the desk phone. "I'm sorry, son. But we need to get this over with." He dialed our home phone number.

We all waited in silence. Nothing. No answer. Jackson placed his finger on the button to end the call. He glanced aside, still holding the receiver, and checked the number before dialing again. We waited. Still no answer.

He hung up and shook his head. "Does your mom usually go anywhere on Sunday afternoon?"

My voice quivered. "No, sir. Nowadays she just sits on the back porch and watches birds on our birdfeeder. Sometimes she even talks to them."

Officer Parker shifted his weight on the corner of the desk and raised his eyebrows. "Can she hear the phone ringing from the porch?"

"Yes, sir, the phone is on the wall next to the back door."

"Do you have a neighbor we could call to check on your mom?"

"Mr. Charlie could do it. He's a good friend. He lives next door." I had to think hard to recall his last name. Then I remembered—Charlie Harris.

Officer Jackson pulled a phonebook from the desk drawer. I knew the thick paperback volume contained everyone's name, address, and phone number for the entire city, organized alphabetically. He flipped through and stopped to scan a page. "Here's a Charles Harris next door to your address."

He dialed the Harris's residence. Mr. Charlie answered, and Officer Jackson introduced himself. He explained the situation and asked him to go next door to check on Mom. He gave the number to their car phone. "Can you call me back and tell me if she's home?" Officer Jackson asked. He then thanked Mr. Charlie and hung up. "Okay, boys, let's ride."

We stood. Lucas looked like a whipped puppy. I felt like a convicted criminal.

The front door to the substation slammed against the reception area wall. Detective Thorne walked with authority into the office area. He nodded at me as he hurried to the desk where we sat. He shook hands with both officers and exchanged greetings. It shocked me to realize they worked together and knew each other well.

Turning to me, he smiled. "Well, Michael, you're a tough one to find. I've been looking for you and your mother since Friday afternoon. I've got an update for you." His eyes twinkled. "The missing bullet made the difference." He smiled.

I took a deep breath, and Jackson and Parker looked at each other.

Thorne continued, "We've been trying to phone your mother to let her know, but she hasn't answered. The receptionist radioed to tell me you're here, so I came by to tell you in person. The missing bullet remained our only unresolved question. Your dad had no other leverage. Then you and your mom found that bullet. So"—he paused—"on Friday afternoon, we declared the investigation permanently closed. The case file reads accidental shooting."

A slow smile warmed my face. Lucas managed a relieved grin and slapped me on the back.

Detective Thorne shook my hand and said, "Okay, Michael. I'm counting on you to share this good news with your mother. I'll call her in the morning to answer all her questions. Let her know." He turned to the officers and chuckled. "Ten-four, gentlemen, these two dangerous criminals are all yours. Time for me to clock out."

Officer Jackson escorted us out the front door behind Parker and Thorne. We headed for the police car—and home.

Please God, let this good news heal Mom's pain.

And yet, I wondered what had happened at home. Why hadn't she answered the phone? Was she okay? Where had she gone?

CHAPTER FORTY

Late afternoon, Sunday, May 18, 1997

We cruised away from the police substation toward the river bridge.

Lucas tapped on the metal screen between the front and back seats. "Sir, did you say you have a phone in this car?"

"Yep," Officer Parker said. "Brand new."

Lucas sat up straighter in his seat. "Can we see it?"

Officer Jackson lifted a canvas bag the size of a car battery from the floor of the car. "Just got it last month. This baby is an actual phone." He smiled with pride and lifted the phone out of the bag. The big square body had a handset receiver on top. He put the receiver to his ear and mouth, demonstrating how it worked. "They say lots of people will have mobile phones in years to come. But they're pretty rare right now. The city installed these in police cars for emergency calls. Cool, right? Makes us feel special." He brushed some loose dirt from the bag and placed it back on the floor.

"Definitely cool," Lucas said.

I nodded. Someday maybe I'd have a car of my own with a bag phone. But for now, Mom was my primary concern.

Lucas and I stared out the car windows again in silence. Parker hummed a tune while he drove, and Jackson drummed his fingers on the back of the seat. We passed Ms. Sarah's Soul Food Bistro, closed on Sundays.

I had felt betrayed when Jackson revealed Sarah as their informant. Ms. Sarah had befriended us, then squealed to her cop brother. At first, the thought put me in a funk. But the more I thought about it, the more I came to a different conclusion. If she didn't care for us, she wouldn't have gone to the trouble to keep me and Lucas safe. I took comfort in that.

Another question arose in my mind. I sat forward and tapped Jackson's arm through the screen. "Sir, when you demanded that Strike turn himself in, you said you had an offer for him. What's the offer?"

Jackson pulled down his visor and looked at me in the mirror. "Well, first, Strike likes to tell everyone that we banished him across the river. You need to know that's not true. He moved across the river because he thinks we're chasing him. We aren't chasing him." He took his arm off the back of the seat and shrugged. "We've been trying to talk to him for a couple of months. We want to help him get off the streets. But he won't come in and discuss our offer. We can't get him to listen. He just keeps running. Lots of homeless people have adapted to that lifestyle and are hesitant to change. We get it, but we keep trying." He cleared his throat and looked back at me. "I've been thinking . . . maybe you guys can help us with Strike."

Lucas turned from the window with an inquisitive look. "Whatcha got in mind?"

"Sarah and I have known Strike for about six months. He started coming around asking for handouts at the bistro. He doesn't know we are brother and sister. So first, you gotta swear you won't give us away."

"We won't tell," I said.

"Yeah," Lucas added. "No problem."

Parker flashed the okay sign. "Strike's an intelligent guy. He's smart and savvy about a lot of things. But his father's harshness left him with emotional scars. And his brother's death wounded him forever. Because of that, he has a major trust issue."

I slid forward in the seat. "Yes, sir, I told him about losing my little brother. Then he told me about his crazy family and his little brother drowning."

Jackson whistled in surprise. "Amazing he would share something so personal with you. He's a good guy underneath all that flamboyance. But his emotional issues make him unreliable." He shook his head. "He can't seem to find a way out of his make-believe kingdom. Living in the woods by the river is his security blanket. And he won't let go."

The police car drove across the bridge where our adventure started yesterday. Only a day ago? How could that be? I looked through the trees lining the river and wondered when and where our homeless friend might appear again.

"Well, what's the offer?" Lucas asked. "And how could two kids like me and Michael help the police?"

Officer Jackson turned toward us with a subtle smile. "Good question. Here's the plan. Sarah and I want to co-sponsor him in a job training program. Then we can get him admitted to a halfway house to get him off the streets. Right now, he thinks he's fine out there alone. But his lifestyle makes him vulnerable to all kinds of things. We just want to help him. Strike's got a lot of potential."

Lucas frowned. "But what if God created Strike to be homeless and live on the river? Maybe we should just leave him alone."

Jackson reacted with a hearty laugh. "Another good question

there, Lucas. The choice is Strike's to make, for sure. We're not trying to force his hand. Or God's hand either." He turned to face forward again. "You two have already become his friends and earned his trust. So, next time he comes to work on Lucas's farm or you cross paths along the river, you could talk to him. Maybe influence him to sit down and consider our offer. But, hey, be sure to tell your parents everything you're doing. You hear me? We better not get any more calls about you guys."

Just above a whisper, I said, "Yes, sir."

Lucas nodded and looked away.

A loud sound startled me. The car phone. Jackson lifted the bag phone and put the receiver to his ear. "Hello? . . . Yes, Mr. Harris, this is Officer Jackson. Any news about Michael's mom?" His shoulders hunched as he listened. "Okay, thank you. We'll be there as quick as we can." He replaced the receiver and dropped the canvas bag on the floor.

Reaching over, Jackson tapped Parker on the arm and jabbed his index finger forward.

The car surged ahead, pinning Lucas and me against our seats. Officer Jackson pointed up and whirled his finger. Parker flipped on the flashing lights and siren from the dashboard. He steered the speeding car through the slow-moving Sunday afternoon traffic. The other drivers gave way.

My heart sped up as fast as the car. "What . . . what's going on?"

"Change of plans," Officer Jackson said, his voice tense. "Officer Parker will drop off you and me at your house. Then he'll deliver Lucas to his parents."

My voice trembled as I asked, breathless, "Is Mom okay?"

Jackson flipped up his visor mirror, hiding his face. "Mr. Charlie is with your mom. He found her on the back porch. She couldn't hear the phone ringing from out there."

I thought I had my emotions under control. But here they were again, rising in my throat to strangle me. My mind went crazy with unanswered questions. My pulse raced and the feeling of hyperventilating returned. With each block we traveled, the siren hammered a chaotic clamor inside my head.

I lifted a silent prayer. *Oh God, I've already lost my little brother. Please don't let something bad happen to Mom.*

The police car whisked down the streets of Arradale. A few sudden turns threw me and Lucas against the doors. My mind took unexpected turns too, wondering what could be happening. The police car careened around a familiar corner, then headed down our street. Parker flipped the siren off and slowed as we approached our house.

My head throbbed and my heart seemed to jump several beats. An ambulance sat in our driveway with the back doors open. Its red lights intertwined with our blue strobe in a chaotic dance.

Lucas reached across and grabbed my shoulder. His voice cracked as he whispered, "I hope she's okay. Let me know. I'm here for you."

Nothing could tear my attention from the ambulance. I stared at the terrifying dance of red and blue lights and stammered, "Please, God, not again." My voice sounded far away.

The police car turned into our driveway. I gripped the door handle, ready to jump out and run to Mom.

CHAPTER FORTY-ONE

Early Evening, Sunday, May 18, 1997

J ackson lunged out of the car, unlocked my door, and wrenched it open. I ran past him faster than I ran in the park yesterday.

Jackson shouted at my back, "Wait! Michael. Let me go with you."

Too late. At the back door of the ambulance, I looked inside. No one there.

Jackson slammed his car door and hustled after me. "Hold on. Wait a minute."

I kept running. Up the front steps, through the door, into the foyer, around the den corner, smack into Mr. Charlie standing in the kitchen. My momentum knocked him backward two steps.

My voice trembled. "Where's Mom?" I searched his face for a clue. My body shook with anxiety.

He stepped toward me and grasped my shoulders. "It's okay, Michael. She's okay."

I pulled away. "But where is she?" I got the shaking under control and summoned some courage.

Mr. Charlie dropped his hands from my shoulders. He looked into my face and spoke with calm strength. "The medics have stabilized her. She blacked out on the back porch."

Officer Jackson brushed by and stepped outside. "Let me check on her. Wait here, I'll be right back."

Mr. Charlie and I stood in the kitchen in silence, not knowing what to say.

A minute later, Jackson stepped back inside. "I spoke to the medic. Your mom's very woozy, but she's okay. You can go see her, Michael." Officer Jackson stepped toward Mr. Charlie. "Mr. Harris, I'm Harold Jackson, the officer who called. Thank you for your help."

Mr. Charlie gazed up at the large man standing in front of him. Jackson nodded, and they shook hands.

My legs didn't want to work, but I forced my body to move. Mr. Charlie escorted me through the kitchen to the back door. I stopped in the doorway and stared at Mom lying on the stretcher. An IV bag hung beside her with the tube inserted in her forearm. I glanced at Mr. Charlie for assurance. He gave me the okay sign.

Jackson came around to my other side. "See, Michael? They're taking good care of her. But she's in and out of consciousness. I'll ask if you can speak to her."

The medic overheard and turned toward us. In a hushed tone, he said, "Come on over, son. You can see her."

Officer Jackson ushered me out the kitchen door onto the porch. Mr. Charlie waited at the door and watched. I saw a tear on his cheek. What a good man he was.

The two medics, a man and a woman, stepped back to make room for me, with Jackson beside me. With careful steps, I crossed to her side and whispered, "Mom, are you okay?" I touched her hair, matted around her pale face.

Her eyes fluttered but stayed closed.

Leaning closer, I spoke a little louder. "Mom, can you hear me?"

At the sound of my voice, she stirred slightly. Her eyes opened just enough to see me. A faint smile crossed her lips. She mumbled, "Hey, Michael. Did you enjoy your weekend?"

Guilt took my voice hostage. I swallowed, then the words broke free. "Yes, ma'am. We had a good time. I'll tell you everything about it soon. You rest right now." I stood straighter. "What happened, Mom? Are you sick?"

Mom gestured to the female medic standing beside her.

The lady spoke with gentleness in her voice. "Your mother overdosed on her prescription meds. She may need to stay in the hospital one or two nights. The doctors will let you know."

A tear dripped down Mom's face, and I wiped it away. I leaned my forehead against hers. She mumbled one phrase at a time. "The pills. Lost count. Took too many. I'm sorry."

I stayed face-to-face with her. She lifted her head and gave me a soft kiss on the cheek. Her kiss warmed the depth of my heart.

Mr. Charlie moved beside us, and I turned to him. His eyebrows knit together with concern and he muttered, "I got here just in time. I'm glad I found her when I did."

I sighed. "Me too. Thank you. You've been so good to us."

Jackson nodded. "Might have saved her life."

Mr. Charlie patted my arm and looked up at Jackson. "Officer, Mrs. Harris and I would be glad for Michael to stay with us for a few days. We're in between her cancer treatments, so this should be a convenient week for Michael to stay over."

Officer Jackson nodded. "Thank you, but that's Michael's mother's call. If she approves, I can attest to it as an official witness. But there's still one more issue here." He looked away, then focused again on Mom. "I need to consult with Social Services concerning your drug overdose. I'm sorry, Mrs. Judson, but I want to make sure we provide the help you need." He glanced at me. "I already mentioned it to Michael."

Mom looked at the officer and her chin quivered. "I understand." She extended a weak hand to Charlie in slow motion, and her words came slowly. "Thank you for taking care of my boy. I give my permission for him to stay with you."

He took her hand for a few seconds.

I looked at Charlie. "Thank you, sir. Staying with you two would be great. I don't have anywhere else to go, so that's a relief."

Jackson stepped aside. "Okay, I think we're all set. Let's allow the medical folks to do their job. They need to get her to the hospital." He turned and walked into the house, and Mr. Charlie and I took a few steps back.

The medics moved in fast. They efficiently secured the IV line and safety belts, then rolled the stretcher across the porch.

I spoke up before they got to the door. "Wait. Stop a minute, please. One more thing I need to say."

Mom's eyes flashed open and looked at me.

I took two quick steps to the stretcher and leaned over to look her in the eye. "Mom, promise me you'll get your drug use under control. We need each other."

She stared, blinking away tears.

My voice rose. "Mom, do you promise? I mean it."

A look of realization moved across her face. In a shaky voice, she said, "Okay, Michael, let's all just step back and take a deep breath now."

We shared a loving smile at her joke. Hearing her signature phrase encouraged me. I wrapped my arms around her shoulders and embraced her in an enormous hug. She whispered, "I promise. And I mean to keep that promise. God will help. I saw his face. He wrapped me in his arms just before I went under."

I released her from the hug and stood. "Wow, Mom, that's so good." I took her hand. "And one more thing. Detective Thorne tracked me down today. The investigators confirmed the accidental shooting verdict. The case is closed for good." I stroked her forehead. "We'll never forget Jacob, but we've got to keep healing and move forward. Like you said, God will help."

Our eyes met and she gave me a weary smile. She whispered, "Thank you, Michael. And thank you, Lord." She closed her eyes.

Mr. Charlie looked toward heaven and said, "We're never alone."

One more time, I reached down and took her in my arms. We held each other tight. This was the mother I remembered. I missed her hugs. She had been a wonderful mother until Jacob's death and the drug abuse took her captive. *Lord, please free her and bring her home to me again.*

Officer Jackson returned to the porch, and Mr. Charlie and I stepped aside. Jackson cleared the way. The medics whisked her through the back door. We followed them through the house, out the front door, and into the driveway.

"Stand clear," the female medic said. They lifted the stretcher, swung the wheels under, then slid her into the ambulance. She climbed in with mom and gave us a reassuring smile.

The other medic closed the back doors, then circled around and jumped into the driver's seat. I flinched when the powerful engine roared to life. No siren, but the flashing lights made me shiver when the ambulance pulled out of the driveway and drove up the street.

Mr. Charlie and Harold Jackson stood beside me in silence. My feet felt locked in concrete, and my head heavy as a stone.

A prayer came to mind. *Please, God, don't leave me alone.*

CHAPTER FORTY-TWO

Evening, Sunday, May 18, 1997

Mr. Charlie stood at the door of their guest bedroom. He smiled and looked around the room. "We're glad to have you with us for a few days, Michael. It makes me happy to host you in our daughter's room. It's great to have a kid here again. Brings back lots of wonderful memories."

I sat on the side of the bed. A sense of calmness had filled me since I came into their home. "Thanks for letting me stay here. I sure appreciate you and Mrs. Harris." The bedside lamp cast my shadow on the opposite wall. My shoulders sagged, weary from a long day of stress.

"Well, we think a lot of you too, young man. Don't stay up much longer. Long school day tomorrow after an adventurous weekend. I know you gotta be tired."

"Yes, sir, I am."

"And thanks for sharing your adventure with us over dinner. We loved hearing about it." He hesitated and chose his words with care. "You've come a long way since we lost Jacob. More grown up. Seems like you've grasped the meaning of our song too. I think you get it now."

I sat taller. "Yes, sir, these have been hard days. But I feel like a different person now. The first weeks after Jacob died, the memory of his eyes haunted me." I smiled. "But Friday night beside the river, just as I fell asleep, I saw God's eyes in the stars. Instead of Jacob's dying eyes, I saw God looking at me in love."

A slow smile dawned on Mr. Charlie's face. "That's very inspiring." We savored the moment before he continued, "Now we're praying your mom discovers that too. I have faith she'll get there." His expression brightened. "By the way, you handled her well before they took her to the hospital. I'm proud of you."

I tilted my head and shrugged. "Thank you. That was hard. But I believe she'll make it." I raised my eyebrows. "And maybe she'll let me get a dog when she hears my story."

Mr. Charlie chuckled and nodded, then stepped back into the hallway. "Okay, if you need anything, just call for me. We're right across the hall from you. Good night. See you in the morning."

He shut the bedroom door, and I heard him walk back to their den.

Sitting on the edge of the bed, I allowed the events of the afternoon to replay like a movie in my mind.

After the ambulance left, Officer Jackson, Mr. Charlie, and I had sat at our kitchen table. Jackson explained his legal responsibilities with Mom's drug overdose. He would call a social worker tomorrow to see how to proceed. Meanwhile, he hoped to find someone to walk with us through Mom's recovery. He winked and said he might know of someone who could help.

His obligation to check with Social Services struck fear in my soul. But knowing this big guy had come alongside me gave great relief. And I wondered who he might have in mind to help.

When Officer Parker returned, we walked outside. Parker wouldn't tell us what happened when he took Lucas home. I imagined the worst.

Before the officers left, they reminded me to reconnect with Strike the next time we saw him. I agreed. We shook hands and they headed out.

Once the officers left, I went inside to pack my bag. Before I left my room, I grabbed Stupid Baby and shoved her in my gym bag alongside my clothes. That little doll gave me a sense of Jacob's presence somehow. No way I could leave her behind.

After locking the doors to our house, Mr. Charlie and I stopped by the Jacob tree for a few minutes. We stood beside the magnolia and remembered in silence the day of the snake when Jacob grabbed the gun.

When we went inside, he introduced me to his wife, Helen. How strange to realize I had never met her. She welcomed me with a warm smile and a bright spirit. Her hair had fallen out from cancer treatments, so she wore a wrap. But she had already begun cooking a special dinner to welcome me.

I took my suitcase to the guest room. Memorabilia from their daughter decorated the room. So cool how the song she loved had become our song: Charlie and Helen, me and Mom, and maybe even Lucas.

After unpacking, I called Dad on the Harris's phone. I told him about mom, but Officer Jackson had already informed him. I didn't tell him about my adventure, though. Before we hung up, he said he would see me soon. I couldn't see that happening, but the possibility lifted my spirits anyway.

After we hung up, I wandered to the den to join Mr. Charlie in front of the television, then sunk deep into the couch and snoozed a little. Mr. Charlie switched channels back and forth between a golf tournament and a baseball game. After golf and baseball ended, he called to check on Lucas and talked to Lucas's dad for a while.

His dad wouldn't let me speak to Lucas. No worries. I knew we'd spend all day together at school tomorrow. We'd discuss everything then. That's what best friends do.

Just before dinner, Mr. Charlie called the hospital. I couldn't visit, but they allowed me to talk to Mom. She sounded more awake and promised again she would get the drugs under control. The hospital had already begun an aggressive treatment program. I thanked God that Jackson's phone call to Mr. Charlie saved her life.

We sat down to a homecooked dinner of meat loaf, whipped potatoes, green beans, and apple pie. Comfort food. In return, I told them all about my adventure. They found it amusing and astonishing.

Before we ate dessert, the phone rang. Mrs. Harris answered and held out the receiver. "Michael, the call is for you."

I took the phone and answered.

"Michael?" The warm voice sounded familiar.

"Yes. Who is this?"

"Hello, young man. This is Sister Sarah from the Soul Food Bistro. My brother told me about your mom and gave me your number. Are you okay?"

I gasped. "Ms. Sarah. I can't believe you called me. I already miss you."

She chuckled. "Well, I miss you too. But we're going to see more of each other starting this week. My brother has asked me to come alongside you and your mom for the next several weeks. Because I serve as a guardian ad litem I've helped lots of families. Now I want to help yours. You okay with that?"

Thankfulness overwhelmed me. "Yes!" I almost shouted. "That's more than okay—it's great. I couldn't ask for a better person to help me. Thank you." After discussing the details, we hung up. When I shared the wonderful news with the Harrises, we enjoyed my second pie celebration of the day.

I headed to bed earlier than usual after dinner. "Lucas and Michael's Excellent Adventure" would remain in my heart and soul forever. And so would Strike and all the people he introduced us to. But the adventure ended too soon. Like a baseball colliding with a brick wall. But now I knew God designed my life to be an adventure. Walking and talking with him—even through tragedy.

After a good night's sleep, I would be able to take on anything at school tomorrow, even the bullies. Somehow, I felt older and wiser. God had showed me what I'm made of. And it wasn't junk.

A huge yawn hit me. I turned back the covers and climbed into bed. When I switched off the bedside lamp, the room went dark. Pulling the covers under my chin, I thanked God for Jacob's life. And I asked the heavenly Father to help Mom keep her promise.

As my eyes acclimated to the darkness, my breath caught in wonder. Mr. Charlie's daughter had stuck glow-in-the-dark stars and planets all over the ceiling.

Starry eyes from above watched me with love. Shining in the darkness to say, "You're never alone."

God's eyes.

THE END

RESOURCES

Tell a friend about "His Eyes" to share hope with someone surviving tragedy. And PLEASE leave an honest review of this book on these websites: Amazon, Goodreads, Walmart, Books-A-Million, and Barnes and Noble. Thanks.

If you need a message of hope directly from God, read these Bible verses: Psalm 3:3; Psalm 34:18-19; Psalm 40:1-3; Psalm 42:5; Isaiah 40:28-31; Isaiah 41:10; Jeremiah 29:11-13; II Chronicles 20:12 & 15; and Romans 8:35-39.

For a free gun safety home kit go to: https://ProjectChildSafe.org/in-your-home

For insider info about "His Eyes" and to subscribe to my *Glimpses of Grace* weekly blog, please go to https://Mark CharlesPowers.com. FOR FUN: How many times is the phrase "his eyes" used in this story and how many different people does it refer to? Go to my webpage for the answers.

Email me at Mark@MarkCharlesPowers.com to share stories of your own journey from tragedy to hope. I would love to hear your story. You're never alone, Mark